Idlewild:

Carl Weber Presents

Idlewild:

Carl Weber Presents

Treasure Hernandez

www.urbanbooks.net

Urban Books, LLC
300 Farmingdale Road, NY-Route 109
Farmingdale, NY 11735

Idlewild: Carl Weber Presents
Copyright © 2020 Treasure Hernandez

ISBN 13: 978-1-64556-094-4
ISBN 10: 1-64556-094-5

First Trade Paperback Printing September 2020
Printed in the United States of America

10 9 8 7 6 5 4 3 2 1

This is a work of fiction. Any references or similarities to actual events, real people, living or dead, or to real locales are intended to give the novel a sense of reality. Any similarity in other names, characters, places, and incidents is entirely coincidental.

Distributed by Kensington Publishing Corp.
Submit Orders to:
Customer Service
400 Hahn Road
Westminster, MD 21157-4627
Phone: 1-800-733-3000
Fax: 1-800-659-2436

Chapter 1

Summer Home

Desiree looked over at her snoring teenage son, Tyree, and wondered if she was doing the right thing. For sixteen years, her life had consisted of protecting him from the evils of the world, even from her own family. On the night he was born, she'd whispered in his ear, "I will never let anyone hurt you. You are my soul."

Thinking about it now made small bumps crop up on her arms. She swallowed hard. She'd worked so hard to protect him. She'd been a fierce force in his life, like a superhero swatting away all obstacles every time things got rough for him. She hadn't let kids in school bully him with their insensitive comments about never seeing his daddy. She hadn't backed down when the mothers of his little friends asked too many questions about their situation.

Desiree had never let her son go places without her unless she trusted that the other parents or chaperones were either in her same boat or understood not to pry. Desiree's entire life had changed the day she chose her son over everything else, including her once close-knit family. When everyone had told her having a baby would ruin her life and her family's good name, Desiree hadn't cared. She'd given up an easy life for a hard one, but Tyree was worth it. So worth it. He was all she had. Desiree sighed and battled the tears welling up in her eyes as she thought about the amount of love she had inside her for her only child—from the tight dark curls on his head to the tiny cleft in his chin.

Sometimes she couldn't believe that he was actually hers. She'd actually have to stop and chant, "He is *my* son and *my* son alone," a few times to get her mind back on track. The fact that the older Tyree got, the more obvious his looks got hadn't helped either. He was one of those babies that made old women say to her, "Girl, you ain't have nothing to do with that baby, huh? He must look just like his daddy." Yes, that was the problem. Tyree looked like a complete replica of his father . . . well, her sperm donor. Desiree often wondered if the donor thought about her at all, if he cared about what had happened to her, and if his mind ever wandered to their summers in Idlewild and their sneaky trysts in Chicago during the school year. She wondered. But every time she wondered about him, she made herself sick.

Desiree shook her head now and cleared those thoughts right out. She didn't have time to wonder. She'd told herself years ago—sixteen years ago, to be exact—that wondering about him was detrimental to her mental stability. She and Tyree were just fine and were content to live a modest life in a small, tight-knit suburb in southern Indiana, many miles from where Desiree had grown up. She didn't need the donor, his family, or her own family. She'd carved out a nice life for herself and her son. It was something her family had thought she could never do, since she'd been so pampered and sheltered from the real world while she was growing up. Desiree worked, had what her family would consider a regular job, and made an honest living.

She hadn't asked her family for anything since Tyree was born. There had been many days when she'd gone without dinner just so her son could eat and have things

that other kids in their community had. It was a far cry
from the lavish way she'd grown up, but that was fine
with her. Anything to protect the love of her life. Desiree
didn't consider herself isolated or estranged, as some of
her relatives had referred to her situation. She'd become
used to the fact that Tyree was her only family now. He
was all the family she needed.

As Tyree continued to snore in the passenger seat,
Desiree stared out the car's windshield, and her mind
began racing in a million directions.

"Damn you, Junior," she mumbled, thinking about
the call she'd received a few days ago, the call that had
prompted this long drive.

Desiree had been standing at her kitchen sink, preparing Tyree's dinner before heading to work, when her cell
phone rang. She'd dusted her hands on her apron and
rushed over to the phone. It was a number she hadn't
recognized.

"Hello," she'd huffed after struggling to get the phone
to her ear without getting any of the remaining flour on
her hands on it.

Silence.

"Hello?" she said a second time, her face falling into a
confused frown.

"Um . . . yeah . . . Desi?" her brother Junior replied
awkwardly.

"Junior?" she asked, not sure she had heard right.

For many years she hadn't heard from her family all
that regularly, and Junior hadn't called her directly in
all that time. They had been close growing up, but they
had grown far apart when she announced she was pregnant. Junior had probably been more disappointed in
her pregnancy than her parents had at the time.

Desiree closed her eyes and remembered the sting of
his desertion. She shivered and bit her bottom lip as she
awaited his response.

"Yeah, it's me. Um, look, I . . . I . . . just called to tell you . . . ," Junior said, stumbling over his words.

Desiree sucked in her breath, not realizing that she was squeezing her phone so tight, her knuckles had turned white. "What?" she said almost breathlessly.

"Nobody is dead," Junior said, picking up on her fear. He knew her so well. They knew each other so well.

Desiree's shoulders relaxed. "Okay, then . . . ," she said, almost tapping her foot in anticipation. She was really confused by his call now.

"Pop is sick. Real sick. This summer might be—" Junior said, but Desiree spoke up before her brother could finish.

"I'll be there," she said.

"But there's one more thing," Junior continued. "He wants to be in Idlewild, at the summer home. I know that might be . . . you know . . . for you, it might be . . ."

Desiree was fine until she heard her brother say she had to meet them at their Idlewild summer home. The section of the Michigan lake country known as Idlewild was a historic resort community that got its start as a refuge for Black vacationers before the Jim Crow era. It held a lot of beautiful memories for a lot of people, but for Desiree, it held memories that were both beautiful and ugly.

"Why?" she rasped, her voice barely above a whisper.

Her brother sucked his teeth, and Desiree knew he was probably judging her already. "Because, Desi, that's what Pop wants," Junior replied flatly.

Desiree snapped her lips shut, closed her eyes, squeezed her cell phone until her fingers ached, and mumbled her weak response. "Okay, Junior. I'll be there." Her entire body began to tingle the minute the words left her mouth. She hated herself right after that. She wanted to scream, "Daddy knows I don't want to go there! Especially at this time of year, when everyone is there!" But she bit her tongue and held in her feelings . . . all over again.

Now, as Desiree drove toward familiar yet foreign territory, her head swam with thoughts. What if someone brought up the subject? What if she couldn't explain her son's familiar face? What if her father forced her to announce, once and for all, that she had a child?

Desiree let out a long sigh. More like a cleansing breath. She'd need to employ all her meditation practices over these next two weeks. Being around her family and being in Idlewild this time of year could potentially throw her back into a deep depression and an anxiety state. Desiree swallowed hard, just thinking about the days she'd spent crying in her closet and how she'd sent her son on playdates so she could lie in total darkness and embrace the dark places to which her mind would take her. Tyree was the only thing that had saved her back then.

Tyree stirred next to her and interrupted the negative thoughts that had crept into Desiree's head. He lifted his head and stretched out his long arms.

"Dang, Ma. We ain't there yet?" he said as he peered out the window.

"*Ain't*? What have I told you about that word?" Desiree said, side-eyeing the love of her life.

"We are not in front of anyone right now! You said not to use Ebonics in front of people," Tyree responded.

"Boy, you know what . . . ?" Desiree replied, reaching over and playfully swatting his arm. They both started laughing.

"I mean, ain't that what you said?" Tyree said, needling his mother some more.

"Ew! Only you can get to me like this," Desiree said lightheartedly, unable to remain annoyed with her son for long. "Only you . . . the person I love the most."

"You know I'm just joking, Ma. I know how to conduct myself. I code switch with the best of them. I'm the Jay-Z of code switching," Tyree told her.

"*Code switch*? What the heck is that? Now I have to learn a new term?"

"Yeah, code switch. It's, like, you can be all down and speaking Ebonics one minute, and then somebody white and uptight comes by, and you code switch it to perfect and proper English. Switching the code, faking it till you make it. I'm the best at it. I mean, I only been watching you do it all my life," Tyree explained, with a shoulder shrug.

"Me?" Desiree asked. "What do you mean?"

"Ma, c'mon. We live in a mixed neighborhood, but clearly, you're more comfortable with the people there who obviously have more. It's like you code switch in reverse," Tyree answered quickly, as if what he was explaining to her was obvious.

"Boy, what?" Desiree's voice went high, and her eyebrows folded into the center of her face. She was really confused now.

"You are bougie. There, I said it. Okay. You are a code-switching bougie person, and you can turn it on and off like a pro."

"What? Okay, now you're going too far," Desiree said, dropping her voice an octave. "Bougie? *Me*? What does that even mean?"

"Ma, it is clear to me and everyone else that you grew up privileged but ended up in our neighborhood, for some reason. You don't speak a certain way unless you're around certain people. You have a certain way you do things—even the way you cook! All proper, with an apron on and stuff. And I have seen that you kind of dumb yourself down when you speak to Kyle's mom, since she's clearly not as, you know, smart or polished. But when you speak to Jawan's mother, who is an attorney and grew up probably like you did, you're all smart and, you know, proper and prim, which, I would say, is more like you," Tyree said, his tone getting a bit more serious.

Desiree's eyes grew round, and her eyebrows went up to her hairline. She was struck silent for a few minutes, and that wasn't an easy task. She had never thought of it the way her son had just explained it. She also had never thought he would be as sharp as he was at his age. He was sharp enough to figure her out, despite the fact that he'd seen her steeped in only one social class all his life. She actually had to admit silently to herself that she code switched, and that she was aware of doing it. She just hadn't known it was called code switching.

"I don't know. I think I'm always the same," she replied, slightly defensive.

"I think not," Tyree replied, laughing. "I guess I'm about to step right into your bougie childhood in a minute. Let's see how it goes," he said, rubbing his hands together like a mad scientist.

"Yes, let's see how it goes," Desiree mumbled under her breath.

Chapter 2

Nothing Gained

The sand sparkled brilliantly in the afternoon sunlight at the Johnson family's summer home in Idlewild. The house—a sprawling mansion on the water—sat along the most exclusive stretch of the beach, and so every room had a magnificent view. The property also boasted a private dock. There Carolyn Johnson, the family's matriarch, stood with her arms folded across her chest, staring out at the beautiful landscape. She inhaled the fresh scent of the wind off the lake and let out a long, exasperated sigh.

Each summer for forty-one years, Carolyn and her husband, Ernest, had been coming to Idlewild—a place built specifically for elite African Americans, who had vacationed there since the turn of the twentieth century. With every passing year, the façade they had erected of what they thought was the perfect couple and the perfect family seemed to crack a little more. Carolyn knew that nowadays her children came to the summer home out of a sense of obligation, but no one on the outside looking in knew much about the inner conflicts plaguing the Johnsons.

This summer was already shaping up to be drama filled, and they were barely a month into it. For years, Carolyn had walked hand in hand with Ernest into the high-class house parties of the Idlewild elite, although her family life had been shattered to pieces a long time ago.

Years ago she'd smiled and told several people that her daughter, Desiree, was away in Europe, studying history, although she and her husband had all but banished their middle child for becoming pregnant at sixteen. Carolyn had felt the guilt of that deep in her soul every single day, and no number of happy moments after that had washed away the pain of what they'd done to Desiree back then. Carolyn had cried many nights from just thinking about it, but she'd made the choice back then to stand by her husband, and that was that.

Ernest had fallen ill not so long ago, and Carolyn had dedicated herself even more to the role of doting and caring wife, although for months she had been contemplating how to get even with her husband for all his years of philandering, which had forced her to kill herself inside to hide her pain from her children. Carolyn had put on a brave face for years, but she was tired now. She didn't know how much more of a show she could put on. The fake smiles and all the lies were wearing on her.

She had literally watched her perfect life fade over the course of many years. And now she was in a loveless marriage, one of her children was estranged, one was growing into a version of her husband, and the other was a total disgrace, if Carolyn did say so herself. While he had vengeance on her mind, the fact that her husband was terminally ill also scared her half to death. She'd become so dependent on Ernest that the thought of him leaving her behind terrified her to the point of nausea.

Carolyn closed her eyes when she heard footsteps approach from behind. She flinched as her son, Ernest Junior, placed one hand on her shoulder and pecked her on her cheek.

"Hello, Mother," Junior said, taking a spot right next to her. "Nice weather these days."

The small talk before the bullshit, she thought.

Carolyn cracked a half-hearted smile, her back going rigid and her shoulders stiffening. She knew what was coming next. She'd heard her son stirring around the house earlier, and he never got up early during the summer months unless he was up to something.

"I'm going to get out of here. I have some important business to take care of back in Chicago," Junior announced. He set something down next to him. She looked down and saw his suitcase. She rolled her eyes and bit her bottom lip. She could feel heat rising in her chest, and her hands involuntarily curled into fists. Junior noticed too.

"I won't be gone long. I promise. I'll be back in time for the annual all-white affair. I know how much that means to you," Junior added quickly in response to his mother's body language. He knew that keeping up appearances for his parents' friends was more important to his mother and father than anything.

Carolyn turned toward Junior, abruptly causing him to take a step back. She moved in like a lion toward its prey. "Did you forget that your father is dying and your sister is coming into town today, after years?" she asked, her voice low, almost a growl. She eyed her son evilly, her nostrils moving in and out. She had one shaky finger jutted accusingly toward Junior, and her other hand was balled up so tightly that her nails were digging moon-shaped creases into her palm. She was tired of playing the role of the quiet, sweet wife and mother. The stress was mounting from all sides, and she wasn't about to let her children get away with their shenanigans any longer.

"I didn't forget. I told you I have a very important business meeting in the city," Junior replied, annoyed, pushing her hand away. "I already told Pop. I told him I'd be back, just like I'm telling you." Junior refused to look his mother in the eyes. He immediately grabbed his suitcase and started down the stairs. In his assessment, there was nothing else to talk about. Junior knew how their confrontations would end up. He had long ago grown tired of his mother's constant guilt trips about how she thought he acted around his sister, Desiree.

"So that's it? You're just leaving your family? Your father is dying, for God's sake! Is that what you want on your conscience? You think running away is the answer?" Carolyn barked at her son's back. "She is your sister, and no matter what, nothing will ever change that, Junior! Your family comes first!"

He ignored her and rushed down the front steps.

"Junior! I'm talking to you!" she called out again.

Before she could say another word, Junior flopped down into the driver's seat of his Mercedes-Maybach and slammed the door.

Carolyn rocked back on her heels as she watched the car ease down the long stone driveway toward the road. That was it. Just like that, one of her children was gone again. Carolyn had been through the same thing so many times, she had come to expect it. It had been so many years since she had seen all three of her children in the same place at the same time that it was easy to forget she had three children, that is, until they did things to bring shame to their family's name.

Carolyn could feel her heart throbbing against her chest bone now. She guessed this was what a broken heart felt like. It wasn't a new feeling, and she didn't know why it always felt like a fresh wound. She silently chastised herself for being so emotional all the time. It had been almost seventeen years since their lives had blown up and her children had been ripped apart. None of them had really recovered. She closed her eyes to stifle the angry tears threatening to fall. Then she headed into the house to check on her husband.

"I just hope you are prepared for what you've asked for, Ernest," she mumbled as she entered the house.

Carolyn heard the hissing sound of the oxygen tank even before she reached the doorway to the master suite. She paused, leaned her back against the wall just outside the room, and closed her eyes. Seeing her husband in this weakened state was taking a toll on her. He'd been her everything for so long that she couldn't imagine life without him. Even when he had done things that were contrary to their happiness, Carolyn had still held so much love inside for Ernest. They had met almost forty-two years ago and had been together since.

The day they met, Carolyn, had been working as a server at a posh dinner reception in Idlewild, where she was spending the summer season. She had stepped over to a table full of what she knew were rich people visiting from the city to serve them coffee after their fancy dinner. As she poured the hot drink, her eyes had danced up, and she'd locked eyes with a handsome young man. He had to be the most gorgeous man she'd ever seen in her short eighteen years of living. He was definitely better looking than any boy Carolyn had ever laid eyes on in her tiny Michigan hometown.

Carolyn's perfect caramel face turned red when the beautiful guy cracked a smile at her. His striking grin caused her hands to shake so badly, she'd almost spilled coffee on their table. Carolyn rushed away, embarrassed and scared to death that she might lose her job. It was her first summer season and her first month at the restaurant. In Yates Township, Michigan, there weren't a lot of jobs in those days, and so when Carolyn graduated high school, she knew she would have to try something different. Most of the girls from her town went to work in Idlewild either as waitresses or housekeepers, and Carolyn felt she had won the lottery when she landed a job in a restaurant instead of having to clean someone's house. Losing her job would be a devastating blow.

"Oh my God," she huffed as she rushed toward the servers' area, her heart galloping. Carolyn put down the fancy silver coffeepot, let out the breath she'd been holding, and wiped her sweat-drenched hands on the little white server's apron she wore around her waist.

"You're stupid if you think that city boy was even thinking about you," said a stern female voice.

Carolyn jumped and spun around at the sound of her boss's voice. "Um, no. I . . . I . . . wasn't," she stammered, her eyes wide with fear.

"I saw him smile at you and you look at him with loving eyes. I know that look, girl. That's the kind of cruel shit these little rich bastards do all the time. They try to see how far they can go with you, but they don't really want a poor little server girl. His mama and papa wouldn't even let him toss a nickel at you, much less date you, so just get your head out of the clouds right now," Carolyn's boss said with disgust in her tone. "Keep your head in this here work, so we can get through this night without any mishaps. You want to keep your job, don't you?"

Carolyn shook her head up and down vigorously. "Ye-yes, Ms. Carmen. I . . . I will keep my eyes to the floor from now on," Carolyn assured her, her entire body hot with shame.

"Good. Now it's time to start the cleanup," her boss said, tossing a cleaning chamois in her direction.

Carolyn scrambled to pick up the rag. She was glad to be dismissed from that conversation. She rushed away, ready to work and eager to keep her job.

The gorgeous guy boldly approached her at the end of the dinner reception. Carolyn, being from the country, had no idea who he was. She later found out that everyone who was anyone in Idlewild knew who Ernest Johnson was—the gorgeous and very wealthy son of Bernard Johnson, Chicago's most wealthy black businessman. The Johnsons owned Idlewild's most exclusive club, the Point, and were at the center of the illustrious social scene. It was a well-known fact that Ernest Johnson could have any girl he wanted. Not only was he strikingly attractive, but he was also rich and single, and the opportunities that came his way were abundant. He was twenty-five and number one on the most eligible bachelor list, a fact that was completely lost on Carolyn when Ernest approached her, flashing his perfect smile and displaying the charm of those Prince Charming types that she'd read about in books as a young girl in the South.

Standing together, they looked like the mismatched pair that they were. Carolyn was dressed in a server's outfit, with her dark brown hair drawn into a tight bun and her makeup-free face flushed red. The handsome stranger, on the other hand, looked rich in his custom tuxedo and diamond cuff links. Together they looked like master and servant.

"You are stunning," he said to her. "I'm Ernest. It's so nice to meet you." His smile was electric.

Carolyn felt dizzy, and her legs almost buckled. A whoosh of breath involuntarily left her lungs through her mouth in response to his smooth baritone. She couldn't speak a word. Although she looked like a grown woman, Carolyn was only eighteen years old and had never gone on a date. In that moment, she was overwhelmed by Ernest's beautiful slanted hazel eyes and his neatly trimmed jet-black hair. He reminded Carolyn of a model she'd seen on a billboard. Looking at him made her pulse quicken, so she lowered her eyes, stared down at her feet, and smiled girlishly.

"You probably say that to one hundred girls per day," Carolyn murmured, still avoiding direct eye contact.

"I haven't seen one as beautiful as you in a long time," Ernest replied, using his pointer finger to push her chin up so she was forced to look at him.

Carolyn reluctantly locked eyes with him, and when he smiled, she swore she could feel her heart melting and oozing down her insides. Standing in his presence, Carolyn forgot she was working and might lose her job by fraternizing with the wealthy guests. She forgot everything, and in that moment, she felt like they were the only two people in the large, crowded ballroom. They spent a few more minutes laughing and talking, until Ms. Carmen peeked around the wall separating the servers' area from the reception hall. Ms. Carmen had a powerful gaze that could stop a giant in his tracks.

"Um, I . . . I've got to go," Carolyn said nervously, her words rushing out. She had felt Ms. Carmen's eye slap all too well. She turned and strode away.

"Wait . . . I didn't get your name," Ernest called after her.

She stopped, turned around, and mouthed her name to him, hoping that Ms. Carmen wouldn't catch any of it. Then she turned around again and started walking.

"How do I find you?" he yelled at her back.

Carolyn couldn't turn around to answer, but she dropped something on the floor in her wake. It was a white paper napkin. She could hear his footsteps behind her and hoped he would pick it up. She had quickly scribbled her information down on the napkin. Carolyn didn't see him do it, but Ernest picked up the napkin and pushed it into his lapel pocket.

The next day Carolyn returned to the house she and some friends lived in for the summer season to find a note stuck to the door of the tiny room she rented.

"I paid this month," she grumbled, annoyed to think her landlord was trying to fleece her for extra money again. With her hands shaking, she quickly opened the note. She read it and read it again. She sucked in her breath, flabbergasted.

I can't stop thinking of you. I hope you don't think this is invasive, but I had to find you. Please call. Ernest Johnson. 312-998-4560.

Carolyn rushed through the door and collapsed on her bed, weak with joy. She kicked her legs in the air and squealed. But then Ms. Carmen's words played back in her ears. *That's the kind of cruel shit these little rich bastards do all the time. They try to see how far they can go with you, but they don't really want a poor little server girl. His mama and papa wouldn't even let him toss a nickel at you, much less date you.*

Carolyn's joy quickly faded. She crumpled up the paper and tossed it across her room.

"Ms. Carmen is right. A man like that is totally out of my league," she grumbled aloud, staring up at her dingy off-white ceiling. She sighed and turned onto her side. "When you're poor, you stay poor. The rich stay with their own kind," she said out loud. Those were some of the words her grandmother had told her before Carolyn got in her car to make the drive to Idlewild.

That night, Carolyn fell into a fitful sleep. When she awoke the next day, she had a different thought. She'd decided to call Ernest. When she called, Ernest officially asked her out on a date. Carolyn couldn't believe it. He sounded so excited to hear from her. Even over the phone, Ernest made her feel like the only girl that existed to him.

First, Carolyn felt happy, but immediately after, she became sick with worry about what she'd wear on a date with a rich man. She rummaged through her tiny suitcase, and everything she had looked like rags. Carolyn sighed. Then, against everything she'd ever promised herself, she lifted up her mattress and retrieved the envelope that contained her savings. Her entire life savings was contained in a small, rumpled white envelope. Carolyn sifted through the flattened bills. She flopped onto her bed and stared at the money.

"I could buy a beautiful dress and save the rest," she said out loud to herself. "But to be with him, I will need an expensive dress," she continued. Her mind was a tornado's eye of thoughts. In the end, she rushed out of her room; raced downtown, to a boutique that she had always felt too poor to even look at; and used all her savings to purchase the most beautiful tangerine dress she could find. Carolyn poured every single hour before the time she was scheduled to see Ernest into getting herself beautified. She surprised even herself when it was all said and done.

They went on their first, date and it was magical—dinner at an expensive steak house a million miles out of Carolyn's league, a romantic walk to the lakefront and, finally, a bottle of wine on the sand. Carolyn was smitten. Ernest wanted to know all about her life. He was the first man ever to talk to her without coming across as an old pervert. They spent that first night talking into the wee hours of the morning outside Carolyn's place. He told her he didn't want her to go, but she finally pulled away and went inside.

Ernest was back almost every day. He wanted Carolyn to quit her job, but she refused. He showered her with beautiful gifts. They officially began dating, he called her his woman, and in her mind, he was her man. Ernest made Carolyn feel like she was the only woman in the world. He took her to all of Idlewild's most exclusive invite-only social events and acted as if he was so proud to have her on his arm. People always commented on what a beautiful couple they made. After a summer of dating, Ernest proposed. When he presented Carolyn with his grandmother's ruby and diamond engagement ring, Carolyn almost wet herself. It was so sudden, but Carolyn knew without a doubt.

She jumped into his arms, screaming, "I do! I do!"

"That's what you say at the wedding. Today you're supposed to say yes," he joked.

They embraced and fell over with laughter. Their happiness was palpable. It was like a beautiful rainbow-colored bubble had engulfed them, and they were the only two living inside it. That is, until Ernest brought Carolyn home to meet his parents in Chicago.

Ernest's parents, of course, were not happy with his choice. They would have preferred a rich, cosmopolitan girl for their only son. Their faces literally dropped when Carolyn opened her mouth and out came her distinct Michigan accent, her words slurring together and her vowels drawn out.

"Where did you find her? She sounds like a slave girl from the past," Ernest's mother whispered harshly to him when they had a moment alone.

Ernest, so head over heels in love, quickly put his parents in their place when it came to his new fiancée. Eventually, his parents, defeated by the strength of Ernest and Carolyn's love, relented.

Ernest and Carolyn were married in a traditional ceremony. The wedding took place at the Johnsons' forty-million-dollar mansion in Hyde Park. Over five hundred guests attended the lavish wedding, and only fifteen of them were Carolyn's family friends, mostly people she'd befriended since moving to Chicago. The remainder of the guests she'd never even met. At the time, Carolyn didn't dare complain. She felt like she was living a dream, something far from what she could have ever envisioned for herself. She would never have to go back to the poor Michigan town she grew up in, and when she went back to Idlewild, it would be to vacation on the water, not to wait tables. On all accounts, Carolyn thought she'd walked into heaven, and she never really believed she deserved the kind of life she lived with Ernest. And there were many times when he didn't let her forget it.

"Mrs. Johnson, Desi called. She is close. She stopped a few times and hit some pockets of traffic, so she's a bit delayed," announced Rebecca, the Johnsons' long-time housekeeper, snapping Carolyn out of her reverie. Carolyn hadn't realized she'd been standing there so long, staring into space, remembering. She quickly dabbed at her eyes, lifted her chin high, and turned toward Rebecca.

"I want everything to be perfect for Desi's arrival and Donna's homecoming. It's a lot all at once, but it is what Ernest wants," Carolyn replied, swiping her hands over her face. "Please make sure the caterers are on time. Everything has to be perfect. Her favorite color is blue. The food and cake are supposed to be delivered in two hours. I just . . . ," Carolyn rambled, an edge of nerves apparent in her words.

Rebecca put her hand up. "Mrs. Johnson, I will have everything in order. I know how important these next few weeks are to you and Mr. Johnson," she said with a warm smile, trying to comfort Carolyn.

Carolyn exhaled and thanked Rebecca, then walked into the huge master suite and glanced at her husband, who was lying in bed, helpless. She trusted Rebecca, who'd worked for the family ever since Junior was born. Only Carolyn, Ernest, and Rebecca knew the truth about everything that had taken place over the years. Rebecca knew all the family's secrets. She stepped into the master suite and followed Carolyn around, making sure she didn't forget anything as she got dressed.

"I'll make sure Mr. Johnson is cleaned up by the time everyone gets here," Rebecca assured her as she finished getting dressed.

Carolyn wore a pair of white, wide-legged crepe Versace sailor pants, which complemented her long, slim model-like legs. She shrugged into a short navy-blue Donna Karan blazer to complete her look. Then she grabbed her Hermès Birkin and looked at herself one last time in the long Victorian-style mirror that took up almost an entire wall in the master suite. She was still a knockout, even at sixty-one years old. She had only a few crow's-feet at the corners of her eyes and a few laugh lines, which was nothing compared to her white friends, who had to use fillers to stay looking young. Carolyn ran her hands over her flat stomach and turned sideways to make sure she was fine.

Flat as a board. Perfect.

She smiled at herself and then back at Rebecca.

"Not so bad for a mother and grandmother, huh?" Carolyn asked, posing a rhetorical question.

"Absolutely beautiful," Rebecca answered, praising her employer.

Carolyn smiled. She was still the quintessential kept woman. Through it all, she had managed to keep herself together. As she headed out of the master suite, she stopped and took another look at her husband.

"I just pray what you've asked for is what you really want," she whispered.

With that, she left the room and headed to the front door and the waiting car in the driveway. She was off to fulfill her husband's other request.

Chapter 3

Prodigal Children

People rushed around her, but that didn't distract Carolyn at all. She kept her head up high as she sat on one of the hard wooden seats inside the auditorium of the New Life Rehabilitation Center. Her palms were sweaty, and she couldn't keep her legs from rocking back and forth. Carolyn was clearly out of her element, but she knew she had to be there regardless. She kept telling herself, *It is my duty. This is what Ernest asked for*.

Carolyn looked around at some of the parents there. Most seemed to be well off, just like she was. Carolyn tried not to stare too long, but she couldn't help it. She felt a pang of jealousy when she saw that some of the couples were holding hands and being supportive of each other. Seemingly happy families made her stomach churn. She wished that was her life again.

Damn you, Ernest.

Carolyn shook her head to clear it and tried to focus on why she was there—for her youngest child, Donna. Her third and last child. It had cost them three hundred thousand dollars to get Donna the treatment she needed. This time. This was her fourth stint in rehab, and Carolyn could only pray it was the last. It was an expense neither Carolyn nor Ernest could argue wasn't necessary. Private drug rehabilitation was expensive, but in Carolyn's assessment, there was no amount of money that could keep her from trying to save her daughter, or maybe save face with her friends was more like it.

There was no way Carolyn could stand for any of her socialite friends or any of Ernest's business partners finding out that Donna was addicted to drugs and had been living like a virtual vagabond for the past year. The thought of anyone finding out made a chill shoot down Carolyn's spine. She hunched her shoulders in an attempt to relax, but the dark thought still hovered in her mind. If someone did discover the truth about Donna, it would be like finding out Desiree was pregnant out of wedlock all over again. Or finding out that Junior had begun to dabble in an underworld he had no business dealing in.

Carolyn remembered clearly how devastated she was when she found out their youngest was addicted to heroin. It was Rebecca who'd nervously told Carolyn about Donna's addiction. Carolyn also thought back to how Ernest had screamed at her and had told her it was all her fault that another one of *his* children was an embarrassment to the Johnson name. He had told Carolyn that it was her "trashy" DNA and family lineage that had caused Donna to be such a disappointment. It hadn't been the first time Ernest had used Carolyn's upbringing against her during an argument. He'd also blamed her for Desiree's pregnancy and Junior's arrests. It was all Carolyn's fault if you asked Ernest.

The night Donna was born, Ernest had missed the entire birth—from Carolyn's labor to the minute Donna took her first breath. Carolyn had spent sixteen hours in labor at the UChicago Hospital, and Ernest had never shown up, not even for a minute of it. Both of Ernest's parents had come rushing into Carolyn's private birthing room in a huff after they'd gotten the news that the newest member of the family was about to arrive. They'd left Junior and Desiree with Rebecca at the Hyde Park mansion. Neither of Ernest's parents could explain why their son wasn't around and why Carolyn hadn't been able to reach him when she called. Ernest's parents had long since stopped making excuses for Ernest, because they knew Carolyn wasn't buying it anymore.

Carolyn felt that they were present at the birth only because they secretly hoped they could make sure she didn't get too unhappy and file for divorce from their son. They'd rather die than see Carolyn get any part of their fortune for herself. Carolyn had known for months about Ernest and his philandering. She knew how his parents really felt about her and also how against divorce they were. Carolyn hadn't felt that alone in a room full of people since her days working the restaurant scene in Idlewild. Nurses, Ernest's parents, and doctors circled her, providing for her every need. But no one could soothe the ache of loneliness she felt from Ernest's absence.

After a horrendous labor, Carolyn gave birth to a perfect little girl, her last baby, by cesarean section. She made sure she got her tummy tucked at the same time. She wouldn't have wanted to disappoint Ernest by not keeping herself up—even though she knew that Ernest was stepping out with other women behind her back.

The baby girl was a perfect chubby-faced, screaming bundle of joy. She had Ernest's hazel eyes and prominent chin and Carolyn's long limbs and button nose.

"Let's call her Donna, after her great-grandmother," Ernest's mother said after she had laid eyes on her granddaughter. "Donna Johnson."

Ernest's father agreed, and who was Carolyn to argue with such a powerful patriarch? Whatever the Johnsons wanted, the Johnsons got. Carolyn had learned that the hard way. Still, despite the fact that she physically and mentally exhausted, Carolyn was determined to have a say when it came to her daughter's name. She suggested that they call the baby Donna Bethann Johnson. Carolyn thought it was a fair compromise, given the fact that she had always wanted to name one of her daughters Bethann after her own mother. She had never told the Johnsons of her desires prior to Donna's birth. Instead, she'd let them have full control over naming her other two children.

When Ernest finally showed up at the hospital to see his new baby, he smelled of a woman's perfume and looked like he'd been partying for days. He leaned in to give Carolyn an obligatory kiss, and she turned her face away. It was all she could do to keep from making a scene in front of Ernest's parents and to hide the hot tears that were threatening to spring from her eyes.

Carolyn tried to hold on to the anger and bitterness she felt when Ernest finally came to her bedside, but after witnessing Ernest hold his youngest daughter with such care and sensitivity, and after watching him seemingly fall in love with yet another baby, Carolyn was once again overwhelmed by that old gushy, head-over-heels feeling for Ernest. It was like when they were in Idlewild, falling in love all over again. Carolyn told herself that night in the hospital that for her children and for the sake of her family, she would do anything it took to make them all happy. It was a promise she would endure suffering to keep.

Things were great for a while after Donna's birth. Carolyn felt like she'd finally gotten her husband back. In the beginning, Ernest was a doting father and a caring husband. He showered Carolyn with gift after expensive gift. He told her the gifts were to thank her for giving him his greatest gifts of all—his children. He spent hours holding baby Donna, talking and singing to her. He doted on Junior and Desiree too. So much so that Carolyn grew a little jealous of how much attention Ernest showered on the kids, especially the baby. But once again, Carolyn put her feelings aside and tried to make the best of the situation.

Carolyn saw herself as a mother and a wife. There was no more individual Carolyn. The things she wanted, needed, and liked came secondary in her life. Carolyn spent every waking minute pleasing her children and her husband. She lost herself in meeting the needs of Ernest, Junior, Desiree, and Donna. With the help of the hired hands, of course. At some point, Carolyn grew to resent her life. Each day she would struggle to put on a happy face.

Carolyn felt a sense of security knowing that her children would never want for anything, which was the opposite of her own experience as a child. Just like Junior and Desiree, Donna was a trust-fund baby from birth. She was worth more than some celebrities five times her age before she even turned a year old. Carolyn and Ernest gave her anything she asked for . . . materially anyway. And Papa Johnson, which was what Ernest's father asked to be called, made sure his granddaughter would never have to lift a finger in her life. Just like her siblings, Donna went to private school. She was given dance lessons from the age of two. She had private tennis lessons as soon as she turned five.

Donna was given an allowance of one thousand dollars per week from the time she was thirteen years old. And every year she had a huge, extravagant birthday party, with a guest list of A-list celebrity children. For her Sweet Sixteen, Carolyn flew in dresses from Paris, Milan, and London and threw a party on a yacht that cost more than some celebrity weddings. And once a year Carolyn and Ernest would take Donna and her siblings on vacation to parts of the world their youngest couldn't even pronounce. But as she got older, Donna realized that nothing her parents gave her could replace spending time with them every day or at least having an occasional sit-down dinner with them, like she'd seen families on TV do. Rebecca was the only person who showed up for school meetings, plays, and trips.

Ernest and Carolyn hardly knew anything concrete about their youngest daughter's wants and needs as she got older. Carolyn was too busy keeping tabs on Ernest to notice. After a while, nothing Ernest and Carolyn gave Donna seemed like it was enough. They poured money into any activity she picked up—gymnastics, soccer, synchronized swimming, lacrosse, equestrian sports, golf, polo, and tennis. Donna would grow bored and quit. She had grown spoiled and angry.

By the time she was seventeen, Donna was deep into Chicago's party and drug scene. She fashioned herself as one of the brat-pack socialites from the Gold Coast, the most affluent part of Chicago. After all, she'd grown up with and become best friends with former child stars, the daughters of hotel magnates, and the children of rock stars. Late-night party scenes became her daily life. During those years, unflattering paparazzi pictures of Donna showed up at least two dozen times in *People* and *Us* magazines. When confronted, Donna would scream and throw tantrums. Carolyn had admittedly dropped the ball when it came to paying her youngest daughter the attention she was craving. Carolyn blamed Ernest for it all, and he blamed her in return.

"Mother," a familiar voice called from behind Carolyn.

Carolyn snapped out of her reverie and popped up out of her seat. She cleared away the thoughts of her past life, which had been crowding her mind lately. Carolyn took in an eyeful of her youngest child, who was clearly not a child anymore. She tilted her head and clasped her hand over her mouth. Tears welled up in her eyes immediately when she went to grab for her daughter.

"Oh, sweetheart, you look amazing. This time away has done wonders. I am so proud of you," Carolyn cried, pulling her daughter into a tight embrace. Carolyn felt a warm feeling of relief wash over her. She stepped back and gazed at her daughter for a second. Donna finally looked like someone Carolyn and Ernest could be proud of.

Carolyn hugged and squeezed Donna again. "Thank God," she whispered. She was really thanking God for bringing her daughter back from the brink of death. What would her friends have thought if Donna had succumbed to drug addiction? Carolyn would've suffered the worst embarrassment of her life. Carolyn shook off those worst-case scenarios and tried to relish the moment.

It was a miracle that Donna was even alive. The night Carolyn and Ernest had signed Donna involuntarily into the rehabilitation center, Donna had looked like death warmed over. Her skin had been ghostly pale, and dark rings had rimmed the bottom of her eyes. Donna's dark hair was matted, and her body was gaunt, almost skeletal. She smelled like she hadn't had a bath in weeks, and her clothes, although expensive, were filthy. Donna had been out on a binge for three weeks, and Carolyn and Ernest had been worried sick and had had people out scouring the entire city for her. It had been the first time they'd come together for anything in years, or at least when people weren't around to watch them. Ernest had even hugged Carolyn a few of the nights they'd both sat up worrying about their daughter.

Donna kicked and screamed when she first arrived at the center. She cursed at her parents and told her mother she hated her. She screamed and begged Ernest not to let Carolyn sign her into the center. Donna blamed Carolyn for everything. Carolyn was an emotional wreck that night. She also blamed herself for it all, although she knew it wasn't entirely her fault. Ernest remained cool as a cucumber, as usual. Little did Carolyn know at the time that her husband had already begun his battle with cancer.

"Daddy loves you. Daddy loves you," Ernest repeated to his youngest daughter over and over again that night. He never once defended Carolyn or told his daughter that she needed help. It was something Carolyn filed in her mental Rolodex. The hurt she felt was almost tangible.

All of that was in the past, Carolyn told herself now. Just like all the other hurts she'd suffered at the hands of her children and her husband, Carolyn had swallowed this hurt like it was a hard marble. Seeing Donna now—her cheeks rosy, her body filled out in all the right places, her hair shiny—made Carolyn warm inside. Donna had taken the best of Carolyn's and Ernest's features. She stood almost six feet tall and was built like a runway model. She had long, slender legs, a small waist, and small breasts. Donna had exquisite thick jet-black hair and Ernest's hazel eyes—the only one of their children to inherit them. She had also inherited Carolyn's high cheekbones and perfect nose, and with Ernest's prominent chin, her face was striking. From the time she was a small child, Donna had turned heads everywhere she went. She was more of a showstopper than both of her parents, to say the least.

Carolyn finally relinquished her grasp on Donna and gave her a good once-over. Carolyn smiled wide; she thought her daughter looked perfect. Donna was dressed conservatively in a maroon Donna Karan sheath dress that Rebecca had picked out, a pair of kitten-heeled Jimmy Choos, and a simple cardigan to top off her look. Donna finally looked like a wealthy young woman should. Carolyn was satisfied, but she still couldn't say she was so proud to say that Donna was her daughter. It had always been a struggle to be a mother to Donna. Carolyn squeezed Donna and grabbed for Donna's hand, hoping to get a return show of affection. But Donna impolitely let her arms hang limply at her sides. Carolyn knew right away that her daughter was in rare form . . . as usual. It was the norm for Donna to treat Carolyn like she had no regard for her at all. Still, Carolyn reached out again and took her daughter's hand.

"How's Daddy? Is he really too sick to come?" Donna asked petulantly.

Carolyn released her daughter's hand quickly. She looked at Donna seriously. She wanted to scream in Donna's face and say, "*I* am here for you! Isn't that enough! Isn't anything I do ever enough!" But Carolyn kept her thoughts to herself, and she kept smiling and kept doing what she did best—pretending.

"Oh, Donna, darling, this is your day. Don't worry about him. You look so good, so healthy now," Carolyn replied sympathetically. She cracked a phony smile and hugged her daughter again, hoping they could move off the subject of Ernest. "You are simply stunning. I can't say that enough," she added, flashing her plastic smile again. Nothing seemed to faze Donna.

"I guess you would say I look good *now* since you haven't seen me in nine months. All you have to compare it to is the way I looked when you forced me into this hellhole," Donna replied sharply as she squirmed out of her mother's stifling embrace.

Carolyn felt like someone had slapped her across the face. She inhaled. It was taking all she had to keep it together now. Carolyn ignored the comment. She already felt awful enough about not visiting, but she'd figured that Donna needed time away without the influence of her parents. She also thought her spoiled child would understand about Ernest being sick.

Carolyn had also been afraid that if she visited, Donna would ask her questions about her father's condition, which had steadily deteriorated over the months. Carolyn had always tried to shelter her children from anything negative about their father: sickness, his cheating, his bad business deals . . . everything. But Carolyn's sugarcoating of Ernest's indiscretions had only made her kids see her as the bad guy and Ernest as the hero in their lives. The past nine months had been no different. Ernest had been ailing, and Carolyn had covered it up. Pretending, faking like her life was still picture perfect, had become like a full-time job for Carolyn. But she had reached a point where she could hide Ernest's illness any longer.

"So, are you ready to go home? You must be excited to get back to life. There are so many good things waiting for you. Whatever you want, you can have," Carolyn singsonged, changing the subject while fidgeting with her newly purchased monstrous twelve-carat canary diamond ring. It was one of many things she'd purchased recently. Another thing she did when she was unhappy was making big purchases.

"Yeah, going home. I can hardly wait to get back to that life. I'll see you after the ceremony," Donna droned gruffly before stomping away from her mother.

Carolyn looked around to see if anyone had noticed the strained interaction between them. She smiled weakly at a couple that had been watching. Carolyn's cheeks flamed when she noticed them. She wondered how much of the conversation they had overheard.

"Our children. We have to love them," Carolyn chortled before averting her eyes away from the gawking pair. She turned her face away and dabbed at the tears threatening to drop from her eyes. Even her baby girl hated her.

Carolyn couldn't win for trying. Nothing ever seemed good enough.

Carolyn and Donna's ride from the rehabilitation center was tense and silent. Donna brooded the entire ride, and Carolyn tried to please her, as usual. It was as if a joyous occasion had not just happened. The pomp and circumstance of Donna's rehab graduation had faded quicker than an eclipse of the sun. In an effort to break the silence, Carolyn tried to make small talk about the weather, Donna's clothes, her new cell phone. When that didn't work, Carolyn told Donna how proud she was of her accomplishments—getting clean and sober in nine months, winning an award for her artwork in rehab, and finally getting her GED. Carolyn told Donna that she imagined it hadn't been easy.

Donna ignored her mother, for the most part, though she dropped a vicious insult in response here and there. It wasn't lost on either of them how many times Carolyn's cell phone buzzed and interrupted their tense exchange. After the third time, Donna even raised an eyebrow at her mother and said, "Why don't you stop pretending to be interested in speaking to me and just answer your phone? I already heard that your favorite was coming home. I'm sure you can't wait. I'm sure you have lots of things planned for the two of you."

Carolyn's cheeks flamed at her daughter's comment. "No one of you is more important than the others. I have three children, not just one," Carolyn replied. It didn't make a difference. She was clearly not going to convince Donna. "Why don't you tell me something new about you?" she added.

Donna rolled her eyes and kept her pursed lips shut tight.

"Okay, then, do you want me to tell you what's been going on with me?" Carolyn asked.

Again, Donna rolled her eyes and gave her mother the silent treatment. The stalemate went on for several minutes. Finally, too exasperated to continue practically begging her daughter to talk to her, Carolyn gave up. Donna rudely put her earphones in and turned the volume up so loud, Carolyn could hear every curse word in the lyrics of the rap music her daughter listened to. Donna also took to texting incessantly on her new cell phone, one of the luxuries she had missed while locked up in that place.

Defeated, Carolyn resorted to watching the passing scenery outside the Bentley's darkly tinted windows. She secretly wished she were someplace else. She could think of a million things she would rather be doing than taking her daughter's abuse. Carolyn's mind drifted to things she found pleasurable.

When the car went up the winding road leading to the house, Donna yanked her earphones out of her ears and bolted upright in her seat.

"I'm not going to the summer house. I'm going to Chicago, to the Gold Coast condo," she announced brusquely.

Carolyn's eyebrows shot up, and her pulse sped up. Donna had been practically living alone at their Gold Coast condo when she disappeared and ultimately got herself in trouble. Carolyn didn't think it was a good idea for her to go back to that environment so soon. Carolyn wanted Rebecca to keep an eye on Donna.

"Donna, please," Carolyn said as calmly as she could, given the circumstances. "Your father is asking for everyone to be here. Everyone. He missed you so much. He is looking forward to seeing you. And I want to catch up. You can go to the condo another day." As Carolyn tried to reason with Donna, she touched her daughter's leg gently.

Donna tilted her head and looked at her mother through squinted eyes. The look sent a chill down Carolyn's back. "Please, Mother. Don't start this bull-shit. You don't want to catch up or spend quality time with me. You want to make things good since your prod-igal children are coming home. Junior—the only person who visited me, by the way—already told me Desi was coming," Donna hissed, pushing Carolyn's hand off her knee roughly.

Carolyn snatched her hand back, as if a venomous snake had bitten her. She pinched the bridge of her nose, trying to quell the throbbing that had suddenly started between her eyes. It was starting again already—the hate/hate relationship her kids had with one another. Carolyn often blamed herself for not handling Desiree's situation like it should've been handled back then. Donna had been too young at the time to understand why her sister was sent away, but Carolyn had seen a big change in Donna afterward. Carolyn let out a long breath, which seemed to zap all her energy. Everything seemed to be at an impasse.

Undeterred by her mother's silence, Donna went on. "I don't want to be here. I'm over Idlewild and all your fake friends. I'm sure you have some kind of party planned for your favorite child, but I'm not going to it. I refuse to be like you, like all the people here . . . fucking fake, hiding behind money and designer clothes, all living a big lie." She paused and gave her mother a hard stare. "Now, either you let me go to the city or you get even more embarrassed when I go around Idlewild telling everyone what a wonderful time I had in drug rehab," she spat viciously.

Carolyn coughed, or more like gagged. She felt like Donna had gut punched her. She placed her hand on her chest, shocked by her daughter's outburst. She looked over at her only child, and she swore she could see red flames flickering in Donna's eyes. Pure hatred clouded the girl's face. Carolyn's jaw rocked feverishly, and her pulse pounded. Suddenly everything was swirling around her. She cleared her throat, like she'd done so many times when preparing to speak to Ernest, thinking Donna had grown to be just like her father. Carolyn knew she couldn't let Donna ruin what she had spent years building—the lie that was their life.

"Donna, I have tried and tried. What more do you want me to do? It is not my fault that your father is sick. He asked for you all to be here, and he chose to ask for Desiree specifically to be here, " Carolyn began, steeling herself for more cruelty from Donna.

Donna's face turned bloodred, and her eyebrows folded into a scowl. "I don't care!" she screamed. "Everyone is always making special arrangements for her whenever she decides we are important enough to come around. She abandoned us! She taught her child to hate us! She hates us!"

Donna yanked on the door handle when the house came into view. The driver slammed on the brakes in response. The car screeched to a halt, and Donna scrambled out the door. Carolyn's body jerked forward, then back, and her head slammed into the headrest. Her heart pounded even harder, and her head throbbed.

"Oh my God! Donna!" Carolyn screamed, wincing and holding the back of her head. She opened her car door and hung her head out. "Donna! Wait!" she screamed. Visibly shaken, Carolyn decided against running after her daughter. There was nothing Carolyn could do now. It was too late. And there was but so much she could take. She knew that Donna had been serious when she said she would tell everyone she was in rehab. Someplace deep inside Carolyn, what all her friends thought about her was more important than forcing her daughter to be there.

"Everything all right, Mrs. J?" the driver asked.

Carolyn was terribly embarrassed and equally as flustered. She didn't respond.

"You want me to go after her?" the driver asked, peering at Carolyn through the rearview mirror.

"I'm fine. She's impossible," Carolyn replied, trying to seem lighthearted about the incident but not able to prevent her voice from shaking. "Take me up to the house and come back for her. Take her wherever she wants to go. If she wants to go to the city, let her go to the city," she croaked, her voice shedding the false cheeriness and her words laced with pain and anger. This scenario was better than Donna blowing the whistle on Carolyn's lies and causing a scene when Desiree arrived.

Once the driver reached the front of the house, Carolyn climbed out of the car. She steeled herself for the questions she knew she'd face when she stepped inside her home. Carolyn immediately began constructing more lies in her head. She had become so good at it that it took her no time to think of what she'd tell everyone, including Ernest, about Donna's whereabouts. Carolyn exhaled a windstorm before she entered the house. It was the first time she had acknowledged to herself that she was losing the battle on all fronts, but she had made up her mind that it wouldn't be for long.

Chapter 4

Memories

Desiree's stomach clenched, and she immediately felt like her modest Honda Accord was out of place on the long winding driveway of her parents' Idlewild summer home. The four luxury cars parked along the stone driveway were so much bigger and more expensive than hers, and this made Desiree feel like a pizza delivery person pulling up for a five-minute drop-off.

"Whoa," Tyree exclaimed as they approached the Johnson summer home. "How come this is my first time coming here?" he asked, his eyes stretched wide and his mouth agape. "You've been holding out big-time, Mom. Like, big big-time."

Desiree swallowed hard. "You know I don't do these family gatherings," she groaned. "If I don't come, you don't come. And none of this is mine, so I haven't been holding out on anything."

"I do know you don't do family gatherings, but I'm still trying to figure out why," Tyree responded as he continued to scan his surroundings. "With a dope house like this, I'd gather with my family every day! This right here is baller, for real," he went on, ogling the house and the grounds.

"Boy, just make sure you're on your best behavior. It's one week . . . Let's make it through. Don't do a lot of talking, so I don't have to do a lot of explaining. Got it?" Desiree said, twisting her neck to tamp down her nerves.

"There's a whole lot of stuff you ain't telling me," Tyree grumbled under his breath.

Desiree didn't respond. She knew he had used the word *ain't* to get under her skin, and her skin was already crawling bad enough as it was.

They got out of the car almost at the same time. Before Desiree could fully stretch, Rebecca came barreling toward her, with a huge smile on her face.

Desiree's heart lurched in her chest, and tears immediately sprang to her eyes. The one person she had missed the most all these years was Rebecca.

"Oh my Lord," Rebecca sang, her arms stretched out in front of her. "I cannot believe my eyes," she said, her voice cracking. Rebecca pulled Desiree into her and squeezed her so tight, Desiree had no choice but to return the embrace.

Rebecca had been a part of the Johnson family since before Desiree was born. She had served as everything to the family. She had been the nanny, but she had also kept house, kept Carolyn straight, and assisted Ernest in some things as well. Once the kids had become teenagers, Rebecca had taken on the task of making sure Carolyn's household chores never piled up, especially the cooking. As wealthy as Ernest was, he had never liked to eat out. He preferred Rebecca's home cooking over a fancy restaurant any day. Rebecca still kept things in the house flowing smoothly. She was just a part of their family, period. And she loved Desiree like Desiree was her own child, and in turn Desiree had confided in Rebecca more than she had her own mother.

"Rebecca," Desiree whispered, finally letting her tears fall. "I've missed you so much," she gasped, almost choking on her words. "So much."

Rebecca's body quaked with sobs. Neither of them had been prepared for the rush of emotions that took over them like a tidal wave. As they stood there, seemingly stuck in one another's embrace, memories flooded them both.

Back then, Desiree had almost jumped out of her skin when the soft knocks reverberated through her bedroom door.

"It's me, Desi," Rebecca had whispered.

Desiree had yanked open the door, her heart slamming against her chest wall.

"Did my mother see you leave the house?" Desiree had asked nervously as her stomach did flip-flops.

"No, Desi, I don't think that she did. And now she's gone, I believe, to a hair appointment or something like that. But you know she'll be back soon, and the first place she is coming is right to this room," Rebecca answered, her eyebrows furrowed with worry. She had been doing nothing but worrying since Desiree had taken to hiding out in her room. But now this . . .

"Okay. Did you get it?" Desiree asked, then bit her bottom lip. She was squirming like she had to urinate really badly.

"Yes, I did," Rebecca answered, digging into her pocketbook. "And I didn't like it one bit. Imagine me buying this stuff at my age . . . the stares I got in that store. This is just too much, Desi. Too much," she complained as she pulled a small plastic bag from her pocketbook and extended it toward Desiree. Desiree's hands trembled as she snatched the bag and looked at Rebecca through glassy eyes.

"Oh my God, Rebecca. I can never repay you for this," Desiree said, her voice cracking.

Rebecca twisted her lips and scrunched her eyebrows. It was an expression that was all too familiar to Desiree. She'd seen it over the years: anytime she'd done something Rebecca didn't agree with, that had been the facial expression she got. Rebecca wasn't much on using words to admonish, but her body language, most of the time, said it all.

"Please. Not that face. Not now. Not you," Desiree grumbled, wrapping her arms around herself. "I'm going through enough. And I don't need you, of all people, to judge me, Rebecca. Please . . . not right now, of all the times in my life," Desiree said, tearing up.

Rebecca softened her expression and touched Desiree's hand gently. She hated to see Desiree cry. Rebecca still thought of Desiree as her little girl. She had basically raised Desiree and all the Johnson children.

"I'm not one to judge you, you know that. God is the only one who can judge you. But if this is so, you can't hide it. I won't help you hide it," Rebecca said softly. "I'll be here for you, no matter what, but I want you to think about this long and hard. You are not married. You're a little girl, and you have so much living to do, Desi."

"It was a mistake. I know everyone will hate me, but I'm not perfect. It was a big mistake," Desiree sobbed, lowering her eyes. She hated it when Rebecca was disappointed in her. When she was a child, the idea of letting Rebecca down was the one thing that could be used to punish Desiree.

"Oh, Desi, I don't mean to be hard, but you know right from wrong. You are better than this. I taught you better than this," Rebecca said sternly, but with the hint of softness only she knew how to master. Desiree looked down at the floor. Rebecca grabbed her into a tight embrace, her ample bosom providing a cushion. She squeezed Desiree close. "I will always love you, no matter how many mistakes you make," Rebecca whispered in her ear.

Desiree let out more loud sobs. "I hope it comes back negative," she whimpered into the material of Rebecca's shirt.

"For the good of everyone involved, I hope it does too," Rebecca said with feeling.

Desiree was scared to face Rebecca when the scandal broke, but Rebecca was the only person she could trust with her true feelings. Rebecca told Desiree the truth about how she felt about her pregnancy, but right after that, Rebecca hugged her tight and told her it would be all right.

"Ahem." The sound of Tyree clearing his throat jolted them out of their reveries.

"Oh my goodness," Rebecca exclaimed, finally letting Desiree out of her grip. "I'm sorry. I just . . . I didn't know how much I've missed you."

Desiree giggled awkwardly, trying to squelch her sobs. "I know, right? I missed you so much . . . and the food . . . oh goodness, the food," Desiree joked, trying to break the heartbreak and tension of the moment.

"Don't worry. I'll feed you well," Rebecca assured her, wiping her own tears away too.

"Ahem." Tyree cleared his throat again, his foot tapping the ground.

Desiree and Rebecca both turned their attention to him this time. Rebecca's eyes welled up again.

"This baby has grown up so nicely," she sang, rushing toward him. She pulled him to her. "Goodness, the last time I saw you, you were knee high to a fly," she joked.

Tyree smiled awkwardly, crushed by her tight hug. He didn't remember Rebecca; that was how small he had been the last time Desiree took him home.

"He's a tall beanpole now," Desiree said, smiling proudly at her two favorite people in the world. She wished they had been together all the time. Rebecca would've been great at helping her raise and take care of Tyree. Desiree was sure of it. Rebecca would have been the best grandnanny in the world. The thought tickled Desiree somewhere close to her heart.

Rebecca let Tyree go and grabbed Desiree's hand. "You need to come inside, get settled, and go see him," she said, lowering her voice.

"How's he doing?" Desiree asked, her voice barely above a whisper.

"Well, I won't say. I'll let you go see him," Rebecca said, hanging her head slightly. Desiree's stomach lurched.

"That bad, huh?" she replied.

Desiree paused at her father's bedroom door. She looked down the long hallway and realized she was really alone. She hadn't been alone with her father in years. Her neck tensed, and she clenched her teeth so hard, pain shot up to her temples. Desiree blew out a windstorm of breath and opened the door. Her eyes went wide and she sucked in her breath at the sight of her father lying in a hospital bed, connected to what seemed like a million wires. The blips and beeps of the fifteen machines sounded uncomfortably loud to Desiree. She couldn't stop the tears from pouring out of her eyes and down her face.

"Oh, Daddy," she whimpered, slowly moving to his bedside. "I'm so sorry."

Finally, she was close enough to touch him. She reached down and picked up his limp, wrinkled hand. Desiree hiccupped a sob and her shoulders fell forward as she took in the sight of the man who had always been her first love.

"Daddy," she sobbed out, slowly pronouncing each syllable.

His gaunt body seemed swallowed up by the bed, and he looked as if he'd aged two hundred years since she'd last seen him. His head was covered with fine gray peach fuzz, and his cheekbones jutted against his paper-thin skin unnaturally. He was nothing like the tall, barrel-chested, regal man who was Ernest Johnson, her father, her hero, and sometimes her worst nightmare.

"I'm so sorry, Daddy. I never wanted to disappoint you," Desiree cried, pulling her father's hand up to her face. Then she knelt at his bedside, put her head down at his side, and closed her eyes. She couldn't stop the memories, both good and bad, from revisiting her again.

Fifteen-year-old Desiree had lain curled up in the fetal position inside her bedroom at the Idlewild summer home for over a day. She'd been there since the devastating meeting took place between her parents and Tyson Blackwell's parents the day before. Unable to stop reliving the worst moment of her life over and over again, Desiree had drawn all the curtains, locked her door, and buried herself under a pile of quilts, even though it was ninety degrees outside. She kept replaying his words, their words, everyone's words as they spoke about her like she was some street whore who had sought to trap Tyson. Tyson had warned her, but she had never thought they'd treat her like that, especially her own father.

Since she had revealed that she was pregnant, her mother had tried to be supportive, but her father hadn't said two words to her. Desiree had been his little girl, innocent in all rights, before this. She couldn't even imagine what her father must think of her now. The thought made Desiree cry even harder as she lay on her bed. She was literally sick to her stomach over this.

Carolyn and Desiree had sat together that first night, as Desiree had cried her eyes out over how stupid she'd been to think it was all going to work out with Tyson. She had believed him when he said he wanted to be with her no matter what. Desiree hadn't ever thought about pregnancy, their family names, and Tyson's future or her own while she was wrapped up in their teenage love.

She had been young, dumb, and in love for the first time. Desiree had become the talk of Idlewild, and she knew it.

As she lay on her bed, she realized that it wouldn't be long before the news traveled home to Chicago, where her family would head once the summer ended and everyone closed up their Idlewild hideaways and went back to their high-priced stone mansions on the edge of Lake Michigan. The thought of what people in Chicago would say about her caused Desiree to shudder and gag. *Loose girl, slut, unworthy* were only some of the monikers Desiree imagined people would call her after her pregnancy was revealed.

She had ignored a bunch of calls from friends and family members who had heard about everything through the Idlewild grapevine. Desiree had ignored every single call. Especially since not one call had come from Tyson himself. After Mrs. Blackwell had all but called Desiree a future-ruining slut, Tyson had locked eyes with Desiree and mouthed that he was sorry, but Desiree didn't believe him. She had seen the look on his face when his mother had called her a slut. His eyes had gotten glassy, and his mouth had turned downward. But still, he hadn't spoken up. In that moment he had reminded Desiree of a scared little boy, not the man he'd always promised her he would be.

And Desiree had noticed the pain and conflict in his eyes. She'd gotten a funny feeling that maybe this wasn't the first time Tyson had done something like this. Desiree was devastated by the thought that she was nothing more than another one of his conquests. She had known all along that she was playing with fire by messing with a gorgeous and popular guy like Tyson, but the attraction she had felt for him was so magnetic that she'd lost sight of the consequences. Now, safely ensconced in her bedroom, she tried to erase all thoughts of Tyson, but it was useless. It was all too much to deal with. She wanted to bury her head and never come back out, but then something suddenly got her attention.

A knock on her bedroom door drew Desiree up off her bed. She padded over to the door, barely wanting to pick up her feet. Her usually vibrant face was drained of color. Her always perfectly coiffed hair had turned into a tangled bird's nest atop her head, her eyes were red from crying, and she could surely use a shower. Wrapped in a soft pink chenille robe, she swallowed hard and exhaled as she put her face close to the door.

"Who is it?" Desiree called out from behind the locked door. She was silently praying it wasn't her mother again.

Carolyn had been driving Desiree crazy with her efforts to cheer her up and get her out of bed. Carolyn had even offered her a day at the spa, car shopping, and shoe shopping, which Carolyn knew were some of Desiree's favorite pastimes. Desiree had refused all her mother's offers. She couldn't imagine going out in public right now. The thought made her cringe and feel nauseous. There was no way Desiree could deal with her mother right now.

"It's me, Rebecca," a soft, melodic voice whispered in return. Desiree could tell from the muffled sound of her voice that Rebecca had her face up against the door.

Desiree's shoulders slumped with relief. She was glad it wasn't her mother, for a change. She unlocked the door and twisted the doorknob. She opened the door a crack and looked out in the hallway suspiciously. Then Desiree grabbed Rebecca's arm and pulled her through the doorway and closed the door again. Desiree locked the door behind them. Though she was nervous as hell, she was glad to see Rebecca.

"Thanks for not bringing my mother with you, Rebecca," Desiree said, on the brink of tears for the fifth time that day.

Rebecca's eyes were wide with fear, like she'd committed a crime. She swiped sweat from her forehead and let out a long, pained sigh. Rebecca had prayed all the way to Desiree's room. Desiree could tell something was off. One thing Rebecca was not was a good liar.

"I need to tell you something, Desi," Rebecca said. "First, let me just say, they love you . . . no matter what they're feeling right now." She wiped at invisible sweat again. "I'm sure they just want what is best for you, Desi. I'm sure," she added, fanning at her face.

"Just say whatever else you have to say," Desiree snapped, feeling as if she might throw up.

"They . . . they want you to go to your mother's private doctor and take care of it," Rebecca said, shame making her cheeks flame.

"No," Desiree rasped, feeling as if the word had lit her mouth on fire as she uttered it.

"Listen, Desi—" Rebecca began, putting her hands up in front of her, but Desiree cut her off.

"No!" she barked. "It's my body and my baby! I won't do it!" Desiree brushed past Rebecca, stormed out of her room, and stalked toward her parents' suite. Rebecca was hot on her heels, but she couldn't catch up, because Desiree was moving so fast.

Carolyn jumped and turned on the balls of her feet when Desiree barged into her bedroom suite. Ernest looked over his wife's shoulder at his daughter.

"I'm not getting an abortion," Desiree blurted, and she immediately felt like a weight had been lifted from her chest. She would never be able to live with herself if she didn't at least get that off her chest. Desiree believed the life of her baby was sacred. She believed that the baby deserved to live, and whatever she had to endure, alone or not, she would endure.

Carolyn shook her head and looked at Rebecca for help. Rebecca shrugged; she had never believed in abortions herself. She had suffered the loss of her only child before she started working for the Johnsons. Rebecca had also seen the psychological pain Carolyn had suffered when she miscarried at least four times between the births of her three children.

Ernest stepped forward. "You think you can have a baby out of wedlock with a boy who doesn't want anything to do with you?" he asked in the serious, businesslike, unloving way he sometimes spoke to his children.

Desiree swallowed hard and swayed on her feet when she registered the disgust in her father's tone.

"No one wants to see you in pain and hurt. And the child . . . What type of life would the child have with no father?" Carolyn said, continuing where her husband had left off, not caring to choose her words wisely.

"You can't stay here with a baby out of wedlock, and that's final," Ernest said sternly and dismissively all at the same time. "We have the family name to consider, and we've worked hard to maintain it. This is not what we do."

"So, you'd throw me on the street?" Desiree asked indignantly, scared to death of her father's response.

"Why can't we all sleep on this and talk about it tomorrow?" Rebecca interjected, as if this was her last chance to keep the peace.

"There will be no more discussion about this after today. Either she does what we have asked or she leaves. Period," her father said without blinking or flinching.

Carolyn gasped and looked between her husband and her daughter, pain evident on everyone's faces.

Desiree felt her chest swelling and heat rising to her face. Her cheeks flamed red as she bit her bottom lip, drawing her own blood, before she spoke.

"You have made your choice! That's how it is?" she muttered. She put her hands on her face, in mock surprise. "Oh, no, not the precious Johnson name. There is no way I can have this baby and bring shame to my family, right?" she mocked through her tears. Then her tone turned serious, and she narrowed her eyes into slits. "I guess what people think is more important than me and what I want. I get it!"

Her father didn't budge, his arms folded across his chest and his face stoic. Her mother sobbed but didn't take up for her.

"My mother won't even stand up for me," Desiree growled through clenched teeth as she gave Carolyn an evil look. Then she turned toward Rebecca. "I guess *you're* the only person who truly cares about me!" Desiree screamed.

Rebecca shook her head from side to side helplessly.

"Well, then, you're the only one I'll ever care about from this day forward too," Desiree said with finality. She just wanted the day to be over. She wanted to get away from around her father's judgmental words and disproving eyes. "I guess this is good-bye," she said to her mother.

Carolyn grunted and began mouthing a silent prayer. That was it! Desiree couldn't hold back anymore when it came to her mother's hypocrisy. There was but so much she could take.

"Oh my God, Mother! Praying now! You, of all people. You can't be serious! First, you were trying to convince me to kill my baby, and now you're praying for me! I don't need all your Jesus talk! I thought you would understand and be supportive!" Desiree barked, on the verge of tears again.

Her emotions had been all over the place lately. No one could imagine how she felt being pregnant by a boy who had been a family friend for years, on top of the entire world knowing about it. Desiree was annoyed that her mother was giving her such a guilt trip after promising her that she'd be supportive. Desiree didn't believe in abortion. And although she knew that she had her entire future ahead of her, and having a child under these circumstances was just not how she had pictured her life ending up, she had to protect her baby. Deep down inside, Desiree knew that her parents would probably accept the child eventually, but Desiree wanted her first child to be the joy of her parents' life . . . not a shameful embarrassment. Desiree's mind raced with all these things.

Rebecca fell silent after Desiree's outburst. She knew all too well how tenacious Desiree could be when she was upset. She followed Desiree back to her bedroom.

"Desi, this will blow over. I promise," Rebecca said, trying to comfort Desiree.

But she was wrong. The next morning, Rebecca was the one to break the news that Ernest and Carolyn had arranged for her to take Desiree away. They didn't even come to see her off.

An eerie silence enveloped the interior of the luxury car as it whizzed down the highway, probably going well over the speed limit. Even the sparkling afternoon sun couldn't change the dreary, almost funeral-like mood that hung over the car. Rebecca cleared her throat, breaking the heavy awkwardness that surrounded her and Desiree. Desiree put her hand up to silence Rebecca before she could start. It was all she could do to keep herself from screaming, crying, yelling and, worse, jumping out of the moving car in protest. Desiree shot Rebecca a glance out of the side of her eye and gripped the door handle tighter, so tight her knuckles paled.

Please don't let her start up again. I really don't feel up to this. Why is she staring at the side of my face like she wants to say something? Please just keep your mouth shut, Rebecca. I'm not in the mood, Desiree thought. She was having a hard enough time coping with the situation.

Desiree had thought Rebecca, of all people, wouldn't judge her and would just give her the support she needed at a time like this. Desiree could feel the heat of Rebecca's gaze on her even more intensely. She just wanted the driver to pull the car over and let her push Rebecca right out the door on the side of the damn road. Desiree kept her eyes forward and flexed her jaw in anticipation. Rebecca looked at the side of Desiree's face one more time before she finally mustered up the courage to speak. Desiree braced herself.

"Desiree, your father is a man of very few words, you know that, right? I mean, maybe you can forgive him one day. Find it in your heart to understand him as a parent. I don't know . . . something . . . ," Rebecca said. "I . . . I just want everything to be normal again. I just wish this had never happened." Rebecca squeezed a tissue in her hand. There. She'd finally said what she had been thinking for the past week.

Desiree remained silent.

Rebecca let out an exasperated breath. "You hear me talking?" she asked softly, being careful not to nag. She could feel the heat of Desiree's gaze fall on the side of her face. Rebecca knew she was stepping on sensitive ground with Desiree.

"I'll never speak to him again. He threw me away like trash, and I'll never speak to him again. I don't care if he's on his deathbed. Don't call me," Desiree said with feeling.

The thought of her father's deathbed snapped Desiree out of her thoughts. She jumped at someone's touch. The memories of the past quickly faded as she looked over at her mother now.

"Hey, baby girl," Carolyn whispered, rubbing her hand up and down Desiree's back.

"Mother, why didn't you call me home sooner?" Desiree croaked, her red-rimmed eyes barely able to focus on her mother's face.

"For a while he didn't want anyone to know. He was dealing with a lot," Carolyn said, lowering her eyes to the floor.

"But I would've come sooner. I feel like it's . . . it's . . ." Desiree's words trailed off, and she sucked in her sobs.

Her mother pulled her into a tight embrace. "Shh. He's going to make it through this. He's the strongest man we know," Carolyn said, doing what she did best—pretend.

Chapter 5

Is This Love?

Junior let out a series of animalistic grunts as his newest sexual conquest, Bella, roughly bounced up and down on his dick. Bella had skills, that was for sure.

"Shit!" Junior belted out as he felt himself reaching a climax. Junior had never had such earth-shattering sexual experiences before he started seeing Bella. Just as he let out another series of passion noises, Bella leaned up a little and balanced her weight on her shapely legs. With one hand, she swiped her sweat-drenched locks of long auburn hair from her face.

"Is it good? Is it the best?" Bella panted, her thick Colombian accent making her seem to Junior like she'd just walked out of heaven.

"Oh! Oh! Oh!" Junior screamed as his body quaked all over.

Bella smiled, and then it was her turn.

"I guess it was good," Bella said, satisfied, as she looked down into Junior's smiling face.

"Damn, baby. You have no idea," Junior panted as his body began to relax. Bella eased off Junior and flopped next to him on the bed. They were both winded and satisfied.

"I've needed that all week. I couldn't wait to sneak away from all the crap I have going on," Junior said, still reeling from the explosive orgasm.

Bella laughed. "Glad I could help," she told him, her accent making her words sound heavy but sexy as hell.

She turned on her side and stared at Junior's profile. Then she reached up and moved a cluster of sweat-drenched strands of hair from her forehead. Junior placed his hand over Bella's, halting her movement. He inhaled deeply and brought Bella's hand to his lips. He closed his eyes and kissed the top of her hand as he clutched it close to his face.

"You're so sweet," Bella commented.

Her beauty, her melodic voice, and the accent made Junior's heart flutter. He was falling in love . . . a dangerous idea for someone like him. Junior had been hurt before, and he'd vowed that women would just be for his own personal pleasure and nothing more. But here he was, totally smitten with this woman.

"No. *You* are so sweet, and you have no idea how much I appreciate you," Junior told her with sincerity.

He meant every word. His trysts with Bella had come just in time. Moments spent with Bella had been the one thing that had saved Junior from going off the deep end when he found out that his father was dying and possibly wanted to make his sister Desiree his heir. It was a betrayal that had cut so deep, Junior had contemplated putting a pillow over his father's face before anything could be set in stone.

Bella had changed Junior's mind. When he'd met her, Junior had decided he would work slowly and methodically to get what he wanted. If his family believed he was distracted by a beautiful woman, they would all let their guard down, enabling him to work on things in the background. After all, Junior considered his meeting Bella as fate anyway. It was the one time he hadn't pursued a woman and the woman hadn't been some moneygrubbing groupie. Everything had happened so organically. To Junior, this was a clear indication that they were meant to be.

Junior had been storming through the lobby of the Gold Coast building that housed the Johnson family's condo when he ran smack-dab into Bella—literally.

"Oh shit! I'm so sorry!" Junior had exclaimed when he realized the cup of hot black coffee the beautiful stranger was carrying had spilled all over her white shirt. "Please. Let me pay for your shirt. I . . . I can buy you ten new shirts," he had rambled as he used his bare hands to wipe the coffee off the completely ruined shirt.

Bella had grabbed his hands, stopped him, and smiled at him. Her smile had given Junior pause, and he had had no choice but to stare into her eyes. Junior had felt something inside him move. It was like nothing he'd felt before in his life.

"It is okay. This shirt is old," Bella said, waving her hand like it was nothing and flashing a gorgeous smile.

"Well, at least let me buy you another cup of coffee," Junior said. He blushed, and fine beads of sweat lined up at his perfectly straight hairline. No other woman had ever made him flush like that.

"This was already my second cup," Bella replied, winking. "It is okay. Really. I am fine. Maybe I needed to throw out this old shirt. With clothes this white, it was like I was asking for it," she joked, her accent making the situation all the more amusing.

They both burst out laughing.

"I'm Bella," she said, introducing herself, as she extended her hand toward Junior.

"That's a pretty name for a pretty lady," Junior replied, feeling something in places he shouldn't have. Bella was perfect. Perfect skin. Perfect teeth. Perfect eyes. Perfect hair. Most of all, perfect timing.

"Junior, um, I mean Ernest . . . Ernest Johnson, Jr.," Junior added sheepishly as he wiped his wet, coffee-stained hands on his pants and accepted Bella's invitation for a handshake. Junior's head swirled with all sorts of thoughts. He had a lot going on at the time, but for just one minute, it all stopped. Time seemed to stand still in Bella's presence.

"I like that name. Ernest. Sounds like a strong name," she complimented, flashing the most gorgeous smile Junior had ever seen.

Looking at her beautiful green eyes, shoulder-length auburn hair, and perfect facial bone structure made Junior feel flushed again. He knew Bella was much younger than he was, but she still made him feel tingly inside, like he had a middle-school boy crush. "Where are you from? I mean . . . the accent?" Junior asked, still wearing a goofy, coy smile.

"I am from Colombia," she told him.

Junior was immediately intrigued. Colombia had a reputation for having beautiful people and dangerous streets. It was one of the places Junior hadn't traveled to. It was, however, now on his to-go list. He loved the idea of being with an exotic woman like Bella. He knew right then and there he wouldn't let her get away that easily.

"Wow. I've always wanted to visit Colombia," Junior said honestly, smiling at Bella again.

It ended up being the beginning of an hour-long conversation. Junior agreed to walk up the street and rebuy coffee for Bella. That first impromptu date led to their next meeting three days later. It was instant sexual attraction. They ended up at the Drake Hotel. Once inside the room, their attraction was animalistic. Junior hadn't had sex in close to two months, and he damn near attacked Bella. He forced his mouth on top of Bella's, and their tongues did a wicked dance with one another. Junior hoisted up her skirt and fingered her hot box. Bella gasped at his touch. They kissed passionately until they finally stumbled over to the bed. When Junior entered her, he let the worries of the world fall away from his mind. Bella took him to places he'd been dying to go for years. Something inside him sparked anew, and he knew it wouldn't be the last time he saw Bella. Still, Junior fucked Bella like he might not ever see her again.

In the months following their first date, Junior and Bella's agreement became a two-sided sort of "friends with benefits" deal. Junior paid Bella's living expenses and bought her expensive clothes. In return, she gave Junior the attention he craved, hot sex, and the satisfaction of knowing he was more powerful around Bella than anywhere else. Junior felt a sense of overwhelming power knowing he was spending his father's money the way he wanted to spend it.

Bella told Junior that she was a struggling part-time print-ad model, and that when she made it big, she'd pay him back every dime of the money he spent on her. It wouldn't be a small feat, because Junior spared no expense on his new lover. Junior didn't care about the money. The way he saw things, Bella helped him regain control of his own life, which he'd lost to his father's demands over the years, and more importantly, Bella made him feel he was finally his father's equal as the man of their family. It was a win-win situation for both of them. At least that was what Junior thought. He was happier than he'd been in a long while. But yet again, his happiness depended on the feelings of another person.

"Where are you going?" Bella asked now, as she watched Junior climb out of the bed. She wasn't expecting him to be able to move a muscle after their hot lovemaking session.

Junior smiled. He loved that Bella made him feel wanted. That was a first for him. In the past, he had usually wanted to fuck and run from the women he was with. "I have to go back to Idlewild. My mother is expecting me at our family's annual all-white affair this evening. If I don't show up, inquiring minds will want to know what happened to me," Junior explained, clearly disappointed. He walked back over and stroked Bella's hair. "I wish I could stay with you forever," he confessed.

She pulled him back on top of her. "You can do whatever you want. C'mon, stay longer with me," she said, her expression like that of a sad puppy dog.

Junior smiled again. He had never felt so wanted in his entire life. Bella gave him purpose these days. "I wish I could stay longer. This happens to be one night I just can't miss. It'll be interesting, to say the least," he said vaguely.

Junior hadn't been home since Desiree and Donna returned. He couldn't lie to himself. He was anxious to see how things would play out. He also didn't want to miss the occasion and allow all the Chicago and Idlewild elite who would be in attendance to think there was anything amiss in his family. Not yet at least. Over the years, Junior had been the Johnson kid who was the least interested in pretending the family was perfect.

"What does that mean? You can't miss it, because . . . ," Bella said seriously, looking Junior in the eyes.

He pushed himself up and grabbed the hotel robe from the end of the bed and wrapped his body with it. He walked over to the lounge chair and flopped down. "Look, Bella, I've never really told you everything about me. Of course, you know I'm a businessman, and I have sisters and parents, but my life . . . it's . . . it's complicated," he said gravely, his eyes downcast.

Bella had her head propped up on one hand, and her shapely body and perfect breasts were on display. "So tell me," she urged. "Your family . . . they have a lot of money, no? What problems can that possibly be? In this country doesn't money solve every problem?" She stared at Junior intently.

Junior ran his hands over his shiny bald head. He didn't know how much he should be telling his lover, but he knew he felt so close to Bella that he wanted to pour his heart out about his father, his mother, his sisters, the business dealings . . . everything.

"My father runs his own investment company, Johnson Trading. He is an investment guru to the stars," Junior replied hesitantly. "His father, my grandfather, made money by investing in Idlewild from the beginning. He was one of the people to open the first club in the resort community, the Point. After he made money from his own investments, he decided to expand by helping other people invest their own money. And then my father took over." He shook his head, like he'd already said too much, especially given what he knew was going on with his father right now. "But there is like a lot more to his business dealings."

"Wow. He sounds like a powerful guy," Bella replied, sitting up straighter in the bed. She seemed more interested now. "Big investment banker. Nothing like me. A struggling model," she quipped, smiling, to lighten Junior's changing mood. She quickly realized that she couldn't seem too interested, or it might scare Junior out of talking about his father and his business dealings.

"No. Not a banker. An investor. He's like a fund manager. And believe me, you're better off than he is on any day. Money isn't everything," Junior shot back.

He exhaled, stood up, and slipped into his pants. He'd said too much. As he put on his clothing, he could feel the heat of Bella's gaze on him. Junior needed to clear his head. He shook his head from side to side in an attempt to pull himself together. Then he turned toward Bella, wearing a fake smile.

"I have to go. Are you all right for money? I have something for you," Junior said all in one breath, his words rushed. He picked up his wallet from one of the nightstands. He began digging in his wallet for the gift he'd gotten Bella before they'd met up the night before. It was just like any other time. He wanted to give Bella anything she asked for, not because he had to, but because he wanted to.

Bella sucked her teeth and rolled onto her back. "I don't want to keep taking things from you, Ernest. I really like you, just for you," Bella admonished.

"It's the least I can do," Junior replied mindlessly. He immediately regretted the words as soon as they left his mouth. He could see the look on Bella's face and could tell he'd said the wrong thing. "Bella, I didn't mean it that way," Junior said.

But Bella had already hopped out of the bed and headed into the bathroom. She slammed the door behind her. Junior flinched at the sound. He felt hot all over with anxiety. He couldn't afford for Bella to be mad at him now. She was his only outlet. His family hated him, but Bella couldn't. That would be too much to bear.

"Bella! Please don't be mad. I'm sorry. You know that I really enjoy our time together. I didn't mean it that way," he called from the other side of the door.

"I guess you can leave your payment on the nightstand, if that is what I mean to you. Like a prostitute!" Bella yelled back.

"I'm sorry. I really didn't mean it that way. Please come out and speak to me. Please, I can't have you mad at me too," Junior pleaded, hammering his fist on the door.

Bella slowly opened the door. They locked eyes.

"I want to know everything about you, Ernest. Your life, your family, what has you so stressed out about your father. I will no longer sleep with a stranger," Bella demanded, grabbing him roughly and forcing her tongue between his lips. After a long passionate kiss, they melted against one another. Junior's heart was bursting in his chest. It was something he'd never experienced in his life. He knew then he might be in love, in real love.

"I will tell you everything. Just don't ever leave me," he whispered desperately.

"I won't. I promise, I won't," Bella replied.

Chapter 6

Haunting Grounds

Donna had spent her entire first night out of rehab alone at her parents' condo. Everything inside the condo was different. Her parents had redecorated. Donna was sure that had been her mother's doing. That she was trying to rid the place of Donna's past drug use was probably what her mother had told herself while she had the condo totally made over. The unfamiliar surroundings had made Donna depressed. She didn't know why she'd gone there to be alone when she knew that what she really craved was to be around her family, the old version of her family. The version of her family that had existed *before* her sister was banished from her home, sent away from them all.

That night Donna had toyed with the idea of calling her sponsor from the rehab and speaking up about how desperately alone and abandoned she felt. How useless and neglected she felt because her sister Desiree was returning to reclaim her spot as the golden child. Donna had picked up her phone several times to call, but in the end, she'd decided against it. It would make her look weak, like she couldn't handle being back in society without falling apart, she had reasoned. The loneliness had gotten to be too much to bear. Donna had decided she wouldn't spend another night like that.

The next night Donna pushed her way to the front of the line outside the Racine nightclub—one of her old haunts from her wild party scene days. It seemed like ages since she'd been at the club. She'd been gone for a little over nine months. Not even a whole year. But nine months away was like years in the party world. Things changed so fast, even the clothing trends. So now everything looked so different that Donna felt so out of place, like she was in a foreign land. But she was confident that the club bouncers would recognize her as the VIP that she once was and allow her to skip the long line that wrapped around the front of the building. Maybe *confident* was too strong a word to use, Donna decided. She was *hopeful* the bouncers would recognize.

"Excuse me. Excuse me," Donna huffed as she jostled her way through small and large clusters of bodies—different groups of friends huddled together, waiting to get inside. She surely wasn't used to that. Waiting in line with the general public wasn't something she had done back when she lived the fast life. She'd had money, influence, and popularity. She was so lost in thought, she ran right into someone.

"Um, sorry . . . um, excuse . . . ," Donna mumbled.

"Hey, bitch! Watch where you're going! There is a god-damned line, you know!" barked a girl with green hair, black lipstick, and safety pins for earrings, drawing angry murmurs from other impatient partygoers on the line.

Donna ambled forward, stumbling a little bit. Her eyes were wide, like those of a lost puppy. She realized she had never visited the club unless she was high out of her mind. She had never known what the crowd was really like there. Being sober was definitely sobering. Donna wished she had something to take the edge off. She hung her head and walked faster through the crowd. Her mind raced. She realized that she'd never been to any of the clubs in Chicago sober. Everything had always been a blur, even the potential dangers out there. Being clean was opening her eyes to an entirely different world than the one she was used to.

When she finally reached the front of the line, the giant, 350-pound bouncer at the door did not recognize her. He looked like a mountain compared to Donna. There was nothing small on the man at all. His arms looked like two tree trunks, and his neck like a thick side of beef. He was surely going to be an obstacle. Donna wasn't used to obstacles. Things had generally come easy to her or had been given to her due to her family name, influence, and money.

"Shit," she mumbled, her pulse quickening, as she took a really good look at the bouncer. She pulled out her cell phone and dialed the number she'd been calling incessantly for the past twenty-four hours. *Maybe he will answer this time. I hope he answers this time*, she said to herself as she listened. But she got the same result she'd gotten all last night and today. No answer. Voicemail box full. Her shoulders slumped.

"Hey! You! This look like a place for you to stand and make a call?" the bouncer barked. With his double chin and dark, hairy face and deep-set eyes, he resembled a grizzly bear. He was scary as hell.

Donna blinked rapidly, her heart thundering in her chest. This was her chance. It was be brave now or never. She swallowed the lump that had formed at the back of her throat. A strong desire gave her imaginary courage and propelled her forward.

"Um, do you know . . . ? Um, can you get Tommy for me? Can you tell him Don . . . um . . . Donna is outside to see him?" Donna stammered, her tongue seemingly not cooperating with her brain. Donna hated feeling like a scared little girl. Being sober fucking sucked. Had she been high, she would've had the confidence to march right up to that fucking monstrous bouncer and demand she be let into the club. She might have even been "drug courageous" enough to slap his ass. Not now. Donna had nothing in her system that could bring her old Donna back. She hated it.

The bouncer scrunched his eyebrows and flexed his neck. He looked down at Donna like she was crazy. "I look like an errand boy to you? Get the hell out of the front of my line. You want to get inside to see Tommy, you get to the back of the line like everybody else," the bouncer spat, dismissing her.

Doesn't he know who I am? I am Donna Johnson, the sister of Ernest Junior and the daughter of Ernest Johnson! Donna screamed inside her head. Her father and brother weren't powerful names just in Chicago; they threw their weight around all over. She'd used her affiliation a million times to get what she wanted, but not tonight. The frustration felt like a large hand choking her neck. She could feel tears welling up at the backs of her eyes.

Donna didn't know what to say next. She stepped closer to the door, her teeth chattering because she was so angry. She tried to dial the number again, but her hands were trembling too badly. She needed a hit, a pill, anything to take the fucking edge off. Now that she was out of the safe environment of rehab, all her desire for drugs was back. The cravings had returned the minute she walked into her parents' condo. That was the reason she'd come out tonight, to fight the urges. *Yeah, right.* Who was she fooling? She'd come out to see the person she'd longed for the entire time she was gone.

"What? You can't hear!" the bouncer barked, moving his mountainous body toward her menacingly. "I said this ain't no place for you to be standing around to make no damn calls! Get your ass to the back of the line, or get the hell out of here!"

The bass in his voice startled Donna, but she wasn't giving up. She bit her bottom lip, swallowed hard, and stepped up again.

"I really, really need to see Tommy. If you just give him the message, you'll see that he'll let me inside. Please, please, it's an emergency," Donna pleaded, clasping her hands together like she was about to pray. It wasn't in her nature to beg or plead. All her life she'd generally gotten what she wanted, even on the party scene. And if she didn't get her way, she was used to resorting to tantrums to turn the tables. However, she figured the temper tantrums she usually threw or the rude way she spoke to those who stood in her way wasn't going to work with this guy. She tried something different.

"Pretty please," she added for good measure.

It was clear to the bouncer that this little nuisance wasn't going to give up. He didn't have time to keep arguing with her either. The bouncer exhaled a windstorm of breath and rolled his beady eyes. "All right, all right. Just hold up, because I see you ain't going to give up, and you are fucking up the order of my line here," he muttered. He let three more people through the blue DO NOT CROSS barricade, and then he looked at Donna one more time and turned toward the nightclub doors. She stood trembling, the uncertainty killing her inside.

"Aye, JoJo. Run inside and tell Tommy a little hot piece of ass is out here to see him. I'm not letting her inside unless he gives the okay. Names Dee, or some shit like that," the bouncer yelled over his shoulder.

Donna's shoulders slumped with relief. Tommy was still hanging at his usual spot, which was good. The bouncer turned back toward Donna, his face twisted, as if he smelled something that stunk.

"You must really need to see Tommy. Don't look like his usual type. You look too clean for the likes of Tommy," the bouncer commented, eyeing Donna up and down.

She wasn't wearing club clothes, so she assumed that was what the bouncer meant by Tommy's "usual type." Or did that mean Tommy had moved on without her? Donna's mind raced a mile a minute.

"I did you the favor. Now get out of the way. Stand to the side until I see if Tommy wants to be bothered with your ass," the bouncer instructed, using his huge hands to push her aside. "Next!" he screamed, waving at the next three people in the line.

The eager club-goers rushed toward Donna, causing her to stumble backward a few steps. The world really was so strange to her without drugs in her system. Donna didn't know how she would survive without medicating herself. She shifted her weight from one foot to the other as she waited for her boyfriend, Tommy, either to come outside or give the beefy guard the word to let her inside.

The last time she'd seen Tommy, he'd given her a fix in exchange for her American Express Black Card. All she remembered about that night was regaining consciousness in the back of an ambulance, surrounded by chaos and screaming EMTs. A day later, she was released from the hospital to the care of her parents, who drove her straight to the rehabilitation center. She was forcefully dragged inside, and after a lot of futile kicking, spitting, screaming, and crying, she was signed in involuntarily. Donna believed it was all her mother's doing. At the rehab center, she was cut off from the world . . . and Tommy.

"Yo, Tommy said to come inside," the bouncer grumbled, interrupting Donna's thoughts.

I knew he would be excited to see me! She smiled, and her insides began churning from fear and excitement.

"I told you he'd let me in," she admonished the bouncer, rolling her eyes at him.

He just shook his head at her. "Yeah, whatever. That might not be a good thing," he muttered.

She stepped past the patrons on the line with her nose in the air like she was an A-list celebrity. Suddenly, she had that old entitled feeling back. The old Donna wasn't far away from the reaches of her mind at all. *This is how I'm supposed to be treated. I am from an important family. These people better recognize.*

Once she was inside the club, the smell of marijuana immediately shot straight up Donna's nostrils. She swallowed hard as her mouth filled with saliva, like that of a hungry dog hearing the dinner bell. Donna could hear the voice of her substance-abuse counselor, Ms. Laura, ringing in her head. *When you go home, any exposure to drugs or the old scene you were used to will cause you to relapse. It will be too dangerous for you if you go back to your old habits. Find new friends and new places to hang out.*

Donna was glad when the blaring music filled her ears. It made it that much easier to shake off the warnings ringing in her head. What did those counselors know about her after just nine short months? Donna felt like she could control her desires to get high if she wanted to. She told herself she was a big girl and she could handle herself. She didn't want to get high right now; she just wanted to see her man, who she'd missed for the past nine months. With all the restrictions placed on telephones and with telephone calls being monitored, Donna hadn't been able to reach out to Tommy while she was locked up in rehab. Donna was sure it was her bitch of a mother who'd added Tommy's name to Donna's "no contact" list. She often wondered if Tommy had ever tried to find her or visit her while she was away.

Be strong when you see him. He is going to be so happy to see you. You'll see, Donna thought, giving herself a pep talk, as she waded through swaying club patrons.

Donna navigated the crowd and reached the back of the club. She spotted Tommy right away. How could she miss him? It was like they were kindred spirits. Made for one another. Besides, Tommy was unmistakable, even in a club packed with people. No matter what the weather, he always wore the same close-fitting black T-shirt that exposed his muscular chest and huge biceps. His dark brown skin, dark brown doe eyes, and obligatory low-cut wavy hair gave away his West Side upbringing. Those same features also made him the bad boy that all the girls loved. Tommy was a wannabe black gangster who hung around real gangsters and did their flunky work. He was also a two-bit drug dealer who preyed on young women with money, his specialty being homemade methamphetamine. He had introduced Donna to the drug when she was just sixteen.

Seeing Tommy after all this time, Donna felt her heartbeat speed up until it was hammering against her chest bone. She felt hot all over, and sweat beads popped up on her forehead seemingly out of nowhere. Tommy had spotted her as well. He squinted his eyes and put his drink down on the bar. Donna let a goofy smile spread across her face as she rushed toward him. Tommy didn't move, but for the frown that caused his thick eyebrows to come together and dip so low between his eyes that they almost touched the bridge of his nose. Donna was oblivious to his reaction to her. All she knew was that she was seeing her man and that something deep down inside her had come alive, like it had just been resurrected from the dead. Donna felt a dizzying rush of emotions, which she hadn't expected.

"Hey, T," Donna sang, her shaky arms outstretched, ready to embrace him.

Tommy twisted his lips and tsk-tsked. He moved to avoid any contact with Donna. She felt pain flash through her heart, like he'd just stabbed her there. Tommy had always welcomed her with nothing but open arms.

"Well, well, well, if it isn't poor little Miss Rich Bitch. I thought my eyes were fucking with me. Out of jail, I see. Looking good too . . . good and rich," Tommy replied bitterly.

Donna dropped her arms at her sides. She didn't know how to react to Tommy's treatment. "Hi, T," she said weakly, at a total loss for words.

"And the first person you come see is me? Wonder why," he continued cruelly, letting a sly smile spread over his face.

Donna's throat tightened. Hadn't he missed her? She had missed him terribly. All she had thought about in rehab was Tommy. No matter what the counselors had said about drug dealers, she had never attributed any of those horrible things to Tommy. In her assessment, Tommy was different, nothing like the rest. It didn't matter that he had got her hooked on the worst drug to hit the streets.

"T, I missed you so much. You are the first person I thought of when I woke up each morning and the last person I thought of when I went to bed. I have missed you so, so much," Donna sang, her voice rising and falling with emotion. Her underarms itched from sweat. Her mouth became cotton-ball dry.

Donna really wanted to run to Tommy and hug him as tight as she could. However, something told her it wasn't a good idea, so she settled for keeping her distance, her body language and tone pleading with him. It wasn't long before reality hit. Donna saw a slim dirty-blond woman with deadpan eyes move close to Tommy and kiss him on the neck. She was wearing a skirt so short, it looked like a loincloth. The scary girl looked at Donna and then ran her tongue down the side of Tommy's face. Donna's legs buckled slightly, and her stomach knotted.

Oh my God! He has moved on. He is with someone else! Donna screamed inside her head. Donna felt another wave of sharp pains flash through her stomach. She swallowed hard and tapped her foot. She suddenly felt an overwhelming urge to urinate. She shifted back and forth on her feet as she watched the girl enjoy what was hers. Donna folded her arms across her body, willing herself not to scream and cry. Tommy spread that notorious sneaky smile of his across his face, pulling the girl closer to him.

"What do you want, li'l rich girl? As you can see, I'm busy," Tommy said to Donna, then chuckled like she was a big joke.

Donna opened her mouth to speak, but the words wouldn't come. Then Tommy turned toward the gaunt girl hanging on his neck and planted a deep tongue kiss on her.

Donna closed her eyes for a long second. She felt like her legs would just give out. Donna hadn't felt a deep pain of disappointment like that since the day her sister was sent away without so much as a good-bye to her.

"Tommy, you know it wasn't my fault. My mother and father, um . . . I didn't want to go. I would've called you. Please don't do this to me—" Donna pleaded, on the brink of tears, her voice cracking some more.

Tommy emitted a shrill laugh that interrupted her and sent her words tumbling back down her throat like hard marbles. Donna could feel tears burning at the backs of her eye sockets. She didn't know how much longer she could hold them back.

Please, God, don't let me cry. I cannot look weak. I cannot look weak, she thought.

"Tommy, just give me a minute to explain . . . alone," Donna croaked, darting her eyes to the skinny girl's face. Donna was moving back and forth and didn't even realize it. She wasn't used to this type of rejection. She was anxious. She wanted to get high so badly now, she could actually taste it on her tongue.

"Look, li'l rich girl, I've moved on. You can crawl back to your daddy and mommy and leave me alone. I don't have time for you anymore," Tommy snapped irritably. He pulled the blonde closer to him for emphasis. "I have no time for the rich girl chronicles anymore. As you can see, there's a new sheriff in town. I only got you in the club tonight to see if it was really you. Shit, I thought your rich daddy had whisked you away to some remote paradise somewhere," he continued, taunting her. "Other than that, I really have nothing to say." Tommy was laying the rejection on thick. He'd always known how to get inside Donna's head. He knew she would do just about anything to get him back at this point.

"Let me just talk to you alone," Donna pleaded again, then stepped over to him and touched his arm boldly.

The ugly skeleton of a girl moved in front of Tommy and blocked him with her gaunt body. Donna's jaw rocked as she snatched her hand back.

"Aye! You can't fucking hear? He said he doesn't have anything to say to you! Now get the fuck away from my man before I get angry! I don't have much sense when I get angry!" the girl hissed, pointing a pale, bony finger toward Donna's face.

A pang of fear shot through Donna's stomach, but she held her ground. "Tommy, just give me a minute," she said, totally ignoring the warning from the girl.

Tommy chuckled, almost to the point of belly laughing. He kind of liked this attention—two women fighting over him was a life goal for him.

"It's all right, Lee. I'm not going anywhere," Tommy said, comforting the girl, as he grabbed her around her waist to move her out of Donna's face.

Donna backed down for a minute. She could feel tears stinging the backs of her eyes. She was trying to think fast, desperate for Tommy's affection.

"Tommy . . . I'm back. Me. Dee, your girl. Remember, you promised me that we would always be together? Remember? The money. The shopping. Remember? Everything we had together? All the things we shared? I just want to be with you. I don't care if she's here. I just want things to be like before. I need you, T," Donna droned pathetically.

She was shameless with her begging, but the truth of the matter was, Tommy was the only person that had made her feel like she really existed. Her parents had always gone about their busy lives like she was just an added burden. Her siblings had got all the attention, and she had literally fallen by the wayside in everyone's lives. They had thrown money at her in hopes of buying her whatever would take the place of their love and attention. Tommy had paid her the attention she had craved, especially when she had things like money and credit cards to offer him. All Donna wanted now was to feel loved again, needed again. She wanted someone to be all hers again.

Tommy looked at her now with intense interest. It was like Donna had said the magic buzzwords—*money, shopping, things,* one or all of those words had piqued his interest. It was as if Tommy had almost forgotten how easy it was to get large sums of money from Donna during their time together. Tommy moved his new love interest aside. He looked at Donna, a devious line streaking his brow. Donna knew she had gotten his attention now. The yearning she felt inside grew bigger. The anticipation of having him again made her sway on her feet involuntarily.

I knew he would remember what we had! I will always be his number one! Donna said to herself, a satisfied look on her face.

"Lee, baby, let me just talk to her for a minute. It's the only way I'm going to get rid of her," Tommy whispered to the girl, loud enough for Donna to hear.

Donna smiled and bounced on her toes. She didn't care what excuse Tommy used to get rid of Lee. Donna longed for his attention . . . his touch. Donna's hand shook uncontrollably, like Tommy was a hit of some powerful drug that she was dying to get high on. She felt like if she could just get a few minutes alone with him, he'd be hers again. Lee sucked her teeth and folded her arms across her chest. She eyed Donna evilly. Something inside Donna felt vindicated, powerful even. Donna smirked at Lee as Tommy walked toward her. Who was Lee anyway? She didn't understand what Donna and Tommy had had. Their love had been powerful. It had been Donna's life back then. It wasn't so long ago that she had had all Tommy's love and attention. Donna was hell bent on getting that back, no matter how long it took.

Tommy brushed past Donna now, but not without Lee's stony gaze on them both. "Follow me," Tommy huffed as he stalked toward the back of the club. He knew damn well he couldn't speak to Donna with Lee so close by. Not the way he wanted to anyway.

Donna turned and gave Lee a squinty-eyed grin. Her facial expression said, "I have him now, bitch." Donna wanted to stick her tongue out too, but she figured that would be way too juvenile. Lee rolled her eyes and flipped Donna the bird. Donna could see Lee's nostrils flaring. Donna fell in step behind Tommy and followed him into the men's bathroom. She felt extra special. She would be *alone* with her man, the way it was supposed to be. Once inside the bathroom, Tommy didn't give

Donna a chance to say a word. He knew exactly what to do. He grabbed her by her arm, turned her toward him, and forced his tongue between her lips.

"Mmm," Donna moaned, a bit caught off guard. It didn't take her too long to match his efforts. She melted against him. She kissed him ravenously. Oh, how she had missed him during her time in rehab.

"Mmm," she moaned some more as tears leaked out of the sides of her eyes. They were definitely tears of joy. Tommy groped her as he pressed his body into hers roughly. Donna wanted him so badly. She wanted to feel him inside her. She slid her hand down to his crotch and felt his manhood against her hand. It was just as she remembered it . . . just right. She could barely breathe now. They didn't even care that someone had entered the bathroom as they feasted on one another for another ten minutes. Donna was all in now.

"I missed you," Tommy said cunningly in between kisses. It was like he wasn't even the same mean, disdainful person from a few minutes ago out on the club floor. Donna held on to him like he was about to run away. She wanted to savor every moment with him. She looked into his face. His beautiful hair and those deep eyes were so sexy. Donna's heart rate sped up.

"I missed you too, T. I'm sorry I had to leave and go away like that. I didn't know what happened to me. They said I almost died, so they got all spooked. I tried to fight it. I really did. I would've never left you like that for one minute. Then my mother . . . ," Donna said, rambling. She finally let the tears stream down her face. She was so happy to be back in Tommy's embrace that she never wanted to leave his side. "I would've never left you like that. I just want things to be the way they used to be. Please, I need you. I want you so bad," she whined.

Tommy knew he had her now. He liked seeing her like this. At his mercy was right where he wanted Donna to be. It was so easy to get her there again. Lee had been a much harder nut to crack.

"Shh." Tommy put his finger to Donna's lips. He didn't need to hear all about the past. He was interested in what she could do for him now. He wasted no time getting to the real point. "So what's up? You said you got your money back and everything?"

Donna was too blinded by her own desperation to see through his scheming and manipulation. She shook her head vigorously in the affirmative. "Yes. My access has been unblocked. I called my father while I was away, and he gave me back all my access to every account. I can get anything I want right now. Just like before. Of course, my bitch of a mother doesn't know anything," Donna told Tommy, nervously wringing her hands.

Donna tried to grab him again. She wanted to feel his touch again. But Tommy was too busy pacing now. She knew that meant his mind was racing, calculating. Whatever it took to keep him around, she would do it. "If you get rid of her, it'll be just like it used to be for us, T," she said, her tone serious.

Tommy came straight out and asked, "Can you get your hands on, like, ten thousand dollars?" He acted as if she hadn't even mentioned getting rid of Lee.

Donna's eyes popped wide open and goose bumps came up on her arms, given the fact that she'd just lied to him about having access to her trust fund and her father's accounts like before. Her heartbeat sped up. Donna shifted her weight from one foot to the other. She had to think quickly. There was no way she could let Tommy slip through her fingers now. Not after she had just gotten him back where she wanted him. A lie popped into her mind so fast, it was like second nature.

"Probably tomorrow. Not tonight," Donna replied uncomfortably. "I can get it first thing tomorrow. Are you going to see me tomorrow? Without Lee?"

"All right, yeah, yeah. You need to come to the crib and see me tomorrow. Bring the cash, all of it," Tommy said sternly. "I'll make sure she's not there when you come. But you got to bring the cash. I'm depending on you now." He touched her chin gently and urged her to look him in the eyes. "I want to be able to trust you again, so don't fuck this up. If you ever leave me like you did before, I don't know what I'll do with myself," he said, puppy dog eyes and all.

"What does this mean, T? I mean . . . for us. You know, like, are we . . . ? What . . . are we?" Donna stammered, blinking rapidly.

Tommy grabbed her head and pulled it to his and kissed her deeply again. The kiss was so forceful, it left Donna breathless. Huge bat-sized butterflies flitted through her stomach.

"It means you never stopped being mine," Tommy replied, looking into her eyes seriously. Something inside Donna seemed to melt. Tommy was the only person who had ever made her feel like that. It was like they were the only two people that existed in the world when she was with him.

"Here. This is for you. On the house. A welcome-home gift," Tommy said, shoving a foil-wrapped bundle into Donna's hand.

Donna stumbled back a few steps, clutching the package. She knew right away what it was. She felt like throwing up right there on the spot. Blood rushed to her head, and the room starting swimming around her. Immediately, an intense throbbing started at her temples. It was too much to handle. Having Tommy back. Being exposed to drugs. It was a lot to handle.

"Tom, I'm . . . I . . . I'm clean. I can't . . . I don't . . . ,"
Donna stammered, the vein at her left temple pulsing
fiercely. It was her first test as a clean and sober person.
Just like that, she had drugs at her disposal again. It
hadn't even taken her any effort to get them. Donna
clutched the little bundle so hard, the center of her hand
began to sting. She wanted to give it back to him, but her
hand would not unfurl to release it. It was a gift from
her one and only love—a gift from Tommy. She couldn't
bring herself to let it go, although she knew what it could
do to her.

Tommy walked up to her and kissed her again. This
made Donna clutch the bundle even harder.

"Just take it. If you don't want it, then throw it away.
But consider it a gift from me. I always want to do nice
things for you. Besides, one little hit like that ain't going
to do shit to someone like you. You used to do at least
three or four of those a day, remember? Those were the
good days—me, you, and that shit right there," Tommy
said smoothly, knowing exactly what he was doing to her
inside. "I don't even give that chick out there gifts like
that. Only for you. Someone that will always have first
place in my heart." He pecked Donna on the lips again
and left her standing there.

Tommy was right. Donna did remember when it was
him and her. She remembered doing so many bundles
in one day that she would start feeling like she could
conquer anything when she was high. She remembered
feeling better about not having her parents around
like she had secretly wanted her entire childhood. She
remembered forgetting all about how much she missed
her sister and how much she couldn't stand her own
brother. She remembered feeling loved by Tommy most
of all, because he cared enough to give her drugs and a
place to get high.

Donna could remember everything about how she felt when she was high. In her mind, there seemed to be way more benefits to being high than being sober. It was like Tommy had said: This little package was light work for someone like her. She could probably take the drug and still be clean. Donna's hand stayed curled around the foil bundle. Suddenly the room was spinning around her, and she felt faint. She had a choice to make, only she didn't feel like her decision-making ability was solid enough.

Chapter 7

Unhappily Good Times

All of Chicago's black elite knew that Ernest and Carolyn Johnson's Idlewild home was a magnificent sprawling mini-mansion that sat adjacent to the shore. It was one of the biggest homes in all of Idlewild. Sand dunes surrounded the grounds, which made the house look as if it was suspended in the air when you gazed at the property from the street.

Carolyn had thrown the family's annual all-white affair in her home many times, and so she had the whole operation under control, but today she broke out in a sweat as the appointed hour for the party approached. It definitely wasn't the same feeling she'd had over the years, when things had been right with her and Ernest. She shook her head, trying to rid herself of the thought that this might be her husband's last party. Her mind drifted to her children. Carolyn was a stickler for family traditions, and she'd warned all three of her children that they needed to be present on this occasion and on their best behavior. Their father was sick, and she wasn't going to make any exceptions for them or their bad behavior, like she'd done many times in the past.

Junior squeezed Bella's hand as his Bentley eased toward his parents' circular driveway. Bella glanced over at him. Her eyes seemed to sparkle against the crisp whiteness of her newly purchased Dolce and Gabbana dress. Junior felt warm inside under her gaze. He wondered then if he was really falling in love with Bella. He turned his head toward the window so she wouldn't see him blushing. He was a man; men weren't supposed to feel this head over heels for a woman.

"Are you as nervous as I am?" Bella asked, her tone more serious than Junior had ever heard it.

He chuckled, trying hard to tamp down his own nerves. He knew this was one of the boldest things he'd ever done in all the years his parents had thrown this party, but he also knew it was necessary. He knew his mother wanted all the attention to be on his two sisters, for different reasons, but he was coming with a surprise of his own. *Why not? Why not make a scene too?* he thought.

"Nah, you're bugging. I'm not nervous at all. If I was going to be all shaky about this, I wouldn't have invited you, now would I?" he said, lying through his teeth. "I am looking forward to the reactions, honestly. Especially my mothers." He leaned over and kissed Bella on the lips—a bold display of affection that she wasn't expecting. Bella flinched when she caught the eye of Junior's driver, who had been watching them, in the rearview mirror. The driver seemed surprised and a bit angry at Junior's bold conquest. Junior saw him watching, and he knew his loyalties lay with his mother, but Junior didn't care. He needed to do this . . . for himself.

Junior had decided to bring Bella along to the party after they'd had a long talk at the hotel. He knew full well all his friends and family would be there. The same friends and family who never expected him to be with a beautiful, classy woman like Bella and who had always written him off as some rich playboy that would never settle down. Junior was tired of his sisters always having the limelight and all the attention, as if he didn't exist. He knew his mother would try to make the party all about Desiree, but he had a different idea. With Bella by his side, Junior felt powerful, bold, and vengeful.

The Bentley finally stopped in front of the house. The Johnsons' hired help rushed over, and one of the servants opened the back door of the Bentley to allow Junior and Bella to exit. Bella extended her long, slender legs and grabbed the servant's hand. Junior waved off the help and climbed out by himself.

Bella looked around and became instantly enamored of the posh property. *So this is how the rich and shameless live? Wonder what crooked investor lives here?* she thought, feeling like a little kid in a huge candy store. Junior gave her a half-hearted smile. He could see that she was both impressed and scared to death. Her eyes told him she was nervous but was playing it as cool as she could.

"Here goes nothing," Bella said with a chortle, though she was really about to fall apart inside. Junior didn't know how he felt about this anymore either.

Bella smoothed down the bottom half of the shocking white dress she wore. The dress fit her perfectly and made her look like a goddess, especially the way it pushed up her D-cup breasts. Junior did the same with his white Gucci slacks and his shirt. Then he stuck out his hand, and Bella took it in hers. He gave her one last once-over, and then they nervously forged ahead to the house. When they reached the front door, it opened before them, and they stepped inside.

"Mr. Ernest Johnson, Jr., and guest!" a white-gloved butler announced, his voice reverberating off the walls of the grand foyer.

Carolyn Johnson seemed to appear like magic. It was as if she just materialized out of the walls. She glided over to Junior, her wispy white Nicole Miller dress flowing around her like fake angel's wings.

"Junior, thank God," Carolyn sang, giving her son a hug. "You look fabulous! So nice as usual," she added, continuing her phony act. Then she kissed her son on the cheek. Junior had watched his mother do this same act so many times, he had memorized the steps and the words.

"You look amazing, Mother," Junior replied, playing his part impeccably in the fake ritual.

Junior gave his mother the once-over. He could tell by the semipermanent plastic grin on her face that she'd had a fresh round of Botox, and probably that very morning, if he knew his mother as well as he thought he did. Carolyn's hair was freshly dyed, and her makeup had been painted on in layers, as usual. Junior had often joked with his mother and told her she looked like an older version of one of those chicks on the TV series *Desperate Housewives*. He had never meant it as a compliment, and he had had no idea his mother took it as one until one day he'd heard her repeat it with pride.

Junior really wished his mother would let herself age naturally. He thought she should just wear her age like a badge. One that she could be proud of. She was beautiful to him, with or without artificial fillers. But he understood that his mother had been friends with some of the women who would be in attendance at her annual affair for almost forty years, and the competitiveness between those women when it came to who was the most glamorous seemed to intensify with each passing year.

Underneath it all, Junior resented the fact that his mother had been putting on airs for so many years. He resented the fact that, although the family had literally fallen apart, his mother and father still navigated through their social circles as if everything was perfectly fine and intact. There had always been rumblings about his father having affairs, but his mother had always pretended she didn't hear them. In fact, among the Idlewild elite, his mother often bragged about how faithful and dedicated her man, Ernest Sr., was. Junior still cringed when he thought about how stupid his mother looked half the time as she floated around, faking that she was the happiest woman in the world.

Bella stood off to the side and watched the perfunctory exchange between the mother and son. For the first time, an ominous feeling crept into her gut that Junior didn't really want her by his side. After all, he acted as if she wasn't standing there. She fiddled with the stitching on the side of her dress, wishing she'd declined the invitation to this affair. It was a dumb move to begin with. She'd known that she would be out of her league there.

"Well, the party is out back, as usual. You know the drill, Junior. Eat, drink, and be merry. There is plenty of the finest food and libation. We always want our guests to feel at home! Enjoy! Enjoy!" Carolyn sang some more. Then she turned away from him.

Junior smiled and raised an eyebrow. He was waiting for his mother to ask. He started counting down in his head. *Five, four, three, two . . .* Suddenly his mother turned back toward him. *There she goes. I knew it!* Junior said to himself.

"Oh yes, before I forget, I thought I heard them announce you with a guest. Is there someone with you?" she said, her eyes darting over to where Bella was standing, looking into space, her hands fiddling nervously with anything she could grab on to. Carolyn looked back at Junior, then shifted her gaze one more time Bella. Junior knew that his mother had figured out that Bella was with him, but wanted to hear it from his own mouth.

"Oh, yeah. I did come with a guest. I decided not to come alone this year and have you shoving your version of acceptable women in my face. This year I wanted to save you from the task of trying to find me a Johnson family–approved wife," Junior said snidely.

Carolyn's fake smile started to fade. "Oh?" she said, her eyebrows furrowing a bit. She blinked rapidly as she tried to play it cool, despite the fact that her son was being sarcastic and deserved a cursing out.

"I am here with a good friend of mine. Her name is Bella," Junior announced smugly. He let a huge smile spread across his face. He felt the heat of satisfaction wash over him.

Carolyn gazed once again at Bella but didn't say a word.

"Bella! Bella, baby, come let me introduce you to my mother, the ever beautiful, ever classy, ever popular Carolyn Johnson," Junior said, smiling from ear to ear while waving Bella over to his side.

Bella blinked like she'd been splashed with cold water. Moving like the scarecrow from *The Wizard of Oz*, she stepped closer to Junior. The fine hairs on her arms stood straight up, and her heart thundered. She felt awkward, to say the least. Junior grabbed her arm proudly and pulled her closer to him until his hand was on her waist.

"Yes, Mother, this is my love, Bella," Junior declared, beaming.

Carolyn's mouth hung open. She didn't even realize that her perfectly drawn red lips were agape.

"Hello, madame. I am Bella Rodriguez. It is very nice to make your acquaintance," Bella said, introducing herself, her accent more pronounced than Junior had ever heard it.

Bella stuck out her hand toward Carolyn for a shake. Carolyn was too shocked to notice. She was also too busy eyeballing the woman her son had dared to bring to her annual event without asking and without first getting her and Ernest's approval. With her hair down and her dress hugging her curvy body, Bella was a bombshell in a video vixen kind of way. Carolyn couldn't close her mouth or hide her shock. She felt a bit light headed. When she didn't return the handshake, Bella pulled back her hand and let it drop to her side stiffly.

Carolyn fanned her face with her hand. She had to admit, her legs felt a little weak. She couldn't even pretend her way through all the feelings she had going on inside. "Well, I . . . I . . . I mean, it's very nice to meet you, Bella. Very nice to meet you indeed," Carolyn gasped, like someone had taken the air out of her lungs.

Junior smirked, a blanket of vindication settling over him. *Desiree Johnson is not the only Johnson kid who has some shock factor in her. I can still shock them too. I'll be the talk of the town, too, now,* Junior thought as he watched his mother come completely undone over Bella.

"It's not polite to gawk, Mother," Junior chortled.

He grabbed Bella's hand boldly and headed toward the party, leaving his mother standing there, with what he was sure was a sweaty hairline and cheeks red as strawberries.

The Johnson party scene was simply stunning. Desiree and her date—who was her son, Tyree—stood at the great-room doors leading out to the party for a few minutes to take in the beautifully decorated estate. There was no doubt that the Johnsons had tried to outdo every other Idlewild party that summer.

"Wow," Tyree said to Desiree. He found it hard to close his mouth.

"Yes, yes, I know. Since I was a kid, each year she has tried to outdo the year before. I'm not at all surprised by any of this," Desiree replied, a hint of sadness apparent in her tone.

As usual, her mother had spared no expense on her annual all-white affair. And it seemed like she'd gone a bit more overboard than usual this time. Desiree knew that was because she was home after so long. Or maybe it was because they all feared it might be her father's last party, although none of them would say those words out loud. Desiree knew her mother was probably trying to make this party something so special that none of them would want to leave in a few days, which was inevitable.

This year's theme at the Johnson estate was Asian fusion. There were round white-linen Chinese lanterns hanging in clusters on invisible wire around the huge backyard. Enough lanterns to cast a heavenly glow over the entire place. The poolside was adorned with glowing square candles with Asian inscriptions on them. The light from the candles glinted off the crystal-blue water in the pool. All-white calla lilies floated in the pool's glistening water. Wind chimes hung from the large oak on the left side of the yard. The sound was soothing. There was a band on the right side of the yard, but the Asian music they played was just loud enough to be considered party music.

Carolyn had also spared no expense when it came to the food. There were several food stations—including a seafood station with huge lobsters on ice. A gorgeous ice sculpture of a dragon sat like a museum piece in the middle of the chafing-dish stations. There were servers walking around with silver trays piled high with vegetable spring rolls, sweet and sour shrimp, crab wontons, and lobster hors d'oeuvres, just to name a few. All the patio and pool furniture was covered in freshly starched white linen perfect for dining on. The entire place seemed to glow.

"Wow. This is a big deal," Tyree whispered to his mother as he took it all in. It was far more than he was used to. The things rich people spent money on never ceased to amaze him, and he'd been noticing this since they arrived at the house. He could definitely see that his suspicions that his mother had grown up privileged and rich had been on the money. Her family spent money like it was growing on the trees around them. It kind of made Tyree feel a little resentful. He couldn't understand why his mother had chosen for them to struggle like they had when her family, whom he still had a hard time considering his family, clearly had more than enough money to share with them.

"I told you so. There is nothing she wouldn't do to impress others. We better grab some food and a spot to sit before everyone else arrives. This is not even half the folks that will show up. Trust me," Desiree whispered back to Tyree as she fielded the stares they received from some very familiar faces.

As Desiree and Tyree stepped into the backyard, her eyes scanned the people that were already there. Her shoulder slumped with relief when she saw that none of the faces belonged to any of the Blackwells. Desiree flashed a plastic smile and waved to a few of the Chicago elite she recognized from the city. She was dying from all the attention. She waved and nodded to the other people, but she never stopped to have any face time with any of them.

"Are all these people rich?" Tyree asked, astonished at how many people were milling around, dressed in all white, and acting like this was something they did on a regular basis. He was trying to store this scene in his long-term memory so he could go back and tell his friends what he had experienced. Tyree's interest was piqued.

"Some are rich, some lie, and most are like a lot of people in this pretentious capitalist society of ours, living off the fat of the land," Desiree answered furtively.

Tyree seemed to contemplate what his mother was saying. *Living off the fat of the land*? he thought. He would have to follow up on that later. If this was what living off the fat of the land looked like, he wanted in right away. He could definitely get used to this lifestyle and would never go back to the cramped little house he and his mother lived in.

He grabbed a huge glass of shrimp cocktail off one of the beautifully decorated tables and devoured it. Desiree took her time sipping her drink. She usually didn't indulge around her son, but at this event, she would need constant distraction. She was just counting down the time until the Blackwells arrived and things got very interesting. She was silently praying that her mother had miraculously failed to invite them this year, but she knew better. Desiree knew her mother's social circle and knew that what those people thought meant more to Carolyn than her own children's well-being. Desiree had seen that firsthand when she got pregnant out of wedlock. This would be no different.

It didn't take long before Desiree and Tyree had become the hot topic of the party. Hushed murmurs and sideways glances proliferated around the Johnson estate. All aimed at Desiree and her "baby." Desiree knew they were talking about her and Tyree; nothing had changed. Her close childhood friend Carly and Carly's husband, Chris, refused to come over and speak to Desiree after they spotted her. Carolyn noticed this and pointed out to Carly that Desiree was there. When Desiree turned her head abruptly, Carly and Chris were staring right at her, but they never came over. She knew she was the topic of their secret conversation. Carly cracked a fake smile at

Desiree and then chastised Chris for looking at Desiree and Tyree too quickly. Desiree smiled back and waved, but Carly just pushed her lips out and turned her head like she hadn't seen Desiree.

Everyone knew about Desiree's banishment and her baby, but the nerve of Carly! Carly had been Desiree's best friend for many years when they were younger. Hadn't she matured enough over the years to let go of her judgment by now? Desiree shook her head in disgust. Carly was out of line in Desiree's eyes. How dare she act like that in Desiree's parents' home!

An hour later it seemed to Desiree that she and Tyree had been at the party for an eternity. She had quickly grown tired of the stares, snickers, and fake smiles. She looked at her watch impatiently. She wondered when her father was going to show up, give the obligatory toast, and take their stupid family photo, so she could leave. Just as Desiree picked up her fourth drink, she heard what she'd been dreading all night.

"The honorable Mr. and Mrs. Tyson Blackwell!" the butler announced loudly.

Desiree's heart jerked in her chest. Everyone seemed to turn toward the great-room doors at once. Smiles and cheers abounded for Judge Tyson Blackwell. But Desiree did not join in. Her reaction was different. She almost dropped her drink when she heard the butler announce Tyson's arrival. He might be a judge now, but he was the same old Tyson to her. She looked around frantically for Tyree. Her heart jabbed her chest bone so hard, she instinctively put her hand on her chest. She spun around aimlessly a few times. Then she spotted Tyree standing and laughing with Junior. Desiree almost put jets on her feet. Breathing hard, she rushed over to her brother and her son. She fake smiled, her nostrils flaring.

"Hey, um, Tyree. You want to go inside with me for a minute?" she gasped, her voice rising and falling. "I . . . um . . . want to show you something."

"Aw, Mom, I'm good here with Uncle Junior. He's telling me so many good stories about y'all as kids," Tyree replied, almost whining. He seemed fully engaged in conversation with his uncle Junior.

Desiree shot Junior a look. Of course, he had a smirk on his face. Only God knew what types of stories Junior was telling, although he and Desiree had had some good times together as kids. But she knew her brother loved to stoke fires, and after she'd been sent away, their relationship had soured, then had become virtually nonexistent.

"What's wrong, sis? You look like you've seen a ghost," Junior said snidely, shifting his gaze to where Tyson Blackwell and his wife were standing and laughing with other guests. "Don't worry. I'll keep him occupied if you want to *run* inside for a while. You seem flustered. See something that threw you off?"

"Junior, stay out of this please," Desiree said, shooting Tyree that motherly look that said, "You need to listen to me." "Tyree, I said I wanted you inside for a minute."

Tyree went to move, but Junior didn't stop his furtive taunting.

"Oh, Desi, look. Isn't that an old friend of yours?" Junior said, pointing at Tyson Blackwell and his wife, who were still making their rounds.

Desiree's nostrils opened wide, and she bit the inside of her cheek until she tasted blood. Then she froze, and so did her son. They all turned to look at the same time. Then Desiree shook her head at her hateful brother and smiled and chuckled with fake joviality.

"I want to meet all your old friends, Mom," Tyree said innocently.

"Well, he's not exactly a friend of mine, per se. He was someone I grew up with a long time ago," Desiree said sharply, speaking through her teeth as she kept fake smiling. She never took her eyes off Tyson. "We lost contact, and there's no need to introduce anyone to anyone. It's been so long," she added.

Junior, Desiree, and Tyree watched as Tyson meandered among the partygoers, amid oohs and aahs, and gave obligatory air kisses to the women and exchanged firm handshakes with the men. Tyson seemed to glide and glow at the same time. There was no doubt, he was still as gorgeous as ever. And as charming and bold as she remembered him being. Tyree watched with rapt attention, a fact that made Desiree completely uncomfortable inside. Desiree didn't want to seem too interested, but she had to agree that Tyson and his wife were definitely noticeable.

"Don't worry. She is not as beautiful as you," Junior quickly interjected, interrupting Desiree's thoughts.

With arched eyebrows, Desiree looked at her brother and then rolled her eyes. She knew he was being cruel. Her gaze returned to Tyson and his wife. She tried not to stare at Tyson's wife, who looked adorable in a silk strapless one-piece shorts jumper. Her long tanned legs were accented by a pair of sparkly rhinestone-covered Christian Louboutin D'Orsays. Her hair was pulled back in a sophisticated chignon, with a few loose strands purposely left untamed to fall around the sides of her oval-shaped face. Tyson's wife worked the backyard like a first-rate socialite. She looked as if she'd learned how to smooze and be fake from the best—like Carolyn or Tyson's mother, Beth. She kissed a few people, gave out hugs freely, and garnered lots of attention. Desiree watched Tyson as he proudly watched his wife. Envy built up inside Desiree like air in a pressure-filled pipe.

I should've stayed away! I knew I wasn't ready! What do I do now! she thought.

Desiree moved closer to Junior and dug her nails into his arm as she pulled him close to her face. "Don't start no shit. I'm warning you. This is my son's life, and I will protect it to the death of me. This is not a little game for your entertainment," Desiree hissed in Junior's ear, the drinks she'd had erasing her reticence.

She suddenly regretted bringing Tyree to the event. Who was she fooling? Even though she'd been gone as long as she had, everyone still remembered what went down. The uncertainty she felt now about how things might play out as soon as Tyson laid eyes on Tyree was making her crazy. What if he realized that Tyree was his son? What made matters worse what that not only was Tyson's wife young, popular, and gorgeous, but she also had the man that Desiree had always envisioned herself being with. She was all the things Desiree felt that she was not anymore. Desiree felt like crying and screaming and running away.

"I hear you, sis," Junior said, still chuckling like he thought everything was one big joke. "I only want what's best for little man here. I can see you're doing a great job raising him. The kid is smart as a whip, and he's got some swag to him too. Just like his uncle." Junior patted Desiree on the shoulder reassuringly.

She exhaled and shook her head. She wanted so badly to grab her son and run away, this time for good. But she knew that would just bring more attention to her and Tyree. "I'm sorry for talking to you like that—" Desiree began, but her words were cut short.

"The man of the hour! Mr. Ernest Johnson!" the butler announced.

It felt like someone had rung a bell in Desiree's ear. She and Junior turned at the same time. Their father had arrived. Desiree thanked God for the distraction, but that didn't change the full gamut of emotions she was still experiencing over seeing Tyson. Watching her father, who was a frail shadow of his usual self, being pushed in a wheelchair took the wind out of Desiree. She flopped down in one of the white chairs, her legs suddenly too weak to allow her to stand. She looked at Junior, and he looked at her, and they exchanged knowing, despairing glances. This was it. The moment she'd come home for. The last party her father would probably attend. Desiree steeled herself for what was to come, but she was not so regretful about attending this party now. Instead, looking out at the expansive estate, at all the guests, at her past and maybe her future, she felt flashes of fear, confusion, and anger all at the same time.

Desiree picked up her newly filled martini glass and downed another drink. No more hiding from Tyree and nursing drinks. It was all too much. She needed more than liquor, if you asked her. This thought made her realize her baby sister, Donna, hadn't shown up at all. *No surprise there*, Desiree thought to herself. Although she'd been gone, her mother and Rebecca had periodically kept her abreast of her siblings and their lives. Desiree had heard all about Donna's drug addiction and stints in rehab.

Junior made a snide chuckle. "How long you think he got?" he said, looking at his Rolex. "I give him about two more weeks," he added heartlessly.

"Shut up, Junior," Desiree grumbled, shaking her head in disgust. It was very apparent that her brother thought everything in life was a joke. She tried to appear as if nothing that was happening was bothering her, but that was far from the truth. Desiree darted her eyes around the backyard nervously.

"Keep your composure," she mumbled to herself. She needed to be on her A game to protect her son. She needed to keep him out of Tyson's eyeshot and her father's too, for that matter.

"Well, our father doesn't like to bested, and that is why he is here, though he is barely able to sit up. A shame, if you ask me," Junior commented. "He can't just be a sick old man. He just has to come put on airs. You'd think by now he'd be tired of this scene, literally."

Junior was sure there would be a show of praise, and all the fakes in attendance would act like their father didn't look like a literal skeleton in a wheelchair. It was the moment Junior was looking forward to, as it would be proof that this was definitely his father's last annual Idlewild all-white affair.

Carolyn saw her husband coming toward her. She tapped her hand on the side of her leg. It was all she could do to tamp down her wired nervous system. Carolyn had watched her husband come through the great-room doors like he owned the night, wheelchair and all. Ernest still had the presence of a world leader and the allure of a king. He waved and smiled. To her, he was still strikingly handsome, even in his failing physical condition. Carolyn felt something inside her chest tighten. She still loved Ernest, and she couldn't help but admit that to herself silently.

All eyes were on Ernest. What was left of his hair was neatly trimmed; he wore an all-white Ralph Lauren Purple Label button-up that Carolyn had given him as a gift on one of the many occasions they had exchanged thoughtless obligatory gifts. She couldn't even remember now if it had been a birthday, an anniversary, or some other special day that didn't mean shit in their marriage anymore. Ernest had his once muscular, toned legs covered under a crisp white Louis Vuitton throw. Rebecca had done a good job dressing him for the event. Carolyn swallowed hard as people surrounded Ernest in his wheelchair. He shook hands with the men, kissed the women, and greeted a few of their other friends with waves. His attention was soon directed toward his wife.

Some of the partygoers could hardly control their excitement as they watched a man who clearly was on his last lap mill around the backyard with a commanding presence. Ernest smiled, laughed even. He had to show his friends that it didn't matter that he was on his death-bed; he was still the strong man he'd always been. What mattered most to Ernest was that he would not look weak to anyone, including his wife and children. He was still the man of the Johnson family, and he wanted that to be clear to everyone, including his son, who he knew was clamoring to step into his shoes.

Junior's jaw rocked as he took long, confident strides around the beautifully decorated estate. Finally, after watching his father's prolonged greetings and hand-shakes for some time, he walked over to him. With a giant's presence, he approached the table at which his father, which was his way of competing with his father. He smiled as he pulled Bella along, hoping to elicit the same reaction he'd gotten from his mother. Junior loved to shock his parents. He'd already been pegged as irre-sponsible, so why not live up to it? His sisters had always had excuses made for their bad acts, but not Junior: any mistakes he made had always been more egregious and more of a bigger deal to his mother and father.

"Pop," Junior greeted, putting on his fake smile. He extended his hand for a shake, but his father ignored it like he didn't see it.

Ernest simply nodded, his eyes on Bella. He folded his arms across his chest and glowered at his son and his companion. "Junior," he returned dryly, without looking at his son.

Junior's hands trembled fiercely. He didn't know if it was nerves or the rush of disappointment he felt from his father's treatment.

Ernest tilted her head, as if to say, "Can I help you?"

Father and son looked at one another for a long minute.

"I guess you didn't think I'd make it this year, and so you thought it was okay to do whatever or bring whomever you wanted," Ernest said flatly, breaking the eerie silence that had settled between them. Bella shifted helplessly under Ernest's gaze. She didn't know whether to go over and greet the old man or remain standing there awkwardly. Bella felt vulnerable, like an outcast about to be called out in front of the crowd.

"Well, you did make it. Glad to see you. And Desiree should make this year extra special for you," Junior said sarcastically, sidestepping his father's dig at Bella. Junior lifted his glass to his lips. Bella shifted on her feet. That was enough of a signal to alert Junior that she was getting impatient with him. There was no telling what his father was thinking either.

"Excuse me," Bella said and turned to walk away. She was clearly uncomfortable in the midst of this unspoken father-and-son power struggle. It was eye-opening for her, to say the least, despite the fact that Junior had told her a little bit about his father.

"Need to go to the little girls' room, do we?" Ernest hissed, sizing up Bella.

Bella turned back around and returned Ernest's eye fuck, showing no signs of the fear that was banging around in her chest. Bella chuckled. She wasn't going to show Ernest that she was scared or intimidated.

Junior cleared his throat, and the two men exchanged another long, heat-filled gaze.

"I'll leave you to talk to your son. Seems to me you have a lot to talk about," Bella replied, still eyeing Ernest boldly, before walking away.

"Why did you need to do that?" Junior growled, his free hand curling into a fist on its own, once Bella had disappeared in the crowd.

"This is my home, and I do as I want," his father replied, looking unfazed by his son's bared teeth and scowling face.

Carolyn stepped between father and son. "Enough," she whispered harshly. "You think this is the time and place for this pissing contest that you two can't seem to stop having lately?" Her cheeks were flushed, to say the least. She could feel her foundation cracking under the heat.

Ernest Sr. bit his bottom lip. His nostrils flared, and suddenly he felt tension rise in his neck. He cleared his throat so that the phlegm he felt building up wouldn't make him sound like a weak old man. "You thought bringing someone like that here was wise, Junior? You thought that would make you look strong? Or did you want our friends to think you're some pimp with whores?" Ernest growled, giving no fucks about Junior's feelings.

It was the open door that Junior had been waiting for. With the alcohol swilling in his system and his father's indignation setting his temper ablaze, Junior squinted his eyes into dashes. It was as if time stood still. All the activities of the party seemed to freeze, and everyone stared at Junior and Ernest like they were watching a movie. Junior bent slightly to meet his father face-to-face. It was the first time in years he'd stood up to him and stopped pretending that he was the doting son, the heir apparent. When he'd found out that his father was thinking of leaving his sister Desiree in charge of all the businesses and financial affairs of the family, Junior had stopped worrying about being the good son in his father's eyes. In fact, ever since he'd been wishing that his old man would die.

Now Junior's gaze was filled with the fire of disdain. Carolyn saw that look and realized there was nothing she could do about it; the anger train had already barreled out of the station. But she refused to budge when Junior took a step closer to his father.

"You have some nerve questioning me! Did you think you were the only one who could have beautiful, exotic women that didn't pass the Johnson sniff test? You think I don't know about you and all the women, Pop? You think I am that stupid!" Junior snarled. "Well, as you can see, two can play your game. I guess I'm not the perfect son anymore, huh? I guess, judging from the fact that you're planning to cut me out of everything, you got a taste of who I really am. Get used to seeing her, because for the rest of your miserable fucking days, she's going to be right by my side."

Ernest bit into the side of his cheek until he could taste his own blood. He knew everyone was watching them. He hated to be embarrassed. His children, of all people, knew this about him. Their family had a name to uphold, and he didn't care what it took to do that. Even if it meant that in the end, he had no children left, he didn't care. So long as his children acted unworthy of the family name, he'd call them out or, better yet, send them away and cut them off.

Ernest reached up and grabbed his son's arm roughly. "I don't care what you know. You will not disrespect me in public. You have some nerve bringing your little whore around our friends to embarrass me. And then you want to speak to me in this way? You've made a deadly mistake," he hissed, his fingers digging into Junior's arm.

Junior was too riled up to feel any pain, but he quickly realized that his father still had a little bit of strength. Things had changed for Junior since he'd met and fallen in love with Bella. He wasn't backing down this time.

There would be no running away and brooding for days. Not today. He was standing his ground.

"What do *you* care? Did you say you were embarrassed when Desiree returned with her illegitimate kid?" Junior shouted just as the band stopped playing. His voice carried over the backyard, as if he'd screamed into a microphone.

Loud groans from some of the partygoers echoed throughout the expansive yard. Junior finally wrestled his arm away from his father's grasp just as Desiree dropped her glass with a loud crash and ran into her parents' house. The damage had been done. Everything had been revealed now. Grumbles and groans continued to spread among the partygoers like the plague.

Carolyn's face was as red as a cooked lobster now. Her lips were pursed. She stomped over to Junior, and in a knee-jerk reaction, she slapped him in the face. Junior held his cheek, in shock.

"Inside the house, Junior! You bring your vile, nasty, hateful drama to our home! How dare you!" Carolyn spat.

"No! How dare you and your fake-ass husband and all your fake-ass friends!" Junior retorted, his face stinging.

"Get off my property! Get out! Take your whore and go!" Carolyn screeched, the veins in her neck bulging. She was mortified by her son's outburst. Carolyn spun around on her heels to see who had been watching this nightmarish scene unfold. And as she suspected, it was the entire party.

"Oh, I most certainly will! But not before everyone here knows the truth!" Junior spat as he got eye to eye with his mother. "I think everyone here would love to know just how imperfect the Johnsons are. I wonder how all Pop's new business ventures will fare then. I wonder if you would look like the perfect, doting wife and the mother with the perfect children then," Junior hissed as he shoved an accusing finger into Carolyn's chest so hard that she stumbled backward, clutching her chest like she'd been shot.

Carolyn could see a few people clasping their chests and placing their hands over their mouths. Others whispered to one another and acted like they didn't see what was happening right in front of them.

"Now, dear mother, we'll see who wins or loses this time!" Junior added. With that, he stomped away and stormed into the house. He headed straight for the foyer and the front door. When he was about fifteen feet from the door, Bella rounded the corner from the guest powder room. She whipped her head around because Junior was moving so fast. Bella changed course and dashed after Junior.

"Junior! Wait! Is everything okay?" she called out as she ran after him. Bella didn't know what the hell was going on, but she could just imagine. "Junior!" she called out again.

"Ms. Donna Johnson!" the butler shouted just as Junior made it to the front door. Seconds later Bella came to a halt beside Junior.

Carolyn almost fainted when she saw her youngest daughter walk through the door. Carolyn suddenly had the urge to throw up. She hadn't really expected Donna to show up there. This was all too much. Carolyn would never have allowed Donna to enter the house without first having Rebecca take her something to wear and make sure she was presentable. The last thing Carolyn wanted was for people to see Donna in anything other than perfect condition. Carolyn's cheeks flamed as Donna stumbled around the foyer, giggling. She was clearly high. Carolyn closed her eyes. She exhaled a windstorm of breath. Carolyn wanted to usher her youngest daughter right back out the door. She stared at Donna, unable to speak.

"What's wrong, Mother?" Donna asked rudely.

Carolyn looked at her like she was a monster. There was nothing Carolyn could say in response.

Donna smirked at her, knowing just what she was doing. "Mother, what is going on?" she asked, quickly folding her arms in front of her and laughing.

Carolyn's face turned dark. She was sick of Donna and Junior, of all her children, for that matter. "Ask your father. You'd prefer to speak to him over me anyway," Carolyn hissed before she turned and walked away from her youngest child.

Bella tried to mind her own business, but she couldn't help looking back at Donna. "So they have another kid too?" Bella mumbled under her breath, realizing there may be some very important things she had yet to find out about the Johnsons. How had she missed that? she wondered as she followed Junior, like she'd been doing for months now.

A high-tech Nikon camera clicked in rapid succession, capturing each high-class partygoer as they exited the Johnson estate. The extended lens sat outside the cracked car window and caught close-up shots of both men and women. No one was spared.

"Did you get him yet?" Special Agent George Craski asked his counterpart, who was adjusting the focus on the camera's lens. More clicking, more adjusting, more clicking.

"Well, if the information Agent Martinez—oops, I mean Bella—called in is correct, then we got our man and a few of the other players we've been watching," Special Agent David Shore replied as he lowered the camera onto his lap and began unscrewing the extended lens.

Both men laughed at their running joke.

"Shit, I've been working for the FBI for fifteen years, and I have never got to go undercover and be the love interest of a rich man," Shore snorted. "Can I get an assignment where a rich, spoiled-ass brat takes me to Saint-Tropez? And buys me Gucci, Prada, Fendi?"

"Hey, let's face it. Martinez looks the part. I can't see you passing for a Colombian print-ad model," Craski taunted, rubbing Shore's pale, balding head.

Shore slapped his hand away and shot him an evil look.

Craski shrugged. "Well, it's the truth."

"What other information did Martinez provide on the call?" Shore asked, changing the subject. He wasn't much in the mood for being teased today. They'd been sitting in that cramped car for hours, while the spoiled rich bastards had sipped Moët and munched on caviar.

"Martinez said the son told her that our guy runs his own trading company for the elite. That he is known among the wealthy for bringing in an eighteen to twenty percent return on investments," Craski said. "But she thinks there is something fishy about the father's business dealings. He told Agent Martinez, or Bella, as he knows her, that he found some documents that his father had doctored to show profits when he knew his company had suffered losses during the stock market crash. He knows his father has been putting money and assets in his mother's name, but he doesn't think that his mother knows."

Craski went on. "Now, the son seems to think that Ernest Johnson is collecting more and more so-called investment money, but he is faking the returns. So, it looks like the elder Johnson continues to collect millions from his clients under the guise that their money is growing. A Ponzi scheme at its fucking best. Judging from the returns we received from the grand jury subpoenas to the banks, Mr. Johnson has been living tax fucking free off his clients' money. A one hundred percent loss for those poor unsuspecting bastards."

Shore whistled and shook his head. "A black Bernie Madoff, huh? Robbing Peter to pay Paul."

"I think he might have Madoff beat. Ernest Johnson has swindled more than the sixty-five billion Madoff got away with," Craski replied gravely.

The two men fell silent. They both seemed to contemplate the gravity of what they were saying.

Shore broke the silence. "And to think he'll be going down all because his son wanted to be loved by a beautiful woman. I guess I have to agree with the saying that life begins and ends in a pussy," he chortled as they pulled away from the curb and began trailing the Bentley that held their female undercover agent.

Desiree splashed water on her face and then looked at herself in the expansive powder-room mirror. She couldn't believe what Junior had done in front of her son. How could he? It didn't matter what he had said about her, but he should not have said it with Tyree standing right there. Desiree sighed and hugged herself. She knew she couldn't hide in the bathroom all night. She made up her mind to make a run for her bedroom.

Desiree opened the main-level powder-room door and peeked out. The coast was clear. She put her head down and rushed toward the winding staircase in the center of the grand foyer.

"Desiree?"

She froze at the sound of her name spoken by a familiar voice.

"Desiree Johnson, is that you?" Tyson Blackwell called.

Desiree couldn't move. Suddenly, it was like her feet had grown roots into the floor. She swallowed hard and held her breath. Before she could turn around, Tyson had rushed around her, and there he stood, right in front of her eyes, looking like an older but otherwise identical version of her son.

"I knew that was you," Tyson said cheerily. "I didn't know you'd be here. It's been years," he said casually, flashing his megawatt smile. The one that had always melted her insides and got her out of her panties in seconds.

Desiree cleared her throat. "Ty, ahem, Tyson," Desiree said, stumbling over his name as if it burned her tongue to say it. "How . . . how are you?" she managed to add, smiling like a starstruck teenage girl.

"I am well. Doing very well," he chimed, smiling back.

"That's great," she said curtly. "I'm so glad to hear it."

"I, um, I always wanted to find a way to contact you. You know, to tell you—" It was Tyson's turn to stumble and stammer over his words.

"No need," Desiree said, interrupting him. "That is all behind us. It was ages ago, and from the looks of it, we have both moved on," she said.

"Yes, yes. You're right. I just never knew what to—"

"Again, no need," Desiree said, cutting him off again. She put her hand up. "It's really fine."

He nodded and blushed a little bit. She could tell he felt just as awkward as she did. "What have you been up to? Do you still live in Chicago?"

"Look, Tyson. We really don't have to—"

"Mom! There you are," Tyree shouted, rushing over to where Desiree and Tyson stood.

Desiree's eyebrows flew up into arches on her face, and her heart literally seized in her chest. She and Tyson turned toward Tyree at the same time. He was barreling toward them too fast for Desiree to stop him.

"Mom, why did you leave the party?" Tyree asked when he reached them. He didn't wait for an answer. "There was some commotion, and Uncle Junior stormed out. What's going on?" he said, his words rushing out as fast as the blood rushed through Desiree's ears.

"I . . . I . . . my head . . . a headache," she stuttered.

Tyson stared at Tyree and then darted his eyes over to Desiree. They locked eyes for several long, telling seconds.

"Is this your baby . . . I mean, your son?" Tyson asked, barely able to get the words out.

Tyree turned toward the strange man. "Tyree," he said, extending his hand for a shake like the gentleman Desiree had taught him to be.

Tyson blinked a few times, completely dumbfounded. He took Tyree's hand and shook it strongly. "Nice to meet you, Tyree," he said, looking over at Desiree as he held on to Tyree's hand longer than a normal handshake would allow.

She lowered her eyes, telling him the answer to the question he was asking with his eyes.

"Mom, do you need me to get you anything?" Tyree asked thoughtfully.

"No, baby. I am going to be okay," Desiree answered.

"Okay, well, I'm going back to talk to Aunty Donna. She's supercool, and I don't remember her from the last time we came around," Tyree told her.

Desiree was too caught up in a tornado's eye of emotions to warn her son away from her baby sister. At that point, she just wanted him to leave so that Tyson would stop staring at Tyree and then at her and then back at Tyree.

"Yes, she's my funny baby sister," Desiree confirmed without saying too much.

Tyree kissed her cheek and rushed off. He didn't bother to say anything to the man standing there, looking like he'd seen a ghost.

Just like he'd come, in a flurry, Tyree was gone. Desiree was alone with Tyson again, but this time something pulled them together, like a rope tethering them to the past.

"Is he . . . ? Is that the . . . ?" Tyson couldn't find his words.

"Listen, we will be gone in a few days. I've never asked for anything, and I won't start now," Desiree replied, fighting back tears. Her throat burned, and her head pounded.

"That's not the point," Tyson said firmly. "He is my . . . I'm his—"

"No," Desiree said firmly. "He is *my* son. *I* am his mother. I am his *only* parent, and the only one he will ever know," she said pointedly.

"That's not fair. I am an adult now. I realize that I made a mistake. I let my parents speak for me back then," Tyson said, his eyes pleading.

"I'm also an adult now, and I also let you and your parents and my parents speak for me. But I don't anymore. Like I said, he is my son, and no one else's, and that is final. I don't compromise when it comes to my son's well-being," Desiree said firmly, not backing down at all when it came to protecting Tyree. "Besides, you're a big criminal court judge now, with a beautiful wife and probably two children or more. You don't need my son to make you whole."

Tyson shook his head. "I am a judge. You're right. But I don't have children. My wife . . . she can't . . . It's not like you think, Desiree," he tried to explain.

"Oh, well, if your idea is that you and your wife will get to play house with my son, you're wrong. Dead wrong. We will be gone again soon. I'm here only because, as you can see, my father . . . ," Desiree shot back, her voice trailing off at the end.

"Please, let's make time to go somewhere and talk before you leave for years again. I'm begging you . . . please," Tyson pleaded, softening his voice in the way he used to do back then.

"I don't think so," Desiree said. With that, she stormed off, leaving Tyson standing there watching her.

As soon as she was no longer in front of him, she finally let her tears fall. She couldn't help the memories from invading her brain.

"Pregnant?" Tyson had asked, shocked. "I thought you said you were on the pill?"

"I . . . I was . . . I mean, I am. Well, I . . . ," Desiree had stammered, wringing her hands in her lap.

Tyson had let out an exasperated breath as he paced in front of her. "How do I know it's mine? I mean, can it happen that fast? We've only, like, done it once or twice."

"I'm sure it's yours, Tyson. I told you. I have never been with anyone else," Desiree said through tears.

Tyson sucked his teeth and contemplated what she'd said. He palmed the sides of his head and squeezed. "Right before the end of high school, Desiree? Really? I didn't want to be a fucking stereotype, one of those dumb-ass guys that knocks up their girlfriend and gets stuck," Tyson said, panicking. "You know that my parents are going to be upset. This will break their heart. It will embarrass them."

Desiree sucked in her bottom lip and swallowed hard. "I'm sorry," she cried. "I didn't do it on purpose. It just happened."

"I don't know what they'll say. I want to be with you, but they won't be happy. They'll say you tried to trap me. I know them. They won't be happy at all. They'll make me stop talking to you for the sake of my family's image . . . for my future's sake," Tyson said. Then his words became accusatory. "You knew that I built my reputation on being an upstanding dude. You knew it. You knew I wouldn't just leave you if you had my kid. Now I have to marry you."

Desiree lowered her face into her hands and sobbed. That certainly wasn't the type of response she had envisioned from the love of her life. The boy who'd professed his undying love for her to get her in his bed.

Now, as she rushed into the same bedroom she'd rushed into back then, Desiree shook her head and swiped at her tears. She sniffed the snot threatening to run from her nose and used the back of her hand to dry her nostrils.

"I'm sorry, Daddy, but I have to go. I have to take my son and go," she said out loud, as if her father was standing in front of her.

Desiree knew it might be the last time she laid eyes on her father, but she hadn't worked that hard to protect Tyree for sixteen years just to let Tyson Blackwell come into their lives and turn them upside down, like he'd done so many years before.

Chapter 8

Nothing Is What It Seems

The day after her alter ego caused a dustup between Junior and his father, Special Agent Liana Martinez rushed through New York's Penn Station, her long hair blowing behind her like a cape of confidence. She was dressed differently than she had been during the past few months, when she'd been undercover. No European-cut jeans, close-fitting shirts, or uncomfortable, expensive high-heel shoes today. Instead, Martinez had donned a pair of loose, dirty blue jeans, a grungy, worn black motorcycle jacket, and her black riding boots. No Colombian model today. She looked at her watch and sucked her teeth. She was late for her meeting with her two case agents, Craski and Shore.

Martinez had overslept after spending another night holed up with Ernest Johnson, Jr. She had comforted him the entire night, after the spectacle at his parents' party in Idlewild. Junior had begged her to stay with him a little while longer. How could she have said no? Junior thought she belonged to him, given the fact that he believed she was his model girlfriend now. Last night Junior had asked that they become exclusive with one another. A request that her alter ego, Bella, had had no choice but to agree to. It was either that or risk the whole case.

Martinez had managed to break away from Junior by telling him that she had a model booking that she couldn't miss. It had even taken her more than an hour to convince Junior that she had to go. He'd offered to pay her whatever the gig was paying, but she'd refused because she had to get out of there for her meeting with her case agents.

Liana Martinez had hurried to her government-commissioned apartment and had changed, picked up her evidence, and then rushed to her meeting. She was sure she would take a bunch of slack from the guys for being late. It was part of the job. Finally, Martinez reached the small pizzeria inside the bustling train station and ambled to the back. It had been their meeting spot since the inception of the case. Agents Craski and Shore were already there, digging into greasy slices of the best pizza in the city. Martinez caught their attention as she approached. The digs began immediately, full mouths and all.

"Aye, if it isn't lover girl, Bella Luna herself," Craski called out sardonically, his Italian mafioso bravado coming through in his words. He wiped his mouth with the back of his hand like a caveman and threw his half-eaten slice onto the greasy paper, as if he'd just lost his appetite. "Is that some kind of womanly glow I see on that face? Must be all that fancy living you've been doing lately, huh?"

"You finally grace us with your presence? I guess you couldn't pull yourself away from your lover boy. Cupid must have bit you in the ass," Shore said, making his own dig. Craski and Shore both laughed.

Martinez rolled her eyes as she took a seat at the table. It was going to be one of those kinds of meetings. Bullshit, bullshit, and then a little bit of work and more bullshit again. She didn't think she'd ever get used to working with these goofballs she called case agents. They were definitely old-school, good ole boys, and they drove her nuts all the time with their chauvinistic comments and schoolboy locker-room antics.

"All right, guys, enough. I'm sorry I'm late. Damn, I couldn't just leave him like that," Martinez replied, her words now totally devoid of a Colombian accent. She had left Bella, her undercover persona, behind, just like that. Martinez had become very skilled at turning that personality off and on.

"You think it's easy playing Bella, the sexy, exotic Colombian model, when I really want to be home eating pussy, riding my Harley, and picking up young hotties on a highway somewhere?" Martinez said sagely. Being undercover wasn't as easy as her colleagues thought it was. She resented the fact that they believed she was just living the high life. She couldn't stand it when Junior touched her sexually, especially because she preferred women. But to get what she needed, Martinez knew it was all par for the course. She likened it to undercover narcs who had to sniff a line or two of coke to get their case evidence.

"I guess we can give you a pass. I mean, I wouldn't know what it's like to kiss a young, handsome rich guy if I liked women. That would be like a guy kissing another guy, but one guy was pretty, right? Or something like that," Craski joked, frowning, as if he'd envisioned something repulsive.

Martinez shook her head in disgust. She wanted to curse Craski out for his crass-ass jokes that weren't the least bit funny, but she held her composure. These were the guys that were assigned to trail her and protect her out there. She also had to get on with the meeting in order to get back to Junior. It wouldn't be long before he started blowing up her cell phone, looking for her. One thing about him, he wasn't going to let a certain number of hours pass without worrying about her whereabouts. Also, for Martinez, missing a day might be missing another piece of the evidence she was collecting to take the Johnson family down. Definitely couldn't afford to miss anything. She had to remain Junior's whole world, or she risked losing the entire case.

"I'll have you know he is a very nice guy. Nothing like the bad boy he portrays himself to be in all those videos you all have of him. A little emotional, in fact. He is desperate to be loved and wanted. Apparently, the parents are shells of the people they portray themselves as in public. Don't show their kids any real love. They just pretend to be the perfect family," Martinez said, defending Junior as calmly as she could.

Craski looked at Shore with a raised eyebrow and then back at Martinez. The two men were both thinking the same thing. Craski cleared his throat and shifted uncomfortably in his chair.

"So, to clarify, you ain't sleeping with that guy on the job, right?" Craski asked as he leaned in close to the table.

Martinez's face flamed. She balled up her toes in her boots. She smirked and shook her head. It was all she could do to take the heat off herself. "What? You think I'm stupid?" she replied, reaching for a slice of pizza. "Would I fuck a man when I like women? I have to make him think I'm his girlfriend, though, don't I? Nothing more than a lot of hot petting and kissing," she lied again. "I hope you all don't think I enjoy even that," she added for good measure. Breaking eye contact with Craski, Martinez chewed her pizza. After a few bites, she looked up to find both men staring at her.

Her eyebrows shot up, forming arches on her face. "What?" she grumbled, tossing her slice down on a paper plate and throwing her hands up. "C'mon, I think my un-

dercover manual says that's all on the up and up. I have
to do what it takes to get all the information. Remember
those words? Besides, I spend most of the time with him
shopping for expensive shit and going to banks so he can
give me cash. All in a day's work, right?"

Craski and Shore seemed to relax a bit. They'd followed
Martinez during most of those shopping and bank trips.
She had shut both men up. Since the day they'd set Junior
up to meet Martinez, she'd brought them tons of great
evidence against Ernest Johnson, Sr., and his son. They
couldn't argue about that. Whatever method she was using
was working. It was the only way they'd been able to find
out which banks Ernest Johnson, Sr. used to further his
schemes, who his clients were, and more importantly, it
was the only way they had been able to keep track of his
and his family's every move without alerting any of
them that they were being investigated. In their years as
criminal investigators, they'd quickly learned that wives
and children were the easiest route to a suspect, and in
this case, they'd learned just how complicit the wife and
the son were in all the senior Johnson's schemes.

"So give us all the new stuff you have," Shore said,
throwing down the crust from his fourth slice of pizza.
He leaned back in the chair, his gut struggling against the
small buttons on his dress shirt.

Martinez pulled up a black bag from near her feet and
sat it next to the pizza box on the table. With the hand
gesture of a game-show host, she presented the bag.

"That's everything from the past two weeks. I was able
to get five more account numbers . . . the Black Card, the
Plum Card, and some new start-up bank Johnson is dealing with, Life State Bank in Miami. I think the manager
is in Johnson's pocket. The son complained about not
having enough access ever since some of the accounts

with larger balances were switched over," Martinez relayed between bites of pizza.

Craski picked up the bag and brought it to his lap. He unzipped the top just enough to peek inside. He looked back up at Martinez with wide eyes.

"A fucking Rolex and a Hublot in just two weeks! He bought these outright?" Craski asked, incredulous.

Shore and Craski both looked long and hard at Martinez.

"Either you got a powerful hand job, or he's stupid and out of his mind," Craski finally commented.

Martinez knew she had to play it cool. She swiped a lock of hair from her face and shook her head.

"No, I can't take any of the credit. It's not anything special that I'm doing, trust me. Junior Johnson just wants to hit his father where it hurts. In his pockets," Martinez replied, her legs swinging back and forth nervously under the table. That answer seemed to put both case agents at ease again.

Martinez hated the fact that these meetings were becoming more and more uncomfortable for her. She wondered if she was really starting to have feelings for Junior, but in a more platonic than romantic way. She actually thought he was a good person under all the layers of emotional baggage that had been passed on to him from his family.

"We need to get his computer or the father's. Since you were able to convince him to take you to that party in Idlewild, which got us some great stuff, maybe you can coax him into taking you to whatever residence houses his home office, maybe his father's . . . the computers they both use the most. I'm sure there are loads of files and, better still, e-mails," Shore said, his tone serious. "Just like Madoff, these white-collar crooks always, always perpetrate their fraud through the wire. We are close, very close, but we need the whole cigar. Understood?"

Martinez dropped her half-eaten slice of pizza and reared back in her chair. She scrubbed her hands over her face and leaned into the table with a grave look on her face.

"I will try, but there is no guarantee that he'll pull another stunt like at the party. I think he regretted bringing me so close to his life. I mean, getting even is one thing, but it literally blew up in his face. He thinks Ernest Sr. will come after him or, worse, cut him off from all business dealings and financially," Martinez told them. "That's his biggest bone of contention, not being named heir to the Johnson empire, or at least the empire he thinks still exists."

"I think Daddy bear knows better than to cut baby bear off. I'm sure Mr. Ponzi Scheme himself knows that his son has been sniffing around. He knows the son has dirt on him and has been involved in most of these schemes. So, we better keep a close eye on him and make sure he doesn't have any untimely fatal accidents or doesn't disappear from right under our noses," Craski warned, raising one eyebrow knowingly at Martinez. "I hear old man Johnson was pretty ruthless in his heyday."

They all fell silent. No one had seemed to think at the investigation's onset about the danger they'd put Junior Johnson in when they'd made him an unsuspecting informant against his own father. Ailing or not, they all recognized that Ernest Johnson, Sr., was a smart, powerful man who'd gone to great lengths to stay wealthy over the years, after his family's original businesses, which he'd inherited, had failed. It was likely that his ruthlessness had not faded with time.

Martinez left her meeting and immediately called Junior.

"Hey, sweetheart. It's Bella. I just wanted to check on you," she crooned, her Colombian accent back in full effect. She smiled when Junior told her to meet him back at Le Parker Meridien. Junior made her job way easier than any other undercover assignment she'd ever been on before.

Chapter 9

Love Loss

"What's going on with you? You've been distant since we got back from the party," Selena whined, twisting the ends of her long silky jet-black hair around her pointer finger, which she usually did when she was bothered by something. "I don't like how you've been acting, Tyson. You haven't spoken to me and have barely touched me. I thought by now you would have ripped my romper off and we would be in bed, but no, all you want to do is be on your dumb computer or act like you have a lot of work to do." Selena stretched out her long, slender legs as she perched on the end of their king-size bed.

From his spot on the bed, Tyson looked up from his computer, a little annoyed by her whiny, nasally voice. Times like tonight, Selena being just a pretty face annoyed him to the point of exhaustion. He couldn't have a conversation with her about anything, really. She liked to talk about her nails, her hair, or some new trinket she'd purchased, and their conversations didn't get much deeper than that. Other times, the fact that his wife was an empty shell was perfect. For instance, he could take her to any government officials' event and the whole room would be watching her. All his fellow judges and most of the state senators and prosecutors could only dream of having a beauty like Selena on their arm. Tyson took pride in being the man when he had her on his arm.

He would walk around, proud as a peacock that he had a trophy wife.

But tonight his mind was completely on Desiree and her son . . . *their* son. Tyson had felt unsettled ever since he'd run into Desiree and the boy. There was no way he could have a calm, cogent conversation with his wife about his feelings, or the situation, for that matter. Selena's brain didn't work in the way that an older woman's worked. She didn't have a grasp of the complexities of life. Tyson knew her limitations and his. At the moment he wanted to push her out of their bedroom and tell her he wanted to be alone.

"Fine," Selena said. "I'll just get ready for bed by myself."

Tyson glanced over at Selena, who was still perched on the end of the bed. He quickly dismissed the ill feelings that had been building inside him when he saw her perfect double-D breasts peeking out of her pink Italian lace La Perla bra. Her neatly shaved vulva winking at him didn't hurt either. Tyson placed his computer down next to him on the bed and flashed his winning smile. His blood ran hot in his veins. One thing about Selena was that she still brought out the sexual beast in Tyson. Which was exactly why he couldn't stay annoyed at his wife for long.

"I'm sorry," Tyson said, moving closer to her. "I've been swamped with this new case. It's nothing for you to take personally." Tyson pulled her toward him. She tried to play hard to get, but he knew that trick.

"Well, I do take it personally," Selena whined, but then she allowed Tyson to pull her on top of him. "I want all your time, *all* the time," she said, her voice suddenly thickening and sounding sexy.

"How personally?" Tyson asked gruffly, his manhood sending the message that he was back, was there and present with her now.

Tyson's taste in women hadn't changed; he liked them young and beautiful. He'd spent years trying to find the right woman to fit his public persona, but he'd only ever really fallen in love with one person. Tyson had grown up feeling that he was deserving of the most beautiful, successful women around. It was how he'd been raised. He'd always been like the prince of Chicago, with women at his fingertips and at his disposal, and though he'd often lost himself in the attention, he had never stopped thinking about or wishing he could speak to his one love, Desiree Johnson. Over the years, Tyson had kept himself in good physical shape, thanks to his team of personal trainers. His wealth and now his status as a judge were two other factors that made him one of the hottest commodities on the market. Still, he kept replaying his run-in with Desiree. What could he have said differently? Should he have just apologized and told her he was grown up now and would've done things differently if he could have?

Tyson pushed those thoughts aside and eyed his wife hungrily. Just looking at her beauty kept Tyson harder than any Viagra ever could. Tyson was quite a bit older than Selena, and he had known her since she was a teenager. He'd always thought she was extraordinarily beautiful, so when his mother had urged him to hire Selena as his legal assistant as a favor to her parents, Tyson hadn't hesitated. At the time his intentions hadn't been to date Selena or even give her the time of day after work hours, but things had gradually ended up there. Selena was undeniably sexy, with her perfect hourglass shape and striking mixed race features. She was the complete beauty package, and this had piqued Tyson's interest from the start. And Selena had been fun to be with in the beginning. She had kept Tyson constantly on his toes and preoccupied. She'd been a constant challenge.

But Selena's best attribute then and now was that she made Tyson look good out in public. Even when he felt less than good enough, which he secretly did often, walking around with his trophy would boost his ego right away. Selena served a vital purpose in his life, but she wasn't exactly what he wanted for himself. His parents approved of her because she was really good at being seen, something his mother, Beth, valued more than anything else in life. Selena was essentially a younger version of his mother, a fact that was lost on him at first.

Beth had long since lost her ambition and had become satisfied with just being a wife and a mother. Tyson's father, Court Blackwell, had chosen Beth as his wife because at the time she was a lot like Selena. When they'd met, Court had been struck by the fact that Beth, a model, was the usual vacuous, overly accommodating, "too pretty for her own good" model or actress type he'd encountered many times while partaking of the elite social scene in downtown Chicago. At the time, Court hadn't been much interested in Beth, but then he'd reached the conclusion that he needed someone to put on his arm, much like Tyson needed Selena now.

Court had told his son many times that a woman should be seen and not heard. Tyson had followed his father's advice and had found the "right" woman, but he'd grown increasingly dismayed when he'd discovered that his wife couldn't actually hold an intelligent conversation about anything. Tyson had tried to ignore his feelings about it all, and soon Selena had become enmeshed in the world of the wealthy and had abandoned her own career aspirations. Then Selena had become obsessed with getting pregnant, while Tyson hadn't been interested in having children at first. He'd never gotten over what had happened with Desiree and after she had disappeared, Tyson had wondered about her and what she'd been through getting rid of a baby.

Selena had turned into just what Tyson had spent his entire life trying to run from—a replica of his mother. Tyson secretly despised his mother. He'd grown up watching his father walk over his mother like the proverbial doormat that she was. During his childhood, there were many nights when Tyson had crept to his parents' wing of their mansion and had heard his parents arguing or his mother weeping. When he'd grown into a man, he'd vowed he would get a strong woman, one who had her own mind and would give him a challenge. Tyson had lied to himself. He'd given in to his parents' influence and found exactly what he resented—a weak and over accommodating wife who was just like his mother had been for as long as he could remember.

While Tyson had quickly grown bored with his marriage to Selena, he wouldn't leave his wife. He was too comfortable using his wife as an arm piece, as a trophy, in order to make everyone watching think he had a full life. Despite his inertia, he felt a void so big and deep, and he was sinking in it little by little each day. Now, knowing he had a son out there was going to kill him inside until he could do something about it.

He kept thinking about Desiree and their time together as teenagers. Desiree had been a breath of fresh air in his life back then. She'd always spoken confidently, and although she was the spoiled daughter of Carolyn and Ernest Johnson, Sr., she had carved out her own identity. Desiree was smart and equally beautiful. Tyson loved her mind and her confidence, both of which overshadowed her looks. When Tyson had begun to get to know Desiree, he'd secretly admired her zest for life. Back then, Tyson had wished he could bottle it like some magic potion and give it to his mother to drink so that she would turn into her own person.

He still loved Desiree now, a fact that had been abundantly clear to him when he'd laid eyes on her at the Johnsons' party. Desiree had evolved into the woman he knew she would become. She was still stubborn and sure of herself. She still stood up for what she believed in and what she wanted. All the attributes that had convinced Tyson back then that he wanted to be with her. He knew he'd messed up in terms of the way he had treated her after they found out she was pregnant. He had kicked himself every day since then.

After that first meeting with Desiree and her parents, Tyson had felt distraught and overpowered by his parents. Not only had he not stood up for himself or Desiree or their baby, but he had actually acted like a coward and had stood there with his hands shoved into his pockets, unable to even make eye contact with her. He'd achieved many milestones since that day, but nothing was ever good enough for Tyson. Nothing had ever filled the deep void he'd been feeling for almost seventeen years. Tyson had gone through life doing exactly what was expected of him. Yes, he was successful in his career and owned the beautiful mansion he'd been expected to own all his life. All that was fine, but he still needed to make things right with Desiree and his son, or he would never be fulfilled in life.

Selena touched and stroked Tyson's manhood now, pulling him out of his reverie. She watched Tyson close his eyes and lose himself. She didn't mind entertaining her husband. This was her job. She loved to shop, go out to dinner, and most of all, she loved to fuck Tyson.

"How about we do all the things we love to do . . . but this one first?" she whispered in his ear. Then she giggled as she let her hair fall around her face seductively. Her striking blue eyes mesmerized him.

"Whatever you want," Tyson drawled as Selena straddled him and lowered her head toward his manhood, trailing her tongue down his chest and stomach.

"Anything for you," he grunted when she finally reached her destination and took him in her mouth. She moved her head up and down like her life depended on it. This was another reason Tyson keep Selena around. In addition to being a bubbleheaded trophy wife, she gave him the best sex he'd ever had.

"Ah," Tyson gasped, closing his eyes and letting Selena take him to ecstasy. He didn't have a care in the world anymore. He'd let the invasive thoughts of Desiree fall away from his mind for a moment. But just for a moment.

An hour later, Tyson was roused from his sex-induced coma by his cell phone vibrating on his nightstand. He mindlessly reached over and picked up the buzzing nuisance.

"Hello," Tyson huffed into the mouthpiece, his eyes still half shut.

Seconds of silence ticked by.

"Hello?" Tyson grumbled when he still got no response. He could hear someone breathing on the other end of the phone. His eyes popped open when he finally heard a voice. Tyson felt a rush of heat come over his body when the caller spoke.

"You said you wanted to talk. I think we should, but just once, so we can be done with it," said a woman's voice, which he recognized as Desiree's.

"Hello? Desi?" Tyson said loudly into the phone, fully awake now, his heart thundering.

"Yes. One chance for me to tell you everything about him and to hear you out. No promises and nothing expected," Desiree said firmly.

"Oh, okay. When?"

"In the morning. Our old spot," she said. With that, she hung up.

Tyson snatched the phone away from his ear and peered at the screen frantically. The screen read unknown.

Unnerved, Tyson sat up in the bed and scrubbed his hands over his face. He took in a deep breath in an attempt to calm his heart down. He exhaled and looked at his phone one more time, as if something might have changed. Tyson's movement caused Selena to stir next to him.

"What's the matter, honey?" she asked, her voice filled with sleep. Selena leaned up on one elbow, letting the sheet fall away from her breasts. Tyson looked over at her and managed a half-hearted smile. His bottom lip quivered from nerves.

"Nothing. Go back to sleep. Business call, that's all," Tyson lied, giving the easiest story he could think of.

"Oh," Selena huffed, yanking the sheet back over her. She wasted no time turning back over and returning to her beauty rest.

Tyson stood up from the bed and walked into the bedroom's huge luxury bathroom. He flicked on the lights above the sink and stared at himself in the large mirror hanging over the white-and-gold marble–topped double sinks. He could see worry flickering in his own eyes. Tyson had no idea what to expect from this meeting with Desiree, but now he felt sure the possibilities could be endless. The thought caused a shiver to run the length of his spine. Tyson had finally met his son, and it had reduced him almost to tears to think he'd missed out on so much of his life. Even a man as powerful as he was could lose himself in emotions over something like this. The boy was his own flesh and blood. All he could do was pray that the meeting with Desiree would be good for them all. "What now?" he whispered to himself. "What now?"

Desiree stood on the beach, facing Spring Lake, one of the quieter lakes in Idlewild. It had always been her favorite place in the world when she was a kid and a teenager. Being the oldest daughter in the Johnson family, Desiree had always been expected to be a social butterfly, to be on the scene and, once she was old enough, to be at the family's club, the Point. However, her social anxiety meant that all of that was more pain than it was worth, so her favorite place in Idlewild was a place where no one could find her—the farthest corner of Spring Lake. That little lake held so much of her life in its shell-filled sand and its air, redolent of fresh water and woods. The water came right up to her feet now, and with every new ripple that covered her toes, memories flooded her mind. Desiree closed her eyes.

It was the summer when Desiree had just turned fifteen. She'd snuck out of the house with the help of Rebecca and had rushed to this very spot, Spring Lake, where she had agreed to meet her new love. She had invited Tyson to her secret place. When Desiree had made it to the lakeshore, to the very spot where the lake fed into a tributary and rocks hung slightly over the water, Tyson was there waiting. She skipped over to him. They played tag. They had a rock-skimming contest, and when Desiree's rock skidded across the water for the longest time without sinking, she jumped up and down and teased Tyson for losing to a girl. Tyson grabbed her around the waist, picked her up off her feet, and spun her around. Desiree giggled so hard, her midsection ached.

He suddenly stopped spinning her, held her still, looked up into her face, and said, "I love you, Desiree Johnson." Then they kissed passionately. He laid her down on the wet sand and made love to her. It was her first time. She had never experienced the feelings swirling inside her before.

"I remember this being my favorite place in Idlewild every summer," Tyson said now.

Desiree jumped and whirled around, as if he'd jolted her with an electric shock. "Oh, goodness. You scared me," she gasped, holding her chest. She could barely look Tyson in the face. Each time she did, her insides melted. The memories had been kicking her ass ever since she'd laid eyes on him at her parents' all-white affair.

"Sorry. I didn't mean to startle you," he said smoothly. "I'm glad you called, Desi. I'm so grateful."

Desiree squeezed her stomach and told herself she had to stay strong no matter what she was experiencing inside. She couldn't let her feelings get in the way, not at this very important meeting. She could kick her own ass for coming to Idlewild at all, knowing there was a possibility she'd run into Tyson. Desiree had always known she wasn't over him. The fact that she had refused to date anyone else in all the years since Tyree was born was evidence enough.

"I didn't call for pleasure, Tyson," Desiree said firmly. She quickly wiped her mind clear of the fuzzy memories of love and fun and put her brain in protective mother mode.

"Okay." He put his hands up. "I don't want to push . . . I just . . ."

"This isn't about you. Everything isn't about you," Desiree interjected, making herself clear. She pulled back a little bit. She didn't want to seem like she was angry and bitter. She wanted to be strong but not come across as a wounded, scorned ex-girlfriend. "This is about Tyree and nothing else," she said, softening.

"Okay," Tyson conceded, shoving his hands in his pants pockets.

"He's a good boy," Desiree began, her voice wavering. The tears immediately sprang to her eyes. Tyson went to open his mouth, but she put her hand up to stop him. "He deserves to have a good life. I've tried my best to raise him to be an upstanding man who follows through, tells the truth, and lives up to his responsibilities," she said, making a not-so-subtle dig at Tyson.

She went on. "There is only so much a mother can do. A mother can teach a boy only what she knows, but he needs a man. I've kept him away from my brother and my father to protect everyone else, but it's time for me to think about him. He's growing up. He stopped asking me about his father when he was about twelve years old. You know why? Because he gave up. It pains me to know that my son, the light of my life, gave up on himself and me," Desiree said, the tears falling now.

"I . . . I . . . don't know what to say, Desiree," Tyson said. He reached out for her hand, and she took it. "All I can say is I'm sorry. I was a kid. I was under the influence of my parents, and I never thought—"

"What?" Desiree thundered, snatching her hand away from him. "You never thought I'd go through with the pregnancy and ruin your life? Even all these years later?" She threw her hands up. "I don't even know why I came here," she said through tears. "This . . . this was a mistake." She started to walk away, but Tyson grabbed her arm.

"Wait . . . please," he said softly. In an instinctive act of love, he pulled her to his chest and held on to her.

This wasn't how she had intended their meeting to go, but it felt so right that she didn't bother to fight it.

Chapter 10

Framed

Tommy's apartment was in the center of a newly gentrified section of Chicago's West Side. It was inside a swanky warehouse-style building that had been converted into luxury lofts. The inside of his loft boasted almost two thousand square feet, and Tommy had it decked out with gaudy red, black, and white ultramodern leather couches and chairs, zebra-print throw rugs, and large black-and-white framed art of various parts of a woman's anatomy. The loft and its trappings were just as arrogant as Tommy. Even though it was only a couple of blocks away from the projects he'd grown up in, his new lifestyle was a world away. Tommy had carved out a good life for himself by using women. A lot of the things inside his place had been purchased with Donna's American Express card while they'd been dating before she disappeared into rehab.

"This is so boss," Tyree said, in awe, as he walked into the apartment with his aunty Donna and her cool friends.

"Where you get this li'l nigga from?" Tommy joked. "He is amazed by everything. Where he been living? Under a rock?"

"Basically," Donna answered as she watched her nephew move around the loft like it was a museum. "His mother would die if she knew I took him with me," she added, shrugging and laughing. "You know I'm not worthy of being around the golden child, right?" She laughed some more.

"So how did you get him out of that big-ass house with no one seeing you?" Tommy asked.

"Oh, trust me, we had to wait. My sister left the house, said she had some kind of important meeting before they hit the road back into hiding," Donna explained. "I asked the kid if he wanted to be a rebel and hang out and party with real party people. Of course his sheltered ass was all about it." She chuckled. "Personally, he is way more down to earth than my sister could ever be. She's just like my mother—a faker and a pretender."

"That nigga need a joint," Tommy said, then chuckled. "He is made lame. Good-looking kid, but lame as hell. He acts like he's never seen anything before. I would love to see where he lives. Must be a fucking trailer park."

"Naw, he will not be getting high on my watch," Donna said firmly. "I can't stand my sister, but I love my nephew. No drugs for him. Hopefully, he will turn out way better than all of us," she said sincerely as she watched Tyree with love in her eyes.

Donna and Tyree were at Tommy's place for four hours before the full crowd arrived for the impromptu party. Tyree was having the time of his life. He was partying with an older crowd, his mother wasn't there, hovering, as usual, and most of all, the beautiful girls there were all making him feel like he was the man. He snapped so many selfies with gorgeous faces that he lost count. There was no way his friends back home would believe that he'd partied up on the West Side of Chicago with models and rich people. Tyree had never experienced anything like this in his life. He was confused about why his mother had kept him away from his aunt Donna and his uncle Junior, and the Idlewild and all of it, for that matter. He made a note to himself to ask her what was really going on in their lives.

Donna watched proudly as her nephew enjoyed himself. It had been easier than she'd thought it would be to get Tyree to trust her and leave with her behind his mother's back. He'd been down before the thought had fully left her mouth. In the short time she'd been around him, Donna had felt closer to Tyree than any other person in her family. It was weird, because she was sure he didn't remember her from when he was little, but their bond had seemed to form quickly. As she watched Tyree now, her thoughts turned to her parents.

Donna had seen both of her parents at her mother's annual all-white affair, but it hadn't turned out so well. When her mother had first caught sight of her, she'd reacted like Donna was a beast coming to destroy their good time. Clearly, her mother's reaction meant she felt embarrassed about Donna. Nobody told Donna about her brother's outburst at the party, of course. Donna walked around the backyard and enjoyed the party as if she was perfect. She knew her appearance and the chitter-chatter of her mother's pretentious, self-serving friends was driving her mother to drink, but what did Donna care? She picked up several alcoholic drinks as she went and gulped them down right in her mother's face. Donna figured that if she was the black sheep, she was going to live up to it from that day forward.

As she stood in Tommy's loft now, Donna kept watching her nephew from a distance. She smiled. Things at that moment were perfect. She had someone there who actually acted like he loved her. And Lee wasn't there. Donna had Tommy all to herself right now. Things were perfect, if just for a moment. It didn't matter how much money she'd spent on Tommy since their reunion, as he still kept Lee around. It had gotten to the point where Donna had just accepted it. It was like they were all in a relationship together. When Donna had first come back

from rehab and had found Tommy at the club, things
between her and Lee had been contentious, but only until
Tommy had pulled out the drugs. Donna and Lee got
along fine now, so long as they could get high. Tommy
found it amusing, even arousing.

"That boy don't know what hit him," Tommy joked
as he walked over to Donna, smiling. "He is loving the
attention."

"I'm glad I am the one to show him a good time . . .
finally," Donna replied. "My sister acts like he is a baby.
Wait until she realizes he is gone. She's going to lose her
shit." Donna shrugged. "It won't be the first time my entire family is disappointed in me. I don't even care what
they think anymore. At least he will have had a great time
when I finally decide to return him."

"Here. I got something that will definitely help you not
give a fuck what they think," Tommy said. He pulled out
a shiny package and waved it in front of Donna's face.

Tommy stood over Donna as she sniffed the first line of
a new type of crank he'd just acquired from his supplier
up in Humboldt Park. Of course, Donna had agreed to
experiment with him in the name of love and money.

"Holy shit!" she exclaimed after inhaling the first line.
She jumped up on her feet a bit and spun around.

"Right! Who takes care of your ass?" Tommy laughed.
Then he pushed another line of the new strain in front of
Donna and urged her on. He watched her closely, waiting
for the reaction his supplier had told him he should
expect.

Donna sniffed the second line, and the rush went
straight to her head. Donna fell back against the couch
at first, and then her eyes rolled up until the whites were
the only parts showing. Her mind went completely blank.
She wasn't thinking about herself, much less about Tyree.

Tommy watched intently, waiting patiently. Suddenly,
Donna jumped up off the couch like she was possessed

by a demon and began quickly walking in circles around Tommy's S-shaped glass coffee table. Tommy jumped at first. Donna's sudden movement had startled him. He quickly realized she was tweaking on one hundred, just like his supplier had guaranteed. Tommy was elated. Donna was going to be the perfect advertisement for his new product.

The party was going on around them, but Donna had slipped into a private party inside her own head. She didn't even remember that her nephew was somewhere in the loft, doing only God knows what, and with God knows whom. She had quickly chosen drugs over looking out for Tyree.

Tommy smiled evilly, confident that he had bought some good shit. He slapped his hands together at his accomplishment, then watched Donna for a few minutes. She was jumping around now, flopping her head from side to side like a wild rave dancer. Thoroughly amused, Tommy bent over at the waist, laughing.

"Look, Lee, she's tweaking like a fiend! This shit is supreme! I'm going to clock a ton on this shit," Tommy shouted excitedly, pointing at Donna like she was a circus act. His girl, Lee, had finally arrived.

Donna was dripping with sweat just that fast. She had no control over her body. It swayed like she had no bones. She moved like she was in a race for her life. A few partygoers stopped what they were doing to watch her. Tommy wasted no time putting them on to what Donna had had . . . for a fee, of course.

"I got to get some more of this shit," Tommy said, thoroughly amused. "Bahahaha! Look at her go! Look at the rich bitch go!" Tommy was satisfied that this would be it. He was sure Donna would be hooked again, which meant his pockets would be padded again. It had been a very small investment with a huge return.

Donna began going even faster around the coffee table now. They didn't know how she hadn't passed out from exhaustion yet. She was soaked with sweat now. Her cheeks were flaming red, and her nostrils flared.

"She better not fuck up my table, or I'll have to charge her twenty thousand this time," Tommy said, laughing even harder.

Lee eyed Donna with contempt. She hated having Donna around, because everything felt like a competition between them.

"That's what happens when you get high after being clean for so long," Lee pointed out dryly, rolling her eyes. "She looks like she about to collapse. Must be some powerful shit. I think I'm going to go make friends with her little nephew while you babysit her. He is supercute," she said, disgusted with Tommy and his games.

After Donna and Lee's first meeting at the club, Tommy had enlisted Lee's help in swindling Donna out of her money. He'd told Lee his plan was to act like he loved the dumb, sheltered rich girl, until he got what he wanted. Lee never thought about the fact that Tommy had been doing the same thing to her at one point. Tommy kept Lee so high that most of the time, Lee didn't think at all. She certainly didn't think about her mother, Carly Shepherd, a famous New York socialite, popular among the rich and famous. Lee's mother, Carly, never missed an A-list event, nor did she ever miss any opportunities to be seen in photos. She had several business ventures, but none brought Carly more attention than being known as the one who'd tell the paparazzi and the tabloids everything that was going on inside those exclusive events. *Move over, The Shade Room and Wendy Williams. Carly Shepherd has you beat*, was Carly's motto. Carly fashioned herself as the pulse of the celebrity gossip world.

The one thing Carly didn't have her finger on the pulse of was her daughter. When Carly divorced Lee's father, Lee Briggs, the front man of Dead Heads, a multiplatinum rock band that toured with the likes of Ozzie Osborne, Carly divorced her child as well. Carly just wasn't interested in being a mother after her husband left. In fact, Carly had never been much into being a mother at all. Even when Lee was a small child, her mother used her as a prop, like the little dogs that rich Hollywood women would keep in their purses. Carly would dress Lee up in the cutest designer clothes and drag her places so she got attention by having the cutest child. But that didn't last long. Once Lee was big and not so doll babyish anymore, her mother had no more use for her.

When Carly and her husband, Lee, finished dragging each other through the mud during their very public, dirty divorce, Lee lived with her father at first, moving with him to California, but she couldn't get along with his new, very young wife. Lee moved back to New York to live with her mother, but the two argued incessantly. Lee hated her mother, and the feeling was apparently mutual. Carly had never shown her daughter any love or affection from the time she was born. She had often told Lee she was just like her father—and that she was destined to be a druggie stoner who'd lose everything to a habit.

Lee finally left her mother's house again, and this time she decided to try something new. Because both coasts had failed her, she figured she might try something in the middle, and so she settled on Chicago. At first, she stayed with friends that she had made through school and the internet, but then she met Tommy. It was then that her journey down the dark path of drug addiction and risky behavior began. Lee often saw her mother on TV, but she acted as if she didn't even know Carly, though she accepted the check Carly sent to her PO box every month so that she, Lee, would stay away. Lee often thought about going to one of those big red-carpet events and letting everyone know just who Carly was—the neglectful parent of a drug addict who lived on the street while her mother rubbed elbows with the rich. Most of the time the only thing that kept Lee from outing her mother was the fact that she was too high to get going.

Now Lee walked over and touched Tyree on his shoulder. He turned around, smiling wide, his face glazed with sweat, overly excited. Lee smiled. She couldn't remember the last time she'd been high on life without needing any substances, like Tyree was now. She found it amusing. He really was a good-looking kid. Lee immediately wondered if he had a big dick. Even at his young age, he stood over six feet tall and had big feet. She could get with him if he had a bigger dick than scrawny-ass Tommy.

"Hey, you're a cutie," Lee said, flirting.

"Thanks," Tyree replied as he watched her touch his chest in a way no girl in his high school ever had.

"You having a good time?" she asked, circling him like a bird of prey.

"Am I! This party is lit," Tyree replied excitedly, whipping his head around for emphasis. "These people are fun."

"If you take this, you'll have an even better time," Lee told him, opening her hand to expose a pill in her palm. She'd wasted no time moving in for the kill. She had already heard Donna say several times that she didn't want her nephew getting high. Lee knew she'd find a way one day to get back at Donna for encroaching on her relationship with Tommy. This was perfect.

"What is it?" Tyree asked, his face growing serious. "I . . . I . . . don't do drugs," he said, putting his hands up in front of him and shaking his head.

"This is not exactly drugs, but . . . okay," Lee said, shrugging. She touched him sexily. She was sure to pop

the pill into her own mouth. "Nothing to it. I thought
you were a big boy and wanted to have a good time," she
said, lifting her skirt a little bit. She knew how to seduce
men and boys. She'd learned at a very young age from
watching her mother. All of them were the same; it didn't
matter their age. Men were fueled by one thing.

"I . . . I . . . do, but without the drugs," Tyree insisted.
"I mean, whatever you want to do," he added, unable to
take his eyes off the first in-person pussy he'd seen in his
entire life.

"C'mon, let me show you something," Lee said, extending her hand toward Tyree. He rushed over to her and
took her hand. She led him through the partygoers into a
back room, but not before she swiped a soda from a table
and slipped another tablet into it. Once Lee and Tyree
were alone, she continued her seduction.

"So, what do you know how to do?" she asked, licking
her lips and dragging her fingernails across his neck
slowly.

"Um . . . every . . . everything, I guess," he said breathlessly. He was slightly embarrassed that he couldn't control his breathing and that his entire body was covered
with goose bumps.

"Let me see," Lee said, tugging at Tyree's belt.

His heart was beating so fast, he felt like he'd faint. His
legs shook, as if he were standing on top of a vibrating
floor. He felt his manhood already pushing against the
hard material of his jeans. He was ashamed, but he
couldn't help it. His imagination had already taken off
like a rocket on its way to space. "You . . . you want to
see?" he panted, then swallowed hard. His head was
spinning, as if he were on a merry-go-round.

"You look like you need to take a drink," Lee said,
laughing at his nervousness. "Here. It's just soda," she
said, pushing the spiked can toward Tyree. She knew that

as bad as he was huffing and puffing, he wasn't going to refuse the drink. Her plan was working just perfectly.

He grabbed the soda and sucked on it so much that he almost finished the entire can in one gulp. He winced as the acidy drink, which his mother would kill him for having, burned a little going down. "Ah," he said and then belched. He shook his head in an attempt to shake off the burning in his chest.

"Oh, excuse you," Lee said, laughing at his nervous belch. "Now back to this." She fell to knees in front of Tyree's waist. She unzipped his pants and dug into his underwear.

"Oh my gosh," he gasped, his chest rising and falling so hard, he had to clutch it to keep himself from hyperventilating. "I . . . I . . . um," he stammered but never got his words out.

"You, what? You're ready to go to heaven?" Lee asked him as she held on to his penis. She was right: for a teenage boy, he had way more dick than Tommy. Lee was excited.

"Mmm," Tyree moaned. It was all he could muster at that moment.

He had never experienced anything like this. He had read about it, had watched porn sometimes behind his mother's back, but had never dreamed this would be happening now . . . at his age. He couldn't think straight. He watched with wide eyes, and she played with him at first. He closed his eyes and let out a long breath when she rubbed the tip of his dick over her lips. But when Lee took him in her mouth . . .

"Oh shit!" Tyree screamed. He felt like he was going to faint or have a heart attack.

Everything around him seemed louder, more colorful; his senses were heightened. The drugs seemed to take effect at the same time that Lee went to work slurping and bobbing up and down on his manhood. Tyree felt like his body was floating. He had never experienced anything like it. He screamed again and shook, like he was having a seizure. He literally felt like he was flying around the room. He could hear the slurping noises and could feel the amazing feeling below his waist, but he couldn't really react. He reached down, but he couldn't grab hold of Lee's head or hair, or anything, for that matter. He couldn't see straight. Nothing seemed real except the sensitive feeling happening all over his body.

"Argh!" Tyree moaned as he reached the first orgasm he'd ever had. He exploded, and Lee lapped up every ounce of him. With that, Tyree collapsed onto the bed, his legs finally giving out. He was asleep within minutes, breathing like a grizzly bear.

Lee laughed. She snapped pictures of Donna's nephew knocked out, with his shirt up, his dripping dick out, his pants down around his ankles. She'd have the pictures on her phone, with the intention of torturing Donna with them later. Lee needed to go back and check on Tommy.

"Sleep tight, lame," she said, snapping her last picture of Tyree, before she left the room.

"Hey! Sit down already!" Tommy yelled at Donna. "Hey! Did you hear me?"

Donna was jumping in place now. There was not a dry spot on her entire body. Her body moved like a rag doll, loose and limp. She looked like she'd run an entire New York City Marathon, with the amount of sweat covering her from head to toe.

"Hey! Don't you fucking hear me!" Tommy yelled again, clapping his hands loudly. Donna kept moving like she couldn't hear him. He stalked over to her and grabbed her around the waist roughly. "Quit moving!" he shouted in Donna's ear, as if he thought she was deaf.

Finally, she stopped moving. Tommy had to hold her tightly to prevent her from starting up again. Donna's face was as red as a cooked lobster, her hair stuck to her sweat-drenched brow, and her eyes were glazed over. She looked like a dead-eyed zombie. Tommy's eyes grew wide, he had finally had the chance to take a good look at her. It wasn't funny anymore. She looked like she was in another place. Her eyes were sunken and vacant. She looked pale, like she would collapse at any minute. Her lips were almost green.

"Shit," he mumbled under his breath. He slapped her on the cheeks. "C'mon, you can't tweak all night," he screamed at her, jiggling her chin roughly. "Snap out of it. Enough is enough."

After a few slaps, the initial rush began to break, and Donna could hear Tommy's voice. Still amused by his handiwork, Tommy dragged her over to his chocolate-brown suede accent chair and plopped her down. Donna stared straight ahead like a real zombie, her eyes stretched to their capacity. Tommy watched her for a few minutes, his mind racing. Then Tommy walked around, thinking. He knew by the looks of things, he had given Donna too much of the powerful mix of new drugs.

"Whoa. That was some powerful shit you gave her, T. Let me hit that," Lee said, stumbling over from wherever she'd been.

It didn't matter that Donna looked like she was about to die of exhaustion and could barely control her breathing. Lee didn't want to feel like Tommy had done something for Donna that he hadn't done for her. And, after taking a good look at Donna, Lee was sold that on the notion that Tommy's new drug was something she had to have for herself. She had never seen anything they'd used in the past do that to anyone else, and she'd damn sure never experienced a high even remotely near that. She was jealous that Tommy had chosen Donna to test his new product and not her.

Tommy blew a puff of air from his lips in response to Lee's request. He wasn't thinking about getting Lee high; he was thinking about the money he was going to make off the new shit. He didn't have time for the jealousy at that moment.

"Naw. That pure, backwoods, redneck-made shit is only for her. Not you. Can't you understand what's going on here? Just reeling her back in until I get what I want from her," Tommy whispered in Lee's ear. "Shit, if your skinny ass takes a hit of this, your rock-star daddy and media-whore mommy will be burying you," he added, chuckling.

That wasn't what Lee wanted to hear. She pushed away from Tommy. She really wanted to claw his eyes out. She hated it when he tried to regulate her like that. She scrubbed her hands over her face and pushed her tangled hair back on her head. Lee began pacing in front of Tommy. She bit her bottom lip until she drew blood. She wanted some of those drugs. Her mouth filled with saliva when she just thought about the high she was Donna experiencing. She wanted to escape too. Tommy was being a bastard, as usual.

"C'mon, Tommy, just give me one hit. A small taste. Please," Lee pleaded. "I mean, you did it for her," she whined like a baby. She was ready to throw herself on the floor and kick and scream for some of that drug.

Tommy's eyes hooded over, and within a minute he was in Lee's face. He grabbed her cheeks roughly and squeezed as hard as he could. She squeezed her eyes shut from the pain. Tears sprang to her eyes too. "I said fucking no! Stop being a fiend and shut the fuck up while I check on her," Tommy said dismissively, releasing Lee's face with a forceful shove.

Lee went stumbling backward. She held her left cheek and let the tears fall. She was embarrassed. People around them had seen the whole thing. She was brooding; her blood was boiling inside. Tommy began walking toward where Donna was slumped over. Lee stomped over to him and got in his face. Her hunger for the drug had given her a false sense of courage. She didn't care anymore. She was pissed now.

"There's but so much I'm going to take, Tommy! You fucking liar! I mean, like, just because I get high doesn't mean I'm going to stand by and, like, watch you fuck her and get her stoned and say nothing about it. I'm supposed to be your girl, not her! You don't even need her money!" Lee shot back, her face beet red, her tears streaking black mascara down her cheeks so that she looked like a sad, dark clown.

Tommy's hands curled into fists, and he rushed into Lee like a bulldozer. Lee grunted and fell back from the force. She hit her ass hard on the hardwood floor. Tommy stood over her menacingly.

"What did you just say to me?" he growled, unclenching his fists and grabbing Lee around her skeletal neck. He lifted her to her feet by the throat, cutting of her air supply. She immediately began gagging. Her feet dangled mercilessly as she tried in vain to get her fingers between Tommy's grip and her neck.

"Close your fucking mouth! You want her to hear you and mess up our plan? Huh?" Tommy snarled through clenched teeth as he squeezed Lee's neck mercilessly. "You can't get another dime out of your mommy and daddy, except for that bullshit hush money your mother sends, so how do you think I've been keeping you high? You think your habit is free? How the fuck you think you have a roof over your dumb head?"

Lee felt like he was mad enough to kill her in that moment. She clawed at his hand some more as she gasped for breath under the tight grip he had on her throat. Her efforts were in vain.

"Now, if I tell you to go along with a plan, any plan—I don't care if it's for you to get in bed with her and have some girl-on-girl action—you will fucking do it!" Tommy growled, then released Lee.

She fell back and landed on the hardwood floor in a heap. She curled up into a fetal position, gasping for breath. This was the side of Tommy she hated to see. The abusive, crazy side. He was showing it more often now than ever. Tears streamed down her face. She was left with the reality that Tommy was the only person she had right now. She scrambled up off the floor, half dizzy, and ran back into the bedroom where she'd left Donna's nephew, but not before she was succeeded at swiping some of Tommy's new drug from the table.

The next morning the sun streaming across her face snapped Donna out of an almost comatose sleep. As she regained consciousness, pain racked her entire body. The first thing she felt come alive with excruciating pain was her head. Donna felt like someone had placed a C-clamp on her head and was twisting the handle, tightening the clamp with each passing second.

"Mmm," she moaned as she fought the pain and turned her head to the left. She tried to move her right arm over her eyes, but lifting her arm was a chore. It felt like it weighed a thousand pounds. The pain behind her eye sockets was unbearable. Donna hadn't been hung over and in this kind of condition in months. "Ouch," she groaned. Her tongue felt as heavy as lead. Donna squinted her eyes, and the pain caused tears to run out the sides of her eyes and pool in her ears. She blinked rapidly, and things started to come into focus. She was on the floor. She could tell that much. Her back ached with a pain that she'd never felt before. So did her legs, arms, neck, and rib cage. She would've sworn someone had stomped on her while wearing combat boots—that was how bad she felt.

Donna swallowed hard; her throat was desert dry. Then she inhaled, trying to get oxygen to her brain so she could think. She remembered she was at Tommy's place. That was a start.

"Ugh," she grumbled. An acrid, metallic smell shot straight up her nostrils. "Ew," Donna said, raising her hand over her lips, as the smell threatened to make her throw up. She swallowed the bile that was rising from her stomach into her esophagus. Then she placed her palms flat on the floor and exerted some effort. She tried to sit up, but the room was spinning, which made her flop right back down. "Ow," she groaned as her head hit the floor. "What the hell is that smell?" Donna moved her head to the right, and the smell seemed to become more pronounced. Then she realized that she had vomited, and it was all over the side of her face and on her chest and hands.

"Oh God," she rasped, wiping her hands on her shirt. Finally, Donna opened her eyes wide enough to see things clearly. It wasn't the same day. She didn't remember shit about the night before, but then it hit her. She had brought her nephew here with her. *Fuck! Where is he now?* She'd kept him out overnight! Panic hit her in the chest like a one-thousand-pound boulder.

"Tyree," she gasped, fighting her pain and struggling to her feet. "Tyree!" she called, louder this time. It hurt her head to yell, but she didn't care. She had to find her nephew. Her sister would kill her if anything happened to Tyree. Donna tripped over a few drugged-out people sleeping on the floor as she beat a path to the bedrooms.

"Tyree!" she called out again, on the verge of throwing up again. Between the adrenaline coursing through her veins from panic and the hangover, Donna felt like death was about to snatch her soul right out of her body. As she stumbled around, everything hurt, but she couldn't give up. She had to find Tyree and get him back to Idlewild ASAP. Donna finally pushed into one of Tommy's spare bedrooms. As she rushed round the room, she fell over something on the floor. Donna hit the floor and rolled over. She hadn't expected anything to be in her way, and her legs were barely steady. Not a good combination.

"Lee?" Donna groaned, using what strength she had left to lift herself up into a sitting position on the floor. She quickly forgot the pain pulsating through her body. She could see the girl lying in front of her. Donna pulled herself up off the floor. When she finally got to her feet, she looked down at Lee, who was lying facedown on the floor. Lee's dirty-blond hair was spread out over her head and the floor and looked like a yellow spiderweb.

"Lee? Lee, wake up. Where's Tommy? Where's my nephew?" Donna croaked, pushing Lee with her foot. "Get up. Why are you lying there like that?"

Silence. And Lee didn't move a muscle.

She pushed Lee harder with her foot this time. "C'mon, Lee. I know you hear me. I need to get out of here. I have to take my nephew back to Idlewild," Donna shouted, a bit more urgency in her tone.

Lee still didn't move or utter a sound.

"Don't play hardball, Lee. Just tell me where Tommy went. He has my keys and my wallet," Donna said, full-on panic lacing her words now. "Lee! Get up!" Donna yelled, raising her voice as much as her sore throat would let her. She finally bent down and shook Lee roughly. Lee's body was stiff. Donna used what energy she could muster to push Lee over onto her back.

"Lee . . . I know you hear me," Donna barked as Lee's head lolled to the side. Donna finally took a good look at the stiff girl. "Oh my God! Lee!" she screamed, her body starting to shake.

Lee's lips were purple, and her eyes were open, staring straight up, glassy and dull. Donna whirled around on the balls of her feet. She could no longer feel the pain pulsating through her body. Her headache was suddenly gone. That was when she spotted her nephew sprawled out on the bed. She rushed over and shook him too.

"Tyree! Wake up!" Donna screamed. "Tyree!"

Tyree groaned as he awoke. "Ow," he blurted, wincing and immediately holding his head. He felt like death. There were bells ringing in his head. "Aunty Dee, what happened to me?" he asked, sitting up like it hurt to do so. "I . . . I don't remember anything." Still holding his head, he squinted his eyes.

Donna let out a long breath, trying to calm her nerves. "Tyree, I need you to listen to me. Was Lee in here with you all night?" she said, trying to keep as calm as she possibly could given the circumstances.

"Who?" Tyree asked. "Lee?"

"Her!" Donna yelled, pointing toward Lee.

Tyree stood up on wobbly legs, took a few steps, and looked down at the girl. He shook his head from side to side and put his hands up in surrender. "I have no idea. I don't know. I've never seen her. I don't know her," he lied, his eyes wide open.

Donna gave him a good once-over. "How did you get blood on your shirt? What happened in here?" she quizzed, grabbing Tyree by the shoulders and shaking him.

He looked down at himself, and his eyes stretched wide. He whirled around with his hands out in front of him. "I don't know! I . . . I . . . I don't know," he said in a panic, his voice rising and falling from fear. "I swear . . . I don't . . . I didn't."

"Did you take anything? Did someone give you drugs?" Donna asked, pressing, as she grabbed his shoulders again and shook him hard. "Did you? Huh? Tell me!" she screamed, shaking him some more. "Tell me!"

Tyree collapsed on the floor and burst into tears. He shook his head while holding it on each side. "I don't remember!" he exclaimed. "Nothing is coming back to me. It's . . . it's all blank. I can't! I don't know!"

"What is the last thing you remember?" Donna asked, trying to calm her voice so he wouldn't be too scared to talk to her. "Tyree, she has blood on her, and you have blood on you. Please, please try to remember. Did you have a fight with her?" Donna whirled around and around, as if searching for an answer.

Her nephew couldn't answer. All he could do was sob. "I really don't know," he told her, his body quaking.

"Oh my God! Oh my God!" Donna cried, flailing her hands in front of her. She looked back down at Lee, whose lips were dark purple. Lee's mouth hung open, and blood covered her chest. Donna couldn't tell what injury she had sustained. There was no weapon around anywhere. Tyree had blood on his shirt, but he wasn't near Lee when Donna found him. He was on the bed.

Donna was frantic. She suddenly had to urinate, and her chest heaved. She touched her own body to make sure she wasn't dreaming. She looked back at her nephew, and it was then that she noticed that he had blood not only on his shirt but also all over the front of his jeans.

"What happened?" Donna cried. She began tugging at Tyree's clothes, getting blood all over her hands. She felt under his shirt for injuries. He wasn't cut. He wasn't bleeding either.

Tyree stood up and did the same. He touched his jeans and brought his bloodied hand up in front of his face. Tyree bent over and threw up. He fell to his knees and started to crawl to a far corner of the room. He rested his back up against the wall. He couldn't control his breathing. His heart was galloping in his chest. He looked over at the body again and sobbed some more. "I swear . . . I didn't do anything to her. I swear, Aunty Dee," he cried.

Donna put her hands up to her head, but that just smeared Lee's blood on her own hair. The room was spinning. The smell. The sight of the Lee lying there, stiff and lifeless. Her nephew covered in blood, with no recollection of what had happened. Desiree finding out. Her parents. It was all too much. Donna held on to the hair on either side of her head and let out a high-pitched scream.

It seemed like an eternity before the police showed up at Tommy's place. Donna sat on Tommy's couch, hugging Tyree and rocking back and forth. She couldn't even remember calling 911. The loft was now swarming with uniformed police officers, a crime scene unit, investigators from the medical examiner's office, and plainclothes detectives. They were all moving like busy bees, and their frenetic movement was making Donna dizzy. Tyree kept his head on her shoulder and his eyes closed. She'd asked him if he wanted to call his mother and let her know he was all right, but he had refused. Tyree didn't know what he would say to his mother now. She would be so disappointed. She would die inside when she found out that he'd snuck off behind her back. Tyree realized now, in that moment, that his mother wasn't some uncool mom. She had always been strict for his own protection. He hated that he might break her heart now.

Donna watched as several of the officers huddled together, whispering and looking over at her and Tyree. Finally, a tall, slender woman detective headed toward where Donna sat shivering and holding on to her nephew for dear life. Donna eyed the woman tentatively. She reminded Donna of the lady cop from *Law & Order*. The scene in front of her was like a television episode in Donna's mind anyway.

"Hi, Donna. I'm Detective Dietrich," the *Law & Order* look-alike said, introducing herself, as she kneeled down in front of Donna and extended her hand. She didn't say a word to Tyree.

Donna looked blankly at the detective and didn't shake her hand. Detective Dietrich was fairly pretty to be a cop, she thought fleetingly. She didn't know why she was pondering that at a time like this, but it was all she could do to keep herself from screaming some more.

Detective Dietrich finally dropped her hand and exhaled. "Donna, honey, we're going to need you to tell us what you can remember about what happened, and then we will have to speak to the boy," Detective Dietrich said softly, patting Donna's knee.

Donna lowered her eyes, clutched Tyree, and rocked even harder. "I . . . I don't know what happened, and I can't let you speak to him without his mother present," she replied. "He is a minor, and he is not old enough." She'd heard during her days hanging in the streets that cops weren't supposed to speak to minors alone, without a parent or a lawyer present. It was within their rights to refuse such an interview.

A streak of frustration flitted across Detective Dietrich's face. She was trying to be patient. Donna could tell that patience wasn't her strong suit, as the detective set her jaw squarely and blew out a windstorm of exasperated breath.

"Listen, the only way we can help you and him is if you help us," Detective Dietrich said, finally getting hold of her calmer self.

Donna didn't say a word. She was truly speechless. Her mind was as blank as the day she was born. She couldn't remember even coming to Tommy's apartment a day ago. She had dropped the ball when it came to watching out for Tyree. The one time she tried to be responsible for someone other than herself and she'd failed miserably. Now it was her responsibility to protect him as much as she could. That was the least that she could do.

"Was there any drug use going on here last night?" the detective asked Donna, raising a knowing eyebrow.

Tyree clutched Donna tighter, and he hiccupped a sob. He'd been crying off and on since they'd found Lee, but hearing the detective ask about drugs sent him over the top again. Seeing him like that, Donna began to cry. She shook her head back and forth. Didn't this detective know how frustrating it was not to be able to remember anything? "I . . . I . . . can't remember anything. Like I told you already," Donna answered weakly.

"You all need to tell us the truth. There is a dead girl lying back there, and he's covered in what appears to be her blood. We're all here to piece together exactly what happened, and trust me, if you don't speak now, they'll come to their own conclusions," Detective Dietrich huffed, pointing toward the gang of law enforcement professionals coming and going from the bedroom where Lee's body still lay. "The only way we get to the bottom of what happened is if you all start talking. I suggest you both think long and hard," the detective added, her patience finally gone.

She got to her feet and hovered over Donna and Tyree like a dark cloud about to rain down on them. There would be no more getting down to their level. In the detective's mind, they both knew exactly what had happened and they were being difficult. Detective Dietrich knew it was important to try to get permission from Donna before she spoke to the kid, or everything he said could be thrown out as evidence. She also knew she had a small window of time to get something before either one of them got their mind together enough to ask for a lawyer. In Dietrich's experience, these little rich, spoiled types always knew their rights. She had to think fast. If she could just get the boy to say something, anything, she might be able to hold on to them.

"I was asleep out here, and he was in the back, asleep. When we both woke up, we found her. He can't remember anything," Donna finally rasped through her tears, her voice barely audible. It was nearly gone from all the screaming.

"So you wake up covered in blood, as you reported, and you don't remember anything?" Detective Dietrich repeated, directing her question straight at Tyree. She furrowed her eyebrows and squinted her eyes.

At that very moment some sort of commotion at the front door got Donna's attention, and then Tommy appeared in the doorway. He had finally arrived back at the apartment. Donna and Tyree both sat up when they saw him.

Where has he been all this time! Donna screamed silently.

"Tommy!" Donna called out as she jumped up from the couch, getting ready to rush toward Tommy.

Donna's sudden movement startled Detective Dietrich, causing her to whirl around on the balls of her feet. Detective Dietrich glanced toward Tommy and then back at Donna. There was no way these two were going to get anywhere near one another to make up a story. Dietrich knew better.

"Donna, sit down," Detective Dietrich ordered, trying to use her body to block Donna's view of Tommy. Donna ignored the pushy detective and watched as Tommy was whisked away to the opposite side of the apartment by two male detectives.

"Wait! I need to see Tommy! I need to ask him what happened," Donna cried, still standing up, ready to run toward Tommy. "He might know what happened. He might've seen something! He had to have seen something!"

Detective Dietrich placed her hands on Donna's shoulders and forced her back down on the couch.

"I need to see him . . . ," Donna began.

Just then, investigators from the medical examiner's office wheeled Lee's body past on a gurney. Lee was covered in a black body bag. All the air in Donna's lungs seemed to rush from her body in a whoosh. At first, she opened her mouth and no sound came out. But then she could hear her own voice at an ear-shattering pitch. Tyree threw his hands up to his ears, and he rocked and sobbed as well. Lee was really dead. If they hadn't believed it before, they knew for sure now.

"Oh my God! Oh my God!" Donna cried as she stared at the body bag.

"What did I do? What did I do!" Tyree moaned over and over, without thinking about what he was saying.

Detective Dietrich shot a look at the uniformed officers standing around the apartment. This was what she'd been waiting to hear. Anything that could be twisted into an admission of guilt was all the detective needed to get someone in cuffs.

"Tyree, how did you get the blood all over your clothes?" Detective Dietrich asked, moving in for the kill while she had the boy's aunt too emotional to protest.

Knitting his eyebrows, Tyree gazed silently at the detective.

"You were asking yourself, What did I do? We want to know what you did too. We want to help you sort this all out, Tyree," Detective Dietrich explained, pushing.

Donna turned toward the detective with her eyes squinted into dashes. What the fuck didn't she understand! "I told you! He doesn't know! He can't remember!" Donna growled, shaking.

Tyree was so emotional, he lost his breath as he punched the leather arm of the couch so hard, he drew blood on his knuckles.

Detective Dietrich noticed that both of Tyree's hands looked pretty rough, like he'd been fighting. She signaled to a male detective to follow her to the other side of the room. Seconds later the two detectives formed a huddle.

"The kid appears to have defensive wounds on his hands and scratches on his arm. I think a fight happened, or maybe even a rape, and things got way out of hand. Add in the meth paraphernalia that we found and, boom, murder," Detective Dietrich said in a low voice, running down her theory to her counterpart.

They both watched Tyree as they whispered about him. He held his head in his hands and rocked feverishly. Looked like he was hiding something to them.

Detective Dietrich shrugged. She thought she definitely had her case in the bag. "I think we need to take him down to the station and get to the bottom of his version of what really happened. Although, I think I already have it all figured out," Detective Dietrich said. "I'll tackle the age barrier once we have him down there. He can ask for his mother . . . but not before I get a little bit of information first."

She nodded her head at the three uniformed officers who were flanking the couch on which Donna and Tyree sat.

"Let's keep the media out of this for now," Detective Dietrich whispered to the detective at her side. With the daughter and the grandson of Ernest Johnson as their murder suspects, and the daughter of Carly Shepherd as their victim, the detectives knew this case could turn into a media circus very quickly.

"Tyree, please stand up," one of the officers instructed.

Tyree's eyes went wide, and his eyebrows furrowed with confusion. He looked over at his aunt for help. Donna shot up onto her feet.

"Wait, I told you he is a minor. He can't speak to you without his parent," Donna insisted.

"Am I under arrest? What is going on?" Tyree asked, his heart galloping in his chest.

"We just want to ask you some questions down at the precinct," the officer said flatly.

"I won't let you take him! No! We know our rights," Donna yelled.

Detective Dietrich stepped over and pushed Donna's shoulder down hard to signal for her to sit down. "We have a partial admission of guilt and enough evidence to take him down to the station, whether you protest or not," she said. "We are well within our rights. This is a murder, not jaywalking or some minor shit."

"You can't arrest him! He's a child!" Donna protested.

"Tyree, you have the right to remain silent. If you chose to give up that right, anything you say can and will be used against you in a court of law . . . ," a uniformed officer droned as he prodded Tyree to stand up.

"Why? I didn't do anything! I mean, I . . . I . . . can't remember! I didn't kill anyone! Aunty Dee, help me! Please! Don't let them take me!" Tyree cried, his face drawn into a pitiful frown.

His pleas broke Donna's heart. She doubled over and sobbed.

Tyree felt rough hands on his arms. He pushed the officer's hands away.

"I can stand up on my own," he protested through his tears. The officer snatched his hands away and waited for Tyree to fall in line. Tyree stood up on shaky legs, and the uniformed officer handcuffed him and began a pat-down search of his person.

"I need to call my mother!" Tyree cried. "Aunty Dee, please! This is not right! Call my mother!"

Donna could not stop sobbing. This was all her fault. As Tyree was being prepared to be led out of the apartment, Donna caught sight of Tommy, who was being interviewed by two male detectives.

"Tommy! Help us out of this! Please tell them what happened! You're the only one that really knows what happened here!" Donna begged as she watched her poor, innocent nephew being led away in handcuffs. "Tommy . . . please! Tell them that Tyree didn't do it!"

Donna's pleas fell on deaf ears. Tommy didn't even look in her direction.

Chapter 11

Crisis Mode

Desiree rode back to her parents' Idlewild estate in shock. She didn't know how exactly to feel after spending the afternoon with Tyson like they hadn't missed a beat in seventeen years. Desiree's head swam as she kept replaying how he had held her and then kissed her. She'd pushed him away, but she had still felt something deep in her soul when he did it. Tyson had apologized profusely, but within minutes, as they sat on the sand, staring out at the water, like they'd done so many times as teenagers, he had put his arm around her again and she'd laid her head on his shoulder.

"You're so stupid, Desiree," she grumbled aloud now. "That man is married. He is being nice only to get close to Tyree." She scolded herself until she pulled in her parents' driveway.

Rebecca was on the expansive front porch, her arms folded across her chest, like she knew Desiree had done something wrong. Desiree parked her car, looked at herself in the visor mirror to make sure nothing was amiss on her face, and got out of the car.

"Hey," she called out to Rebecca.

"Evening, Desi," Rebecca said, a hint of accusation in her tone.

"Everything okay?" Desiree asked, feeling guilty as hell.

"Fine. I was just wondering where you and Tyree went off to so early," Rebecca said, her eyebrows arched.

"I went to a meeting . . . Tyree should be in his room," Desiree said, winded after climbing the front steps. "He likes to sleep late, but not this late."

"Oh," Rebecca said. "He's not here. I haven't seen him since last night."

"What?" Desiree said, her voice going up a few octaves. "What do you mean?"

"I saw him at the party, talking to Junior for a while, but I haven't seen him since then," Rebecca explained. "Of course, I had to tend to your father, so maybe I missed him."

"I saw him right before I left the party for my bed. I had a headache. Tyree kissed me good night," Desiree said. Then she thought about it. When she'd gotten up and snuck out to meet Tyson, she hadn't wanted Tyree to see her and ask her any questions. But she had assumed he was in his room, asleep.

"Oh goodness," Rebecca said, worry cropping up in her voice.

Desiree rushed inside the house and raced up to Tyree's room, which was really Junior's old bedroom in the house. She opened the door and found the room empty. Frantic, Desiree raced to her own bedroom. Empty. Then to Donna's old room. Empty.

"Shit," Desiree panted as she scrambled to the far east end of the house, where her parents' suite was located. As she rushed there, she ran into her mother.

"Desi? Everything all right?" Carolyn asked, noticing the wild, frantic look on Desiree's face.

"Have you seen Tyree?" Desiree asked, her words rushing out.

"He was with Junior at the party, but—" her mother began.

"No! I saw him after that. He was in the house. He is supposed to be here," Desiree interrupted, on the verge of tears.

"Have you called his cell phone?" her mother asked.

Desiree fumbled with her phone and, with shaking hands, hit Tyree's name. She walked around in circles as she waited for his phone to ring, but it never did. Tyree's giggling voice filtered through Desiree's phone as his goofy, playful voicemail greeting played.

"It went straight to voicemail," Desiree said, her voice cracking.

"I'm sure he has to be here somewhere," Carolyn said, a bit too calm for Desiree's liking. "Maybe he went down to the beach. Remember how you kids used to sneak down there and—"

"Mother! Please! This is not the time for memory lane," Desiree shouted, cutting her mother off. "Bad enough I'm here and can't stop these fucking memories from choking the life out of me! I need to find my son!"

Carolyn clutched her chest and stepped back. "Well, I'm sorry. Should we call the police? Report him missing?" Carolyn asked.

"Police . . . missing," Desiree whispered as both words seemed to burn holes in her tongue.

Junior jumped out of his sleep when his cell phone began ringing on the hotel's nightstand. It was strange, since no one ever called him anymore besides Bella, and Bella was lying right next to him in the bed, taking a nap following their afternoon delight.

Junior unhooked his body from Bella's clutch and blindly grabbed for his phone. Barely able to get his eyes to focus, Junior squinted at the small screen. Finally, he was able to see that it read unknown. He sighed and closed his eyes again. Junior started to press IGNORE, but a feeling in the pit of his stomach told him to pick up. Whoever was calling him had a reason, and it had to be important. What if it was about his father?

Leaning away from Bella, Junior held the phone tightly to his ear, hoping that Bella would not hear the voice on the other end, in case it happened to belong to his mother.

"Hello?" Junior breathed into the receiver, his head flat on the pillow. Immediately, goose bumps covered his body in response to the sound filtering through the receiver.

"Hello? Desi? Wait . . . calm down. Wait," Junior said, his voice going high and his eyes widening. He shoved Bella's arm completely off him and shot up in the bed. "Desi! What is it? Please calm down. I can't understand what you're saying!" Junior exclaimed frantically.

His heart immediately started hitting against his breastbone with the force of a jackhammer on concrete. Junior was on his feet in one swift motion. He was no longer worried about Bella overhearing his conversation. Clearly, it was an emergency. His sister was beside herself with grief and panic. Bella sat up in the bed, alarmed at the high-pitched tone of Junior's voice. Her eyes were round like marbles; her mouth was slack with confusion.

"Junior, what is it?" Bella asked groggily, scrubbing her hand over her face in an effort to wipe away the sleep cobwebs.

Junior halted her with his hand and gave her his back. Now wasn't the time to be responsive to Bella. He needed a minute of privacy to speak to his sister Desiree. Only God knew what the matter could be, but Junior couldn't help thinking that it concerned their father, given the fact that their father had been in a fragile physical state of late. Bella was going to have to understand that.

Bella craned her neck and furrowed her brow at Junior's brisk rejection. She was taken aback. She sat back on the bed and watched Junior speak in a panicked tone to whoever was on the phone. Bella listened intently. Everything Junior did was of interest to her. These were the times when she had to put on her Special Agent Martinez hat and leave model chick Bella to the side. If anything was suspicious, Agent Martinez was intensely interested and tuned in. She sat on the edge of the bed listening closely to every word Junior uttered. If the senior Ernest Johnson had croaked, she needed to know that right away.

"No! He's not with me. I haven't seen him since I left the party. He didn't ask to hang out with me or anything like that. Are you sure you searched the beaches and everywhere in Idlewild?" Junior replied swiftly, pacing. "Oh my God, Desi. Okay, sis, calm down. I'm on my way!" Junior exclaimed, his words coming out rapid fire. He had a look of horror painted on his face.

"I'm coming!" Junior cried before he threw his phone down on the bed and raced around in circles. He mumbled under his breath and flailed his arms, like he didn't know where to begin, like he couldn't decide whether he should get dressed, call his mother, or run out of the hotel room.

Bella watched Junior for a few minutes, and then she decided to act. She slid off the bed, swiped her long hair back, and walked over to where Junior was going around in circles. Bella grabbed him around the waist. She wanted to stop him for a minute, help him gather his thoughts.

"No! I have to go! I have to go!" Junior shouted, pushing at her small arms. Bella held him tighter.

"Talk to me, baby," she cooed. "You can tell me anything."

"Not now. My family needs me. I have to get out of here. I should've been there," Junior snapped angrily. He was already blaming himself, when there was no way it could be his fault.

Bella just tightened her grip and pulled him close to her chest. She knew Junior was in no shape to leave like that.

"Shh. Wait. Junior, baby, take a minute to calm down," Bella soothed, holding him tightly, like he was a mental patient in need of a straitjacket. "Tell me what is going on. Please, Junior, please talk to me."

Junior's shoulders slumped, and he finally relented. Bella wasn't giving up, and he didn't really want her to. His body seemed to go limp against Bella's. The rise and fall of her chest and the steady thud of her heart comforted him. Bella eased her grip a little and moved back an inch so she could look up into his face.

Junior's face displayed horror. For the first time, Junior looked less than manly to Bella. It was as if worry lines had suddenly cropped up on his face after the call. She'd never seen him look this helpless and weak.

"Talk to me," she said softly, looking in Junior's glassy eyes. "I want to help. I want to be here for you, Junior, that's all." Bella's facial expression was sympathetic yet serious.

Junior closed his eyes for a minute and put his face in his hands. He didn't know if he wanted to share this with Bella. He'd told her a lot, but nothing about Desiree and the situation with her son. Most of what Bella knew she'd gathered from Junior's cruel outburst at the all-white affair, which he had immediately re-gretted. Junior wanted to stay close to Bella and hated to leave her out of anything. He was torn. But Bella wouldn't give up. She pressed him gently until he finally revealed what had happened.

"It's my nephew," Junior whispered, his mouth feeling like he hadn't drunk water in days. "That was my sister Desiree on the phone. My nephew wasn't in the Idlewild house when she got back this evening. He's missing. No one has seen him since last night, at the party," Junior relayed, shaking his head like a lost child.

Bella's facial expression changed, turning into a mixture of sympathy and shock. She could only imagine what was going on. Junior hadn't told him much about his sister and nephew, but she had thought he was a cute, good kid when she'd met him at the party. Hadn't seemed like the type to just disappear like that. Special Agent Martinez was thinking now. She'd have to find a way to make a call and get some of her people on the case to look for the kid. She'd have to do that secretly. She wanted to help, and she also didn't want this to be a distraction that took Junior out of her sight for days or weeks. She couldn't afford to lose sight of her case at this point. Not after she'd gotten this far with Junior.

"I'm so sorry. Did they call the police? Did anyone see him leave the house? Do they think something happened to him?" Bella asked, her mind racing a mile a minute. She tried to think of all the things Agents Craski and Shore would ask her. This was definitely something that had to be reported. Martinez wasn't too happy about having to deal with the local police either.

"I really don't know what happened, Bella. It's all so much. My sister couldn't talk long. She was so upset. Screaming and crying. She has never been away from him for more than school hours since he was born. That kid is her life . . . literally," Junior said ruefully.

Bella didn't speak. She was a bit dumbfounded.

"Bella, I don't know. But I have to go. I know my family may not be the greatest, but they're all I have. Really, I have to go. I'm sorry for pulling you into my mess of a life.

I'm really sorry that you have to deal with all this. First, the party fiasco . . . now this," Junior told her solemnly.

Bella released him and put her hands up in surrender. She had heard enough. She was itching to call her FBI counterparts to get them started on locating the boy.

"Okay. I understand. I will wait for you to call me," she told him. "You know if you need me, you can just call me."

Junior gave her a half-hearted smile. He finally began getting dressed. He looked around the hotel room, and his legs suddenly got weak. He flopped down on the bed and began sobbing loudly. The sense of calm that Bella had given him a few minutes earlier hadn't lasted long. Bella sat next to him and went to put her arm around his quaking shoulders. The burden of it all had finally settled on Junior like a five-hundred-ton weight. His family really was a mess, but they were the only mess he'd ever known. He had to do better by them.

"Please . . . don't," Junior cried, waving her away. For the first time an overwhelming feeling of shame about how vulnerable he'd been around Bella took ahold of him. *Maybe if I wasn't here with her, I would've been there for Tyree. I've been weak. Like a bitch*, Junior scolded himself. He had a migraine after thinking about it all.

"Bella, look. I've been away from my family, and I've been selfish. I put way too much time into this . . . this . . . us. I need to get my shit together for my family and for myself," Junior said, his honesty sending bat-sized butterflies into Bella's stomach. "I don't know what I was thinking. I've been so busy being shameless, just like my father had been so many times, that I lost sight of everything that should have been important to me. I let my family suffer because I was so hell bent on revenge against my father. I've been reckless. Now look what is going on. My nephew is out there and may be in trouble, and it's all my damn fault."

Bella stood up and walked away from Junior. She turned her back and sighed loudly. Bella knew what was coming next.

"So what does all that mean, Junior? I mean for us? For me?" she asked.

"I'm sorry, Bella, but I can't talk about that right now. I just don't know anything right now," Junior said flatly, trying to get his emotions together. He had to be there for Desiree and Tyree, even if it meant letting Bella and his deep feelings for her go.

"You don't mean that. I know you're upset," Bella replied, grasping at any bit of sympathy he might have left. She was seeing her case fall apart second by second.

"I mean it. If I wasn't here, being all wrapped up in you, with my fucking head in the clouds all the time, my nephew might not be gone," Junior snapped. He meant it. He'd been acting like a bitch, all head over heels for Bella.

"Just go to your family. If you need me, I am always here," Bella told him, still not giving up all the way.

She watched as Junior stormed out of the hotel room. This time he didn't leave a gift or any cash.

Bella rushed over to her pants and pulled her cell phone out of a pocket. She noticed that she had six missed calls. She recalled the last number and pressed the CONNECT button.

"Martinez!" a voice said in a rush.

"Yeah?"

"Don't let Junior Johnson out of your fucking sight. We just found out that he and his father are in deep with the Irish Mafia. They may go after him, and we need him to stay safe, or all of this will be for nothing," Shore belted into the phone.

"Too late. He just left," Martinez said, slumping down on the side of the bed.

"Well, you better find him. Find him fast!" Shore screamed frantically.

Liana Martinez hung up the phone and tossed it across the room.

"Fuck!" she cursed, flexing her jaw. She grabbed her undercover garb and slid into the jeans and tight-fitting top. She had her work cut out for her.

"He said his nephew is missing. There's a fucking million miles of land in Idlewild. He could be any fucking where," Martinez grumbled aloud as she headed out the door. She had to find Junior and tell him everything before something terrible happened, if it hadn't already.

Chapter 12

Guilty Until Proven Innocent

Tyree lifted his head when he heard the locks on the slate-gray metal door click. He rubbed his red-rimmed eyes as they adjusted to the light. He let out a long, exasperated breath when he saw who had entered the room. *Not this lady again*, Tyree said to himself. He had definitely had enough.

Detective Dietrich slammed a stack of files and a videotape down on the opposite side of the small, wobbly metal table. Detective Dietrich's face was stoic and hard lined. She wore twenty-two years of police work like a mask, each worry line that had cropped up near her mouth and each wrinkle branching out from the corners of her eyes telling a different story of sleepless nights, dead people, and remorseless suspects. Detective Dietrich had broken through the Chicago PD's glass ceiling, and she prided herself on her nearly perfect track record. She was known around the department for "always getting her man."

No kids, no family, and no life outside of work had made it easy for Detective Dietrich to be the best of the best. She had dedicated her entire adult life to the police department, sometimes to a fault. Since becoming a detective, Dietrich had not left any case unsolved and had elicited confessions in all but one of her cases. She was not about to let some rich, murderous little brat change that. She looked at Tyree with pure disgust. He was an example of everything Dietrich hated in her life. Here was this little boy, who, she assumed by virtue of his last name, had been born with a silver spoon in his mouth, throwing his life away on wild parties, drugs, and now murder.

Detective Dietrich had already surmised that Tyree had never worked for anything a day in his life, which was the complete opposite of her own upbringing. Dietrich had been born in Rogers Park, deep into the Northeast Side of Chicago, and had been abandoned by two drug-addicted parents, who had never looked back. Dietrich had knocked around in the old foster care system at a time before anyone cared about finding foster children a loving, stable home. She had suffered abuse at the hands of several foster parents and had to work extra hard just to make something of herself. She flexed her jaw now, just thinking about it all. How senseless it was for these rich people to throw their lives away when the road was paved for them. She had low tolerance for the insolence of the rich.

"You ready to talk?" Detective Dietrich asked, placing her hand on top of the videotape. It was a scare tactic that she had been best at using within her unit. It almost always got a suspect talking.

Tyree looked down at the tape and back at Dietrich. Nothing could possibly be on the videotape, Tyree thought. People didn't even use videotapes anymore.

"Well?" Dietrich shifted her head to the side, drumming her fingers on the top of the videotape. Her prop seemed to draw Tyree's attention, like it was intended to do. Dietrich felt a pang of excitement flit through her stomach. Conquering this little rich boy would do so much for her. She could taste the vindication on her tongue.

Tyree looked down at the table, at the videotape, and then placed his head back down on his folded arms. He wasn't going to say it again. He did not remember shit about the murder. All he knew was that he didn't do it.

Detective Dietrich could feel heat rising from her feet and making its way up her body. She clenched her fists. This little boy was really starting to push her buttons. The videotape prop had worked on grown, well-seasoned criminals. How dare this little bastard make her feel stupid! She moved to the edge of her seat, the large vein in her neck pulsing fiercely against her skin.

"Look, Tyree, I am only trying to help you help yourself. What we already know is that a girl is dead and that you were the last person seen with her. You had her blood all over you. Now I'm trying to find out why it happened. Maybe it was self-defense. Maybe she attacked you, and you took a weapon from her, and things just . . . just happened. Maybe everything that happened is all on this videotape, and I am trying to clarify why it happened," Detective Dietrich opined, raising her eyebrows at Tyree.

Tyree didn't budge. He kept his head down on the table, ignoring everything the detective was saying.

Dietrich closed her eyes for a quick second to compose herself. *You get more bees with honey than with shit. You get more bees with honey*, Dietrich chanted inside her head. She had to try to keep herself calm now.

"Ahem," she said, clearing her throat. "Tyree, you know this could be easier than you think. I'm trying to help you. I really am trying to be in your corner. Here's what I can tell you. That building and your aunt's boyfriend's apartment had plenty of cameras around. We have access to all of that when something like this happens, you know, and we can review those tapes." Dietrich retrieved her pen from her shirt pocket and tapped it on the videotape.

Tyree lifted his head and stared at Detective Dietrich with a glazed look in his eyes. "If you have the murder on that tape, then I need to see it, because I already told you I don't know what happened. Maybe I can learn something new from you too . . . since you already think you know what happened. You don't really need my help, Detective," Tyree deadpanned. He wasn't trying to be difficult, but this detective acted as if he didn't understand English.

The line had been drawn in the sand. The tension in the room was so thick now, it was almost palpable.

Detective Dietrich leaned into the table, her face drawn into a tight scowl. "Now listen fucking here, you little bastard—" she began, but the sound of the door locks clicking interrupted her tirade. Both Dietrich and Tyree jumped at the sound of the steel door clanging open. Dietrich whirled her head around so hard, she almost gave herself whiplash. Tyree popped up from his seat. Neither of them knew what to expect.

"That'll be enough, Detective. My client does not wish to speak on this matter until he has had time to consult with me," a male voice announced.

Tyree and Detective Dietrich looked up at the tall, slender black man standing in the doorway, flanked by two uniformed officers. He displayed a smile that showed a perfect set of gleaming white teeth.

"Aaron Collins, Mr. Johnson's attorney. I can't say it's nice to meet you, Detective. Maybe if these were better circumstances," the man said, smiling wide and holding his card out in front of him, between his pointer and middle fingers.

Detective Dietrich's jaw rocked feverishly as she grabbed the man's card, threw it on top of her pile of fake evidence, and grabbed it all up into her arms. Her heart pounded in her chest, and she could feel adrenaline rushing through her veins. She wanted to punch a wall or kick something, and the urge almost overwhelmed her. Before Dietrich left the room, the detective turned toward Tyree with fire flashing in her eyes. Her nostrils flared, and audible puffs of air escaped them. She stepped in front of Tyree's attorney so that Tyree had no choice but to look at her.

"Having money can get you only so far. The truth and its karmic consequences always prevail. You may have had everything laid out for you in life, but one thing is for sure. You will not get away with murder on my watch," Detective Dietrich growled, locking eyes with Tyree.

Tyree averted his eyes and looked for help from the stranger who had just walked in the room.

"That's enough contact with my client, Detective. I think you are one step from being out of line. I know plenty of folks at BIA downtown, so you had better quit while you are ahead and leave us alone," Collins said as he slid into the chair across from Tyree.

Detective Dietrich backed down. She held up her left hand, signaling her retreat, but her face said something totally different. It wasn't over. That was for sure. Dietrich was not going to quit until she had this case all ready for the prosecutors. She would not rest until Tyree was convicted for the murder.

Tyree's shoulders slumped. He hung his head and exhaled. He had never felt so relieved in his entire life. Maybe his mother had found out what happened and had come to save the day.

"Is my mother here with you?" Tyree asked his new friend, the lawyer.

"Your mother? I don't know your mother," the lawyer replied, shuffling through some papers.

Tyree crinkled his brow. "So, if my mother didn't send you, then who did?"

"Let's just say you have friends that you don't even know about," Collins answered, smirking.

***

Tommy's hand shook as he lit the cigarette one of the male detectives had given him. Tommy took a long drag on the cigarette and blew the smoke out in a long huff. He had had enough run-ins with the law to know that the goodwill gesture of the cigarette was part of their buttering up. Tommy had seen it in movies, too, police giving suspects things like cigarettes, coffee, and food to get the suspects comfortable enough to talk. Tommy was smarter than that. He had taken the cigarette, but they couldn't trick him. He had told them his story, and he was sticking to it. Tommy thought he was way too smart to get caught up in his own story. Playing it cool was his plan. He blew out another long stream of smoke.

"So let's get this straight. The boy we're holding down here, Tyree Johnson, a sixteen-year-old kid, is the nephew of your ex-girlfriend, who told you the night before the murder that if she couldn't have you, no one else was going to have you? *You*? Really? *You*?" Detective Ron Parker repeated, his fingers steepled in front of him.

If he had it his way, Detective Parker would've had a little roughing-up session with Tommy before talking to him, but he knew the case was going to get lots of media attention real soon. Parker didn't like anything about Tommy. He knew the little slimeball was a weasel that preyed on rich girls. He also didn't believe a thing that came out of Tommy's fat, puffy, lying lips.

Tommy blew more smoke from between his lips. "Look, man. I told you this story ten different ways," he said, sitting up straight on the hard wooden chair. He thought if he looked straight at the detective, that would somehow make him more credible. "It's like I said before. Donna came home from rehab, but she still wanted to get stoned. Once a stoner, always a stoner. You know what I mean? I was her supplier when I used to deal. I don't sell drugs anymore, you know," Tommy explained, looking directly at the detective to see if his story was making a dent in the doubt clouding the detective's face.

Parker let out a long sigh, then a grunt.

"I mean, we messed around here and there, but she's jailbait in my eyes. She came to the club the other night, searching for me. You can ask the bouncers. They'll tell you. I didn't even want to be bothered, but she begged them to let her in to see me. She stormed in on me and my girl, Lee. Donna started cursing at Lee, telling her that she wanted to be with me, and that if she couldn't have me, no one would. Lee got in her face, but being that I am the man that I am, I came between them. No sense in letting two girls fight over a regular guy like me," Tommy said, smiling, like the story was amusing. It was starting to sound good. Half of it was true, so he just knew he had it in the bag.

Detective Parker exhaled a windstorm of breath. He knew Tommy was full of shit, but he wanted to get him on the record.

"So then what?" Parker asked, tapping his foot under the table impatiently. "She went from proclaiming her undying love for you to having her nephew kill a girl? Just because you are the best dick this side of Chicago? I mean, what is it? You're so good you got girls willing to send someone to kill over you?" Parker said, summing up Tommy's story, his lips twisted in disbelief.

Tommy rolled his eyes at the detective's snide remarks. "Then I told Donna to get lost. She offered me ten thousand dollars to be her friend again. She was known for that . . . buying friends. Just ask any of the rock stars' daughters. They all know the real Donna. She came by my place with the cash, and when she saw Lee inside, she started going crazy. I calmed her down again and told her that Lee was my girl, and that if she didn't like it, she could take her money and go. Donna calmed down. She came inside, and Lee allowed her to hang out with us. They both wanted to get high. I tried to convince Donna that she shouldn't do it. I mean, she had just gotten home from rehab. Must've been the biggest waste of time and money ever."

Tommy went on. "Anyway, Donna had some crank from her new dealer, since I got out of the business. She threw the money and the crank up on the table. All of a sudden, she and Lee were best friends over that crank. They started tweaking together like best friends. Me . . . I don't dabble in that shit. I was watching them for a while, but I got bored with that real quick. Donna had the kid with her, but he had disappeared somewhere in the apartment. Then I got a call from my boy John. John needed me to come help him take care of a problem, so I left the apartment to go see about the problem with him. When I returned, I found all you dudes crawling all over my place, and you know . . . Lee . . . Lee was dead." When Tommy finished, he hung his head for a good show of grief. "That's all I know," he added with a shrug.

Detective Parker tilted his head and glared at Tommy. *This kid's got to be fucking shitting me if he thinks I believe that bullshit story he just told me*, Parker thought.

The detective put his elbows on the table and leaned in. "Something about your story stinks to holy hell, kid. See, what I think is that you know a lot more than what you're letting on. I also believe you're a fucking liar from the bottom of your feet to the top of your head. One thing I know for sure is the truth will come out," Parker said seriously. He wanted Tommy to know he wasn't a rookie. This wasn't his first time around the block on a homicide.

Tommy stayed calm, though. He stubbed out his cigarette on the table and disrespectfully flicked the butt into a corner of the room. "Just tell me if I am a witness or a suspect, so I know whether to call my lawyer or not," he replied snidely. He was sick of this abuse. But Parker was equally tired of Tommy.

Detective Parker jumped to his feet, reached across the table, and grabbed Tommy's collar. Then he yanked Tommy up out of the chair and pulled him halfway onto the table to meet him face-to-face.

"You little piece of shit. I know you were getting those girls high. It was your drugs, and I want to know what you did that killed that little girl. I'm not going to let you send an innocent kid up the river because you're a fucking slimeball," Parker snarled.

The door flung open, and the two detectives who had been recording the meeting behind the double-sided glass rushed into the room.

"C'mon, Park, let him go. It's not worth it," the one named Detective Wayne urged, pulling Parker by the waist.

"Just let him go, man. He's not worth it," said the other detective.

But something inside Parker wouldn't allow him to let Tommy go. He was reliving his own struggles with his drug-addicted daughter. It was a painful topic for Parker, and everyone knew it. "Let me tell you something, you little drug-dealing gangster wannabe. I will find out what role you played in that girl's death, and I will make sure you hang from your balls in the town square for everyone to see. I see your type all the time, and you think you're so fucking untouchable. Well, you got a fucking surprise coming your way," Parker growled, his breath hot on Tommy's face.

"Ron, man, let him go. C'mon, he ain't worth it," Detective Wayne said, still pulling Parker from behind. "He's a punk. Don't get into a mess with BIA over this loser."

By now Tommy had turned as red as a freshly cooked lobster. That was the last thing the detectives needed right now, a police brutality charge.

Detective Parker loosened his grip on Tommy and sent his face slamming into the table.

"Ahh! Fuck! You fucker!" Tommy screamed as his nose busted open and began spilling blood like a knocked-over fire hydrant spewed water. "I'll have your fucking head for this!" he screeched, trying to use his hand to quell the bleeding.

"Get him out of here!" Wayne yelled to his counterpart.

The detective who had accompanied Wayne into the room grabbed Detective Parker and dragged him out.

Just as they were leaving, Detective Dietrich approached. She stood in the doorway and watched as Tommy tried to stop the bleeding from his nose with the sleeve of his jacket.

"What's going on here?" Detective Dietrich asked, looking at the overturned chair and the bleeding witness.

"Things got a little heated," Detective Wayne answered as he walked over to the door. There wasn't much else to say.

"Let me get a few minutes alone with him," Detective Dietrich said.

Wayne stopped right in front of Dietrich and looked at her with a raised eyebrow. "Aren't you supposed to be working on the boy and the other girl?" he asked.

"He lawyered up. I think that's confession enough for me. Especially if I can get this one to officially sign on as a witness," Dietrich answered.

Detective Wayne smirked. Hadn't Dietrich done her homework? Tommy was a well-known drug dealer.

"This guy is as credible as Hannibal Lecter. Put him on the stand and no jury worth their salt will believe him, unless he says he was standing there when the murder happened," Wayne replied.

"Well, whatever it takes. I need to get to this case solved. I'm not going to let my perfect record be tarnished by the fucking rich and shameless. Not by that little spoiled brat down there, of all people," Detective Dietrich retorted.

Wayne shrugged and moved out of her way. Dietrich stepped into the room and closed the door behind her.

"Thomas Marlon Jackson, or Tommy, as your friends call you, I'm Detective Dietrich. I hear you're going to be my star witness against Tyree Johnson," Detective Dietrich said, extending a wad of tissues toward Tommy as a peace offering. Tommy snatched the tissue and started cleaning up his face.

"Where do you want me to start? Oh, I got a lot of shit to say about this," Tommy said, his voice nasally.

Dietrich smiled. Those were the words she'd been dying to hear. She liked Tommy and what he had to say already.

Chapter 13

Sins of the Father

"Fuck," Donna grumbled as she stumbled, nearly twisting her ankle in the dark. She paced in front of the building that housed the Chicago PD's Eleventh District police station. She fumbled with the small silver flask she had, which contained straight vodka. She'd forgotten she had it in her pocketbook until she was brought down to the station with Tyree and then turned away when they started questioning him. Donna really needed to get high, but the liquor was a medicine she could get her hands on easily without Tommy. She had to get her mind off what was going on. Donna wished she could forget everything she'd seen in the past few hours. She wanted so badly to speak to Tommy. She had to know what had happened to Lee.

One thing was for sure, Donna knew her nephew wouldn't harm a fly and he hadn't killed Lee. She wished she had fought harder to stay clean that night so she could've kept an eye on Tyree. Donna blamed herself for what Tyree was going through. Just like everyone else in her life would too. Another sip of vodka and it didn't feel as bad. She scrubbed roughly at her tears. "Oh my God. I did this to him. It's all my fault," she grunted under her alcohol-laden breath. She took another swig from her flask.

"Donna!"

Donna froze. The voice came from her mother, and she could already hear the anger and the judgment in her tone. Donna turned around to find her mother and her sister rushing toward her, their faces similarly folded into angry scowls.

Her sister, Desiree, had been crying. Even from a distance, Donna could see that her eyes were swollen and her nose was red.

Carolyn reached her first. "What have you done? What the hell is going on?" she shouted, jutting an accusing finger in Donna's face. As usual, her mother wasn't going to listen to reason. She had already concluded that Donna was guilty of whatever was going on.

Donna shook her head. She was finally feeling the effects of her libation. "Don't start with me, Mother," she said, slurring a little, and rolled her eyes at her mother. Thank God she had had that drink, or she might not survive this encounter. There was no way Donna could ever deal with her mother sober. She saw that now. In fact, Donna still wanted to tear her mother apart with her bare hands for everything that had ever happened in her life.

"Are you drunk?" her mother asked, waving her hand in front of her face and scrunching her nose. "At a time like this? You can't even control yourself for one minute, can you?"

"Whatever!" Donna said, moving closer to her mother's face.

Desiree stepped between them. "Please . . . now is not the time for this. Where is my son?" Desiree said, getting right to the point. She was shaking all over.

"He's in there with them. I . . . I swear, I tried to keep them from speaking to him. I tried," Donna said, on the verge of tears.

"Well, if you hadn't brought him to Chicago—" Carolyn began, pointing a finger at her youngest daughter.

"Please, Mother," Desiree said, cutting her off. "I just need to know what is going on with my son." She was trying to stay calm and to keep herself from completely spazzing out on her own sister. Their relationship had been strained ever since Desiree was forced to leave the family, and it had never recovered. Desiree had heard things, but she didn't know her sister anymore. Donna looked like a complete stranger to her as she stood there, half drunk, disheveled, and appearing nothing like Desiree remembered.

"He's talking to the detectives. It's been hours now," Donna said, shaking her head. "First, they spoke to us together, then to me, then to him. They, um, they think Tyree murdered a girl at this party we were at," Donna explained, lowering her eyes to the ground. "I know he didn't do it. This is all a misunderstanding."

Desiree opened her mouth to speak, but their mother pushed her aside. Carolyn moved in on Donna like a lion on its prey. Her nostrils flared, and her lips were scrunched tightly. "It's a damn shame the way you carry yourself. You are a total embarrassment to our family. Now your shit may have ruined my grandson's life." Carolyn shook her head in disgust. "You will never change. You were born a loser and will always be one. You get away from Desiree. She has to find out about her child. She has to think about someone other than herself, something you know nothing about," Carolyn hissed, pulling off the kid gloves she'd been trying to use with Donna for a while. Carolyn was tired of pretending. Things were closing in on all of them, and she simply could not hold it together anymore.

"Take her into the police station before things get very ugly out here," Donna said to Desiree. "One thing I'm not

going to allow anymore is your cruel fucking words, and
then the innocent role you play in front of others, Mother.
You're a fucking fake and always have been. You have
your favorite child with you now, so go ahead and be
there for her and leave me the hell alone, as usual."

Carolyn balked, reacting as if Donna had open-hand
slapped her in the face.

"We do not have time for this right now," Desiree said
sternly, coming between them. "Both of you are being
selfish this right now." Then she turned on her heels and
headed inside to see about her son.

"Desiree," Donna called out.

Desiree stopped walking for a minute and turned her
head slightly to look over her shoulder.

"He is a good kid. For whatever it's worth, I will get to
the bottom of what happened and get him out of this. I
am a lot of things, and you all might hate me, but I love
Tyree. I'm sorry for taking him with me, but I would've
never let anything happen to him," Donna said, her tears
falling again.

"But you *did* let something happen to him, Donna,"
Desiree said evenly, trying her best not to break down
again. With that, she walked into the precinct station.

Inside the precinct police station, Desiree was clearly
out of her element and uncomfortable. Her mother, who
had followed right behind her, was really out of place,
which made Desiree even more uncomfortable. Carolyn
was dressed in premium designer clothes and shockingly
sparkly jewels, and so she stuck out like a sore thumb in
this grungy police station on the West Side of Chicago.

An hour passed, but it felt like a hundred hours. Desiree
clutched a wad of damp tissues as she sat on a hard
wooden bench inside the lobby of the station. Desiree
was too lost in her own problems to notice some of the
rough characters floating around her. All she could think

about was her son being afraid, hungry, lost without her, and locked up with people he'd never been exposed to in his entire life. Desiree's legs shook. Her nerves had been on edge since the Idlewild Police Department had taken her missing person's report, then had called a short time later to tell her they'd found Tyree in the Chicago PD's booking system. Desiree had felt like someone had put a huge hand around her neck and started squeezing all the life out of her. She'd literally lost her ability to stand when they'd told her the news, that her son—her baby, her innocent child—had been arrested. It was a wonder she had even made it to the precinct.

Now, sitting with her over-the-top mother, who was of no comfort, Desiree watched as uniformed police officers dragged their evening collars in. Some of the handcuffed perpetrators looked rough, and others looked like every-day people. Desiree watched, knowing her son didn't fit in here. Every few seconds she dabbed at the tears that threatened to escape her eyes.

After the initial shock from the police officer's phone call wore off, Desiree had shared what had happened to Tyree with Carolyn and Rebecca. Carolyn had imme-diately jumped into action and had called their family attorney, Aaron Collins. Collins agreed to rush down the police station and get to the bottom of the matter. Two hours later they got a return call from Collins, and Desiree almost fainted as she listened to her mother speak to the high-priced criminal defense attorney.

"Murder? Am I hearing you correctly, Collins? *Murder*?" Carolyn said during their phone conversation.

Carolyn was completely caught off guard by the news, but Desiree immediately went into a full-blown panic at-tack when she heard the word *murder* repeated. Desiree thought she must be dreaming. This all had to be a bad nightmare, one that she would eventually wake up from.

How could her son be charged with murder? Tyree was a baby in Desiree's eyes. He was a good kid and had never been in trouble. She'd raised him to be respectful and courteous and kind. Desiree knew her son wouldn't hurt a fly, let alone lay hands on another person. There was no way she would believe that Tyree had murdered anyone.

Carolyn wasted no time and asked Collins to represent the boy. He agreed to sign on to the case and to set to work immediately. After ending the call, Carolyn had her driver rush her and Desiree to the precinct police station to meet Collins and see about Tyree. As they waited in the lobby now, the attorney was in an interrogation room down in the belly of the dank old building. Desiree and Carolyn were being made to wait rather than being escorting the interrogation room.

Desiree had argued that she needed to see her son, but after realizing she was losing the fight, and becoming afraid the officers would take it out on her son if she didn't calm down, Desiree had given up. She didn't think she could take much more emotional battering. She also didn't know how her son would react to having her there, and she worried that if he saw her and fell apart, this might cause him more harm than good being. She would do anything to protect her son. There had been many times like this throughout his childhood when she had to make difficult decisions about his welfare, and on those occasions, the fact that she was raising her son alone had been at the forefront of her mind. And during those times she'd been so angry with Tyson Blackwell for not being there. She had wished she could lean on him, that they could stand together for their son.

Desiree dug in her pocketbook and pulled out her cell phone, something she had been doing every five minutes or so for the past hour. With trembling hands, she looked at the screen and contemplated whether or not to call Tyson. He was a powerful judge, and this was his son. Desiree was anxious just thinking about what she'd say if she did call Tyson. *Our son has been arrested. I know you just met him, but he needs you to get him out of this now. I know I said he was a good boy, but he is in a big mess now.* Her mind raced. She let out a long breath. Suddenly she felt sick inside just thinking about what she'd done with Tyson the day before. She couldn't believe she had made herself so vulnerable by going to their old meeting spot like some flirtatious teenage girl.

The time with Tyson had served as an outlet, an escape, and more importantly, he'd helped her get things off her chest that she had never said to anyone since she'd had Tyree. Being secretive and keeping things inside was a defense Desiree had become used to putting up. It protected her, and in her mind, it protected Tyree as well. Now, sitting there on that hard bench in the police station, contemplating her son's fate, she didn't know why she couldn't stop thinking about wanting Tyson there with her or sharing with him what was going on with their son.

Desiree shook off the thoughts. *It is my duty to be here for my child. It is not his duty. He is married. He doesn't want me. It is my duty to be here for my child. It is not his duty,* Desiree chanted silently. The idea that Tyson would rush to her side or care about what was happening to Tyree was preposterous, she decided. She could just picture Tyson pressing the IGNORE button on his cell phone if she called. After all, he might be laid up with his wife, Selena, and the two of them might laugh when Desiree called, like she was a big joke. Desiree cringed at the visual playing in her head. She was completely lost in her own world of thoughts, oblivious to the bustling about her and the noisy surroundings.

"What happened? What are they saying, Desi? Is he all right? Can we see him?" a voice yelled from Desiree's left side. She jumped at the sound of Junior's voice. She had been so lost in thought, she had not realized until this moment that her brother had come inside the station and was standing a few inches away from her.

Desiree furrowed her brow and looked up at her brother, surprised he was there. He was concerned; she could see it all on his face. Junior also read the expression on her face and immediately softened his tone and tried to calm down so he wouldn't upset her even more.

"I'm sorry I couldn't get here sooner," Junior said, touching Desiree's shoulder. "I should've been there for him. I had no idea something like this . . . "

Desiree touched his hand and quieted him. "It's not your fault. Hell, it's no one's fault. I know that my son didn't do this. There is no way he did what they're accusing him of. I gave birth to him. I know him better than he knows himself," she said with feeling.

"What are they saying now? I have friends in high places in the police department. We can get some information from them if we need to," Junior told her, not knowing what else to say. He really didn't know how to comfort his sister, and he'd hurt her the last time they were together, so he was trying to tread lightly.

"They aren't saying much, and I was trying to remain calm, but if they don't let me see my son soon, I am going to act crazy in here, like they expect us to," Desiree said, getting to her feet. This was too much for her now. The Chicago PD didn't know who they were fucking with. She was sure her father still had some clout in the city. Tyree probably felt completely lost by now. He had lived a very sheltered existence his whole life. He had been driven almost everywhere, and if he hadn't been with her, he had always been with their friends, friends she had vetted and chosen to be in their life.

Taken aback by her son's presence after his spectacle at her party, Carolyn stood up, gathered her pocketbook, and stormed past both of her children. Junior didn't say a word to her, nor she a word to him. She disappeared from the lobby.

Junior sighed loudly. "I'm going to step outside for a smoke, Desi. If they come up, let me know," he said.

Junior rushed outside and walked to a darkened corner at the side of the building. He lit a blunt. He needed it to calm his nerves. As he sucked in his first toke, a stranger walked up on him. Junior stepped back a few steps.

"Whoa! You ever heard of personal space, man?" Junior grumbled, his eyebrows dipping low on his face.

The man moved even closer then. He grabbed Junior's arm and dug his large animal-like hand into the muscles of Junior's forearm and pulled him forward.

"Get the fuck off me!" Junior growled, attempting to yank his arm away from this crazed lunatic. But another man approached from the back and then another.

"What the fuck is this!" Junior yelled, hoping to get the attention of a passing police officer, but they were all either inside the precinct station or moving fast with their prisoners or preparing to end or begin their shift, and so no one really paid him any attention.

The stranger who gripped his arm pulled Junior closer to him. So close his breath was hot on Junior's face. Junior was breathing hard himself. He choked out a short grunt. He was forced so close to the stranger that they were standing cheek to cheek. He could feel a gun pressed into his spine from behind as well.

"Fuck off me," Junior growled, the gun pressing so hard into his back, it hurt.

"Hush. Calm down. Don't make a scene, Junior. You should act like we are long-lost friends. Uh, we kind of are long-lost friends," the stranger whispered now.

Junior's heart pounded, and he immediately felt sick to his stomach. He had no idea how this bastard knew his name or where to find him at that moment. This could mean only one thing: someone had been following him.

"The fuck you want? If it's money . . . ," Junior began, so furious he was involuntarily speaking through his teeth. He was too angry even to process the fact that he should be afraid that the men could blow him away right there on that street, with zero fucks to give.

The man replied only by squeezing Junior's arm even harder now. Unbearable pain shot up to his shoulder and radiated through his body.

"Say what the fuck you got to say," Junior snarled, again trying to make eye contact with any of the police officers who buzzed by like he didn't even exist. He heard the guy behind him cock his weapon. Junior was paralyzed by fear now, his entire body rigid. The heat of anger was burning deep in his chest and gut, like lava in the center of a volcano.

"Hush. Don't talk. Keep your punk-ass, rich-boy mouth shut and let me do the talking. I want you to tell your father, Ernest Senior, the crook, that Patrick sent me to see you. Your father will know who Patrick is. He can explain to you why we had to meet like this. Tell that papa of yours, Patrick has a message for him again. The message is Patrick knows you and your whole family, what you look like, where you live, where you shop, where you go to fuck your little Colombian girlfriend, and Patrick will come see you all again if your father doesn't make good on the deals. Understand? Next time, I will do more than just threaten you. Yes, yes . . . it will be much, much worse, trust me," the man hissed, then gave a nasty little chortle at the end of his threat.

This time Junior realized the man had some kind of an accent. He was too shocked to place it immediately, but the man had a heavy accent nonetheless. Junior's jaw rocked feverishly. He knew his father had gotten himself into some deep trouble, but he could've never imagined anything like this. Threats to him and the entire family were a major deal in Junior's book. His father had done awful things before, like neglecting his family for years, having affairs, and the like, but this, this was more than Junior could stand. If his father were in front of him now, he would finish the job that cancer had started.

"You leave my fucking family out of this . . ." Junior began, his words rising and falling.

But the man didn't stay to listen. He quickly loosened his grip on Junior and gave him a shove. And, in what seemed like a flash of light, he, his sidearm bearer, and his second henchman disappeared. It was the craziest thing Junior had ever experienced. He swung his head around frantically, but there was no sign at all of the menacing strangers. Junior placed his hand over his chest and inhaled. He was trying to get his heart rate to slow, but it didn't work. His heart pounded so hard, Junior thought it would jump loose from his chest. His head swirled now with the worst migraine he'd ever experienced.

Junior didn't know what his family had done to deserve all the things that had been happening to them back to back. Even with all their shortcomings and all their animosity toward each other, the Johnsons had prided themselves on trying to live right outwardly. They'd given to charities, gone to church whenever they could, and even sometimes given to the homeless people they saw on the streets of Chicago.

We are definitely being punished for something. Sins of the father, I guess, Junior reasoned. He dabbed at the new line of sweat that had materialized on his forehead. Again, he attempted to calm himself before he went back inside the station. As he braced himself, he slumped over at the waist for a quick second. His legs felt weak, like he'd just run ten miles. It was his nerves.

"What is happening?" he whispered to himself. "What is happening to us?"

Desiree had started pacing after yet another officer had told that she would have to continue to wait. As she made her way back to the bench on which she'd taken up residence and spent the past three hours, a commotion erupted as a group of people moved in her direction. Desiree widened her eyes. She couldn't take much more. The stomping of feet and the shouting gave her pause. Panic stricken, Desiree gazed intently at the scene, frantically trying to spot her son. She noticed Aaron Collins, their family attorney, among the noisy group moving in her direction. Desiree paused and forced herself to stand still. She clenched her fists and bit her bottom lip. She needed to know that Tyree was safe. That no one had hurt him in any way. Desiree seemed to have a newfound strength. A boost of motherly power propelled her forward and toward the attorney. Everything else in the world was secondary in her mind as she rushed right up to Collins, her face consumed by worry.

"Mr. Collins . . . what is it? Is he all right? Has he eaten? Has he been treated fairly?" Desiree fired off the questions in rapid succession.

Collins put his hand up in a halting motion. His paper bag–brown skin was seemingly stretched tight with worry lines. Desiree didn't like the way he looked. Carolyn had reentered the lobby after stomping off, and she suddenly materialized at her daughter's side. She didn't like the look on Collins's face either. She'd never seen him look anything other than cool under pressure.

This time was different; his eyes seemed to say it all. That look didn't bode well.

"What? Tell me," Desiree demanded. It was all she could do to keep herself from slapping him and screaming, "Tell me my son will be all right!"

Collins pulled her by her elbow, leading her away from the crowd of detectives and police officers. Desiree took his cue and moved close to him. Her insides were churning from nerves. Her mother was right by her side, looking like she was about to lose her breakfast as well.

"Look, Desiree, Tyree is okay. I mean, he is in one piece. He is scared as hell, but that's to be expected. He's doing as well as can be expected under the circumstances," the lawyer whispered, his tone serious. Desiree listened intently.

Collins turned toward Carolyn and addressed her. "I've known you and your family for many years, Carolyn, so I'm not going to lie to you. We have our work cut out for us." He broke eye contact with her.

Not a good sign at all, Desiree thought. She threw her hands up to her face and finally let her pent-up sobs escape.

"I'm sorry . . . very sorry. There is nothing more we can do today," Collins said in a hushed tone, like he had already lost all hope. "They will be keeping Tyree overnight, and he will be arraigned by a superior court judge tomorrow morning. I will be in court at nine a.m. I expect that they will set a very high bond. They are charging him with the murder, Carolyn. He was covered in the dead girl's blood."

"Oh God," Desiree gasped. Things were beginning to spin around her. Her ears were ringing. Her head felt like someone had it in a vise grip. It was all too much. Desiree's eyes fluttered.

"Desiree? Desiree, are you all right?" Collins asked, dropping his briefcase at his feet.

"Desi!" Carolyn called out.

Desiree let out a short grunt. She placed the flat of her hand on the pale yellow cinder-block wall for support. The color made her nauseated.

"Desiree . . ." Collins grabbed her by the arm. It was for nothing. He couldn't prevent the natural course of things.

"Desiree!" her mother screamed right before Desiree's world went black as she fainted. "Help! I need help over here!"

Chapter 14

Powerful or Powerless?

Desiree regained consciousness in a cold, sterile room at Mount Sinai Hospital. She rocked her head from left to right as her eyes fluttered open. Panic struck her like a ten-ton boulder. She had no idea where she was.

"Uh," she sighed as she became painfully aware of the bandage around her head. Desiree lifted one weak, shaky hand and touched the gauzy headdress. "Mmm," she moaned. She could suddenly feel throbbing around her injury. Next, she moved her head to the left and eyed the monitor that was making an annoying *beep, beep, beep* over her head each time her heart beat.

"Oh God," Desiree whispered, her mouth so dry she felt her lips splitting as she spoke. She was about to close her eyes, because the pain of having them open was excruciating, when a sudden movement to her right startled her. Desiree jumped, but she knew that if someone was coming to do her harm, she was totally defenseless as she lay there all bandaged up. Suddenly, she saw a shadowy figure, and seconds later it came into focus.

Hey. I'm so glad to see you're awake," said a soothing voice, the words floating over her.

Desiree closed her eyes for a second and took in Tyson's sweet voice. She opened them again, wanting to say something, but she was at an immediate loss for words. Before she could say anything to him, Tyson reached out to grab Desiree's hand. He gave it a soft, reassuring squeeze to let her know he was there for her. She frowned. She wanted to cry.

"What happened? How did I get here? What are you doing here?" she finally managed to croak out. Now that she was looking at Tyson, the throbbing in her head seemed to intensify.

"Shh. Don't try to talk. You had a fall and hit your head pretty hard. I found out from Rebecca what happened to Tyree. I am trying to work on things and am doing what I can. Don't worry. I snuck in after your mother left. I saw her walk out a few minutes ago," Tyson told her, his tone serious yet caring.

Tears immediately welled up in Desiree's eyes. She couldn't understand how she was still so in love with this man after all these years. He was a married man, but he was still there by her side. She experienced a confusing mix of emotions on top of the hazy feeling in her brain. Desiree squeezed Tyson's hand with what little strength she could muster.

"Thank you, Tyson," she whispered, her words strained due to the oxygen cannula in her nose. She really meant it. She couldn't believe that he was still there, after all the things she'd said, after she'd hid Tyree from him, after she had put all the blame on him.

"I should be thanking you, Desiree," Tyson said, cracking that gorgeous winning smile that had hooked Desiree in the first place so many years ago.

What Desiree didn't know was that Tyson was on a mission now. Losing sight of Desiree and his son again was out of the question. To lose them would be a crushing blow to his life now that he knew for sure Tyree was his son. At this point, Tyson needed them just as much as they needed him. If he didn't claim Tyree as his son and give him the Blackwell last name, his family's name was going to die out once Tyson was gone. He couldn't have that. He still had a need to make his parents proud, and if he couldn't have children with Selena, he was going to have to make sure Desiree let him be a father to his son.

Patrick O'Malley was an unassuming man. He stood only five feet, ten inches tall, and had a protruding gut and flat feet. His appearance didn't matter; his power and reputation were what preceded him. Although unassuming to the eye, Patrick was the third man from the top in the hierarchy of the South Side faction of the Irish Mob. He had come to the country specifically to engage in the decades-old tradition of organized crime.

Patrick sat flanked by four of his men, who were all dressed in black. It was like something out of a movie for sure. Patrick took a long pull from an illegal Cuban cigar and blew the smoke out slowly. He seemed to be pondering the information he'd just received. His intelligence was being insulted, he could tell that much. Finally, Patrick looked across the table at Ernest Johnson, Sr., and nodded his head. Patrick wanted to hear it again, in a different way. He wanted to make sure he was hearing it correctly before he reacted. The frail eldest Johnson had been brought to the meeting after Patrick had his men run up on Junior again and demand to see his father.

"So, Johnson, tell me again why I can't draw down the funds you told me for years were in my account?" Patrick asked, his Irish accent thick, his words jumping up and down. Patrick coolly took another long pull on his cigar. He held his breath extra long, letting the effects of the smoke rush to his head.

Patrick had been putting millions of dollars into Ernest Johnson, Sr.'s hands for the past six years, and owing to the statements he'd received from Johnson Trading

Patrick was of the belief that he had earned over six million on his investments. Patrick had been hearing things about Ernest's recent business dealings, and he wanted to collect his money. Both men had their eyes locked on one another, except Patrick was cool and Ernest could barely keep his eyes open and had his toes balled up inside his Gucci slippers. Ernest's stomach was also knotted like a nautical rope. The tension in the room was thick. Junior, who was also at the meeting, didn't know what to think or how to move. He'd thought about bringing some street muscle with him, but he'd been told by Patrick that it would be a bad idea.

Ernest cleared his throat, the sound seeming more pronounced in the eerily silent space. He had thought about what he was going to say, but he just wasn't sure it was going to fly with Patrick. He was clearly dying, so his life didn't matter, but he had to smooth things out to protect the rest of his family.

"I told you, the SEC regulates all the accounts. It is out of my hands until I meet all their requirements. I just need time to get the funds wired back to you. I already have my assistant working on that," Ernest said, fabricating his answer on the spot, his words coming out weak, like those of a ninety-five-year-old man. He was silently praying that his most notorious client bought the story. Truth was, Ernest was silently racking his brain to think of how he would get his hands on that kind of money at a time like *this*. He wiped at invisible sweat on his forehead.

Patrick laughed heartily, and then he looked at his men, and they started laughing as well. One of Patrick's men, Constantine, found it real funny that Ernest thought Patrick was so stupid.

Junior's and Ernest's eyes seemed to grow wide at the same time. Ernest flexed his neck and exhaled, which caused him to cough violently. It wasn't going to be so easy to convince Patrick, Ernest realized.

"Look, he's sick. He's trying his best. There are rules . . . ," Junior stammered, stepping in on his father's behalf.

"Johnson, do you think I am dumb? Eh? You think that because our families have history, you can lie to me? Oh, no, no, no," Patrick said calmly, his face devoid of any emotion. He ignored Junior and stared at Ernest, leaning into the table that separated them. Ernest's lip quivered under Patrick's glare.

"Patrick, I've been dealing with you for years. You know that I wouldn't ever think you were dumb. I have nothing but respect for you," Ernest replied, making a halting motion with his frail, shaking hands. "I will have your money. I have to follow procedures . . . you know. Just give me a few days." He swallowed the ball of nerves sitting at the back of his throat. If he could get up and run, he would. Ernest looked around at the other men, who were all staring at him. He knew why they were there.

Patrick lifted his left hand in the air, signaling to one of the four men who flanked him. A tall redhead with icy blue eyes, a barrel chest, and square shoulders stepped behind Junior. Junior whirled his head around frantically. His heart jumped in his chest. The man was perilously close to him. Junior could feel his breath on him. Patrick made a quick motion with his hand. The redhead bore down on Junior like an attack animal that had been given the order.

"Patrick, listen, I . . . I'm going to . . . ," Ernest stuttered, trying to save his son, his eyes wide as dinner plates.

The redhead grabbed Junior's right hand and held it flat against the table. Junior squirmed in his chair. He could only imagine what was to come.

"Patrick! Please! Don't do this! Please!" Ernest begged, his voice rising three octaves.

"Pop, don't let them." Junior struggled against the redhead's grip, but he was no match for the hulk of a man.

Patrick stood up, amused at the sight. "I don't like to be jerked around. You may play games with your other clients, but not with me. We have been in this too long, my friend. I will forgive a lot of things for the sake of our history, but I will not forgive you fucking with my money, because if you fuck with my money, you're fucking with me," he said calmly, an eerily sinister grin painting his face. He reached down and ground the lit end of his cigar into the flesh of Junior's hand. For a moment, time seemed to stand still in the room.

"Agh!" Junior screamed, jerking his body in the chair. The pain climbed from his hand all the way up his arm. Spit flew out of Junior's mouth, and his chin fell into this chest. "Ahh!" he wailed as he rocked back and forth. The man continued to hold Junior there.

Satisfied that Junior was in excruciating pain, Patrick got close to Ernest's face. "This is just the beginning of what will happen to your family if you don't arrange to have my money go into my offshore account by the end of the week. Your wife, your daughters, they all will be next. I won't bother with you. Looks like God has already taken care of you," Patrick whispered harshly, his stale cigar breath shooting up Ernest's nostrils.

The redhead loosened his grip on Junior, who was having a hard time catching his breath. Junior used his right hand to hold his throbbing, painful left hand. "Ahh!" He rocked back and forth as the pain of the burn continued to radiate up his arm.

"God help me," Ernest murmured as Patrick and his men exited his office. "God help me." He didn't know what he would do now. Things had finally gotten to be too much to handle.

***

"Who is that coming out of Johnson's office?" Agent Craski asked, elbowing Agent Shore on his arm to wake him up. Agent Shore jumped and instinctively raised his professional-grade binoculars and adjusted them. He squinted through the large round lenses and frowned.

"Shit! Hand me the long lens quick!" he exclaimed, his hand flapping in anticipation. Craski scrambled to reach into the backseat for the camera. He grabbed it and hastily tossed it to Shore. Shore held the camera up to his eye and began clicking the shutter button rapidly. They couldn't afford to miss this moment.

"What is it? Who is that?" Craski asked impatiently as Shore continued to click the camera's shutter button.

"Looks like Johnson stepped in shit with the Irish Mob. That's Patrick O'Malley! The number three in the Irish Mob. Dangerous. Fuck!" Shore cursed, punching the car door.

"What? What does this mean?" Craski asked, staring at the men through the windshield. He was confused. *Irish Mob? Johnson? What?*

"It means to save our case and our subject, we may have to go overt on this case quicker than we thought. Johnson probably took money from them, and if he can't produce returns, he'll end up in the Chicago River before we can ever snag his ass or before cancer ends his ass. That blood will be on our hands too. Call Martinez right away," Shore answered as he continued to snap pictures.

Ernest held on to the sides of his wheelchair, too frail to let go. Junior sat across from him on a leather sofa in the bank president's outer office and drummed the fingers of his unbandaged hand on the table next to him. He looked impatiently at his sparkly diamond and rose gold Rolex for the tenth time. The watch made him immediately think of Bella. He'd bought her one just like it. Regret and guilt trampled on Junior's mood like an army on the attack. Each time he thought of Bella, his mood shifted. She was the one who had picked out the watch during one of their many shopping sprees. He missed Bella like crazy. She'd been calling him, but he had been ignoring her calls, opting instead to hide out like a coward. He looked down at his hands again; this time the other hand came into his focus. The large gauze on his other hand made Junior think of Patrick and the fifteen other clients that had contacted his father since then, demanding answers about their investments.

Junior quickly shook off thoughts of Bella; he had to focus now. He couldn't even think about his sisters—one in the hospital, the other on a bender somewhere—or his nephew, who sat rotting in a jail cell. Their family had fallen into despair. Things were all muddled up in Junior's head, but keeping his loved ones at the back of his mind was important right now. It was the only way he could operate quickly and without distraction to make sure they all stayed alive. His father had asked him to put him on a plane so he could go to another country and just die in peace. It was the only way Ernest could make a clean break, for the safety and well-being of all involved. Ernest couldn't take a chance, not with Patrick leveraging those threats against anyone he cared about. Ernest Sr. had told his son if he didn't leave, if he stayed around and died of cancer, he knew he would cause everyone more pain. But really he couldn't think about anyone but himself right now, and it was best that he have no contact with anyone.

Junior's phone buzzed in his pocket. As usual, he ignored it. He had purposely ignored calls from Bella for the past few days. He scrolled through his call log. There were at least sixty calls from Bella. A few times he'd been tempted to answer, but he had thought better of it. He had to sort things out before he could deal with her. Junior pinched the bridge of his nose and let out a long exasperated sigh. His head ached from a million thoughts coursing through his brain. He looked at his watch again, but this time he didn't think of Bella. Instead, he flexed his jaw and balled his good hand into a fist.

The bank president was taking much longer than Junior and Ernest had expected to convert Ernest's assets into cashier's checks, which could be converted back into cash when Ernest was ready. Their family had always had a good rapport with all the heads of the financial institutions he dealt with, so Ernest couldn't imagine what was going on. He was used to getting his way with everything; waiting wasn't one of the things he was used to in life.

"Excuse me," Junior called to the petite redhead who sat behind a shiny ultramodern glass desk right outside the bank president's door.

The doe-eyed girl lifted her head, pushed her stringy red hair out of her face, and looked at Junior, as if to say, "Yes?" She didn't answer him.

Junior locked eyes with her. He thought she was cute, but not as beautiful as Bella. The senior Ernest also watched the girl. As sick as he was, he still flirted with his eyes. In the old days Ernest Sr. would've made a move on a young, pretty girl like her. Knowing his reputation, he would've bedded her the same night. Ernest quickly blinked a few times, clearing his mind of the thoughts. He didn't have the time or the energy right now to even consider having his way with another woman. He probably never would in life again.

"Do you know why this is taking so long? I have a flight to catch, and I've never had to wait this long at any other financial institution, or at this one, for that matter," Ernest grunted, clearing his throat of the phlegm afterward. He seemed a little more agitated after thinking about how much his life had changed in the blink of an eye or, in his case, with the diagnosis of cancer.

The girl stared blankly at Junior, like she didn't really understand what his father was asking.

"I think this is bordering on poor customer service now. I think we have too much money tied up here to be treated this way," Junior announced, pontificating in an annoyed tone, as if the girl could do anything to help him.

She at least listened and let him finish his lecture. Then she broke eye contact with Junior and started fiddling with her hands. Something about her reaction sent an uneasy feeling over Junior.

"Are you just going to sit there, or you going to answer the question? Call someone. Get up and go find your boss. Do something!" Junior barked.

The girl gave him a nervous smile and shakily picked up her phone. It was like she was stalling for some reason. She wasn't responsive or fast enough for Junior's or Ernest's liking. Junior could feel his blood boiling now.

"I can't wait any longer," he huffed. He stood up and found that his legs were shaking involuntarily. His instincts were telling him something wasn't right. Junior hated it when he felt nervous. He prided himself on his cool, calm, and collected demeanor. He heard the girl speaking in hushed tones with someone on the phone. Junior could only assume she had called someone to tell them he was complaining.

"Mr. Becks said he'll be right with you, Mr. Johnson," the girl said, a bit too tentative for Junior's liking. The information she provided didn't put him at ease one bit.

He looked at his watch again. He wanted to make sure the girl saw him this time. He adjusted his Ralph Lauren

Purple Label suit jacket and bent down slowly to retrieve his Hermès briefcase. Didn't these people at the bank know how important he and his father were?

Ernest Sr. cleared his throat, something he did incessantly when he was nervous. Nervous was an understatement for how he felt at that moment. "I have a flight to catch. I guess I will have to have the bank wire the funds to my account. In which case, Mr. Becks will be picking up the tab for all the wire transfer fees. We are talking big money here. I don't know whether you know who I am or not, but I'm sure he'll regret having to pay the fees," Ernest snorted sardonically as he signaled to Junior to wheel him from the seating area of the bank president's outer office to the space where the redheaded girl sat at her desk.

Realizing Ernest and Junior were serious about leaving now, the girl shot up from her desk like she was the figure inside a jack-in-the-box. She rushed around her desk and stood her ground. Mr. Becks had given her an express warning not to allow the two men to leave, but he hadn't said how she was supposed to really stop them.

"Um, Mr. Johnson, I . . . um . . . I think it'll just be a few more minutes," the frazzled girl stammered, rushing toward Ernest with her hands out. She blocked Junior and Ernest's path with her small body. "Maybe I can, um, get you a drink of water or a soda. Oh yeah! We have a lunch delivery coming soon. I can get you a gourmet sandwich . . . Those are so delicious . . . ," she rambled, her voice going high like that of a dying songbird.

Junior used his hand and shoved the girl aside. She stumbled. "Like I told you before, we have to go. My father told you more than once he has a flight to catch," he huffed. Now he was sure something was amiss.

There was nothing the girl could do to keep them there. She was no match for Junior—a man on a mission. "Just a few more minutes, Mr. Johnson!" she called at Ernest's back.

Ernest just ignored her, and Junior grabbed the handles on the wheelchair and pushed his father out of the office. Junior wished they could find a stairwell and take the stairs down, but his father's wheelchair was a hindrance and he immediately nixed that idea. Besides, they were way up on the twenty-first floor. It was where all the wealthy bank and investment clients conducted their business.

Junior rushed his father to the elevator bank and tapped the DOWN button. He looked at his watch again. The large beads of sweat that had broken out on his hairline were lined up like ready soldiers. An elevator had yet to appear, so Junior tapped the button again, as if that would make the elevator come faster. Finally, he looked up at the lights above the elevator doors. The down arrow above the left elevator door lit up white. The doors dinged as they opened, and Junior prepared to push his father inside the elevator, a short-lived feeling of relief washing over him.

"Ah, Mr. Johnson. I'm sorry it took me so long," Mr. Becks sang, as if he wasn't surprised at all to see Ernest and Junior.

Junior, taken aback, jumped at the sight of Mr. Becks. Junior eyed the other two men who were with the bank president inside the elevator. They watched him too. "We really have to go. My father is sick, and he has an international flight to catch," he huffed.

Mr. Becks walked straight into Junior, backing him out of the elevator.

"Nonsense. You all are almost at the finish line now. It'll be only a few more minutes. We'll arrange a car for your father straight to the airport," Mr. Becks said, a silly nervous smile painted on his face.

Mr. Becks and the two men stepped out of the elevator together. They let the doors close before Junior could jump inside or push his father in. Mr. Becks clapped Junior on the shoulder and urged him to turn around and follow him back to his office. Junior pushed his father forward and reluctantly fell in line. The other two men seemed to disappear in the opposite direction.

Maybe I am being too paranoid, Junior scolded himself silently. Just as he began to walk beside Mr. Becks, his cell phone began buzzing in his pocket again. Junior reached inside his suit jacket and retrieved it. He read the screen, and his heart rate sped up.

Junior knew better than to ignore the call again. He cleared his throat.

"Hello," he whispered into the phone. Junior felt confident this would be the last time he had to answer this call.

Silence.

"Hello?" he grumbled again.

"Agh! Help me! Help me! Please someone help me!" The shrill screams coming through the phone made Junior stop in his tracks. He immediately recognized Donna's screams. Junior felt like his heart would stop. He clutched the phone so tight, the veins in the top of his hand bulged against the skin.

"Donna?" Junior rasped, trying his best not to scream. He came to a stop. Mr. Becks stopped walking in response to Junior's strong reaction to the phone call.

A male voice came on the line. "Tell your father she will die if you don't have the money tonight. Then your mother . . . then your other sister. And it will go on and on until, last but not least, you. We are not playing any games with you anymore."

Junior could still hear Donna screeching in the background, like she was in a lot of pain. His heart was hammering so hard and fast, Junior lost his breath. He actually had to inhale deeply in an effort to get his lungs to fill up with air.

"Please don't hurt—" Junior blurted breathlessly, but he never got to finish his sentence before the line went dead.

Mr. Becks was no longer smiling after he watched all the color drain from Junior's face. He stepped closer to Ernest, his eyebrows dipping low on his forehead. "Is everything all right, Mr. Johnson? You look like you've seen a ghost," Mr. Becks said, gazing down the long hallway they were standing in, as if he was looking for someone.

Junior felt like he'd seen more than a ghost. . . . He'd heard the devil himself. "We have to make this quick. We have to go. There is an emergency. My sister . . . she's had an awful fall," Junior said, fabricating a story on the spot. He was glad he was used to quick thinking. He could make up lies so fast, he sometimes amazed himself.

Mr. Becks's eyebrows shot up into arches. He knew right away Junior was telling a lie, but he needed Ernest to sign an important document before he could release the money. "Oh yes, yes. I understand that things sometimes happen. Follow me," Mr. Becks replied as he began speed walking back toward his office.

Junior wasn't happy to have to return to the bank president's office, where he'd just sat for all that time. But he didn't have time to make a fuss about it. He just wanted to take care of his business and get out of there. He wanted to get his ailing father out of there and find out about his sister. Junior's legs were moving, but he wasn't concentrating at all. His mind raced with thoughts of Donna being tortured, beaten, tied up or, worse, killed.

They were so close to finishing up, but suddenly Ernest couldn't breathe, and not even his oxygen was helping. He felt like someone literally had his or her hands around his throat. By the time he made it to Mr. Becks's office, he was drenched with sweat. The room began to swirl around him. He gripped his chest with one hand and the arm of his wheelchair with the other.

"We will make this quick, Mr. Johnson. Neither of you looks so hot," Mr. Becks commented. He slid a release in front of Ernest.

But Ernest's vision was clouded now, and he could hardly hear. Mr. Becks seemed to be speaking in long drawn-out words. Junior watched nervously as his father tried in vain to steady his shaky hand. Ernest let out a strained gasp. Junior wanted to grab him and tell him to hurry up. Ernest felt like things were closing in around him. He knew he needed to get his signature on that paperwork, or this whole ordeal would all be for naught.

"Are you all right? Mr. Johnson, are you all right?" Mr. Becks called to Ernest now, holding out a black and gold fountain pen in front of him. Mr. Becks was just as anxious as Ernest was to get that paperwork signed.

Ernest reached out with a trembling hand and grasped the pen. It was taking everything inside him to fight his shortness of breath and the feeling that his neck was being squeezed. He had the pen in a death grip. Now all he had to do was get his hand to cooperate with his foggy brain. He blinked rapidly, trying to get his eyes to focus on the paper that lay in front of him.

"Are you having trouble? Do you need some water? A doctor maybe?" Mr. Becks asked, his hand on his chest in a "clutching the pearls" manner.

Ernest finally scribbled his signature on the bottom of the paper. He'd finally managed to seal the deal.

Finally! We got him! Mr. Becks screamed in his head. He looked out the door at the girl, and she nodded.

Then it seemed like things unfolded in movie-like slow motion. Junior could suddenly hear the loud thunder of feet pounding toward him. It wasn't long before he heard the loud commands and shouts that followed. He placed a protective hand on his father's wheelchair.

"Don't move! FBI!" It was the final sign that all hell had broken loose for Ernest Johnson and his entire family.

Junior let go of his father's wheelchair, stood, and raised his hands over his head. It seemed like the FBI agents were materializing from the walls. They tramped in from all directions. You would've thought he and his father were public enemies number one and two.

"Ernest Johnson, Sr., and Ernest Johnson, Jr., I am Special Agent Craski from the Federal Bureau of Investigation, and I have a warrant for your arrest," said a white man as he stepped close to Junior. Another one came over and began reading them their Miranda rights.

"My father is really sick. He needs to go to a hosp—" Junior began, but he stopped short when he spotted her. He crinkled his face.

"Bella! Baby, what are you doing here?" Junior asked, his tone frantic. "Did they come and snatch you?" But then he noticed she was dressed differently. She wore an FBI raid jacket. His heart sank, and his legs buckled a bit. "Bella? What? Why are you . . . ? What's going on?"

Bella swallowed hard and wore a sympathetic look on her face. She even had tears wanting to come to her eyes.

"Well, Martinez, I think it is time you tell Mr. Johnson who you really are," Craski said with a snide grin on his face. He clapped Bella on the shoulder, like a father sending his daughter out into the big scary world alone for the first time.

Bella said nothing.

"We'll give you a few minutes to break the news, but don't make it that long. We don't got all day. There is plenty of work to be done here," Craski grumbled, letting go of Bella's shoulder and stepping aside.

Junior's mouth sagged on each side, and he stepped forward a few paces and looked closely at Bella's face. He couldn't grasp what was going on. It was all too much. More like he didn't want to believe what was happening right before his eyes. Pain shot through Junior's chest. He clutched at his collar.

"Wha-what is he talking about, Bella? Why is he calling you Martinez? Who the hell is Martinez?" Junior rasped, his words catching in his throat. He could feel tears burning like acid at the backs of his eyes. He had to be a man. Crying wasn't an option anymore, especially not in front of the woman he had thought was his girlfriend all this time. The only woman he had ever really loved.

Bella still didn't speak.

"What does he mean, tell me who you really are?" Junior croaked. His heart was thundering against his sternum now. He was afraid of whatever he was about to learn. Junior didn't think there was much more he could take. Bella reached out to grab his hand, her eyes low, filled with remorse. Junior snatched his hand back, like she was a venomous snake.

"No! Don't touch me! Who are you?" he screamed, on the verge of hysteria. He moved a few paces away from her. "Tell me! Tell me right now! What are they talking about, Bella! Who are you? Why are they calling you Martinez? Your last name is Rodriguez, so why are they calling you Martinez!" Junior shouted, tears finally springing to his eyes. He already knew the answer, but something inside him wanted and needed to hear it from Bella's mouth.

"Junior. I am so sorry. Let me explain everything to . . . ," Bella said, her accent completely gone. Craski butted in at that moment and pushed her aside. Bella stumbled sideways, caught off guard. Her hands involuntarily curled into fists. She immediately wanted to punch Craski in his face.

"Oh, for Christ's sake! She is not Bella or Rodriguez, or whoever you thought she was. She is Liana Martinez, FBI agent—undercover FBI agent! She has been undercover all this time, and your little girlfriend never loved you one bit. All the shopping sprees, trips, gifts—those were all a lie," Craski shouted cruelly. He didn't care one bit that he had just crushed this rich bastard's entire world.

Junior's head started to spin. Tears were falling from his eyes like a waterfall, and he didn't even care. He felt humiliated. Embarrassed. Ashamed. Like a fool. He hadn't trusted many people in his lifetime, but what he'd had with Bella, he'd thought was real. It had been very real to him. He had even thought that he had fallen in love with Bella.

Craski continued his cruel rant. "See, she was helping us bring you and your father down. She used you to get close . . . real close. Thanks to you and Martinez here, we have just about all the evidence we need to put you and your father away for years."

Junior swiped angrily at the tears on his cheeks, and he exhaled a windstorm. He looked from the woman he knew as Bella to Craski and back again. His nostrils moved in and out as his heart raced. "Is what he just said true?" he asked the stranger he had been calling Bella.

Agent Liana Martinez lowered her eyes, unable to look at him. "Yes, Junior, it is true. My name is Liana Martinez. I am an FBI agent, and I was undercover on your father's case," she said in a low, sorrowful voice.

In a knee-jerk reaction, Junior reached out and slapped Bella, or Agent Martinez, across her face with the force of a hurricane. Bella stumbled sideways, and a bunch of agents descended on Junior.

"How dare you!" he spat. "You bitch! You mean, I was your job? A project for you? A case to conquer? Everything I shared with you was a lie! You used me, just like everyone else in my entire life! I hope you rot in the pits of hell for everything you did to me!" Junior hissed, the pain he felt almost palpable.

Martinez held her stinging cheek as she flexed her jaw. She had never wanted it to come to this. It wasn't supposed to come to this. She was supposed to just disappear from Junior's life one day, before they went overt on the case. Junior was never supposed to know that what he'd shared with her was all a lie. She knew that would hurt him deeply.

Junior shot her one last dagger of a look; then he turned and shook his head. His entire world had really just crashed in around him, and there was nothing he could do now but pray.

Agent Martinez looked at Shore and jutted an accusing finger in his face. "I can't believe what you guys did to me! To him! He may not be fully innocent in all this, but you know he was pulled in by virtue of his father. You know what he has been through these past few weeks . . . and now this! You fuckers could've given me a heads-up that you were going to go overt on the case today! I didn't even get the courtesy of a fucking heads-up! All this fucking work I put in, and this is what you do to me! Don't you two ever ask me for shit! Get your own fucking clues to where the evidence is. At least that way you can truly say you finally did something on this case besides take a few pictures and fucking get fat sitting in your car! You don't even care about the human collateral damage you have caused!" Martinez yelled, the heat of her breath hovering over Agent Shore's face.

"Sure seems like someone fell in love," Shore replied snidely. It was all part of the job. They hadn't anticipated that Martinez might be in too deep.

Martinez stalked out of the room; she had to leave be-fore she ended up assaulting one of her own peers. She had no clue what was going to happen to Junior now. She knew she had to keep following the case and make sure he was all right. There were things she just had to get off her chest. She just wanted to tell Junior the truth. That she had been doing her job and had never meant for him to get hurt. This was not how she had anticipated her relationship with Junior playing out in the end. Martinez knew when she started the case, she'd eventually have to tell him who she really was, but she had wanted to do it on her own terms. Not like this.

She left the building and sped down the sidewalk, on a mission. She would make sure that she tried to fix things, eventually. She'd try to make things better for Junior. Her mind raced with all sorts of thoughts. After all, she had developed feelings for Ernest Johnson, Jr., whether she liked it or not.

Chapter 15

All Falls Down

"Famed celebrity gossip blogger and socialite Carly Shepherd is finally speaking out on the apparent murder of her daughter, Lee Briggs. Lee, who was nineteen years old, is Carly's self-proclaimed love child with wild-man drummer Lee Briggs. Carly broke her silence today with the assistance of her family's attorney. 'My daughter was a perfect girl. She may have had some hard times, but what celebrity doesn't? She didn't deserve to be slaughtered like this . . . murdered like an animal. The person that took Lee's life will pay to the full extent of the law!' Carly shouted at the press conference she held today in front of her Manhattan high-rise.

"Shepherd and Briggs's daughter was said to have been found slain in her boyfriend's apartment on the West Side of Chicago three days ago. The medical examiner's report stated that the girl suffered blunt-force trauma and stab wounds. Police will not release any details of the investigation, but a source inside the department has told News Four that the main suspect in Briggs's murder is sixteen-year-old Tyree Johnson, grandson of famed investment banker Ernest Johnson, Sr. It is believed that Johnson may have taken drugs with Briggs and then attacked her when she refused his sexual advances. Some witnesses have come forward saying they saw Johnson push Briggs into a bedroom. Police have not confirmed this information. We will continue to follow the story as it develops. I'm Dana Park, News Four."

The huge flat-screen that hung over the Italian lacquer–accented mantel in the living room at the Johnsons' Gold Coast condo blared the news. Desiree and Carolyn sat in silence side by side on the plush suede sofa, listening to the reporter's every word. Both were lost in thought for very different reasons. Carolyn was the first to break the quiet, causing Desiree to jump a little bit.

"Look at her! Just look at this shameless wretch . . . all decked out, makeup flawless, talking about her dead child. Does she look like a grieving parent? She didn't even shed a tear during that entire press conference!" Carolyn shouted, looking at Desiree, although she really didn't want her daughter to answer.

Desiree nodded and used the tissue that had lived in her hand ever since her son's arrest. She hadn't talked much in the days since she'd found out her son would be held without bond. They'd actually listed her son as a flight risk.

"Not one bag under her eyes from so-called days of crying . . . wearing bright yellow, as if she's celebrating! Such a media whore. Who wears bright yellow to speak about the dead? Her daughter is dead, for God's sake!" Carolyn yelled as she watched Carly Shepherd and her attorney soak up the world's spotlight. "I can't stand it! She is all dressed up, model perfect, holding a media press conference about her dead child? I don't think so! I'm sure this media trounce is to boost her blog ratings and any other way she can make money off the poor dead child. People like her make me sick to my core! Shameless!"

Desiree picked up the remote control and clicked off the television. Carolyn looked at her daughter. Desiree had tears welling up in her already red-rimmed eyes. "I can't watch that anymore, Mother. I feel bad enough.

I can't deal," Desiree told her mother before she broke down again.

Desiree recognized that her mother had been trying to be supportive in the only way she knew how to be. Without Tyson and Carolyn, Desiree didn't know how she would've made it through all this chaos. They had kept her sane.

"Mother, it's all over the news now. Everyone where we live will know. Tyree's life will never be the same. Everything I worked to avoid is happening. My worst nightmare," Desiree cried as she picked up three tabloid magazines from the floor. Carolyn and Desiree looked at the words on the covers at the same time. ROCK-STAR DAUGHTER MURDERED BY DRUG-CRAZED TEEN. MURDER AMONG THE WEALTHY. JOHNSON HEIR A KILLER.

Carolyn shook her head in disgust and tossed the magazines aside. She looked at Desiree with sympathetic eyes. "Do you see what I mean? This is all Carly's doing, I'm sure! There is no way Tyree will get a fair trial anywhere in Chicago . . . anywhere in the States, for that matter!" she shouted.

Desiree rubbed her own legs, which was all she could do to comfort herself at a time like this. She didn't know why her mother kept bringing her the tabloids and newspapers, since she was already heartbroken as it was.

"This is all so horrible. I still haven't heard back about whether or not Daddy can call in any favors. What am I supposed to do to help my son? I have no choice but to wait for a miracle," Desiree said, then let the sobs start up, her chest feeling tight and her head feeling hazy again.

She had signed herself out of the hospital against the doctor's wishes to be at Tyree's arraignment. The judge, citing Tyree's "wealthy family" and his ability to leave the country, had denied him bond. Desiree had felt like she would faint again when she'd heard the no bond order.

She wanted to scream that her son wasn't rich! He hadn't grown up like she had, and they had nothing. He didn't even have a passport. But she knew that would just get her tossed out of court, and she wanted to spend every moment that she could in the same room with her son. She tried reaching out to Tyree with her eyes. He looked terrified, which broke her heart into a million pieces.

Carolyn tried to comfort Desiree now, but there wasn't much she could offer aside from her company. Carolyn pulled her daughter to her and held her in a tight embrace, although she knew that nothing she could do would ever take away Desiree's pain.

Rebecca stepped into the living room just then. "Ahem. Mrs. Johnson, you have a visitor," she announced, hanging her head after noticing that she'd walked in on a mother-daughter moment. Carolyn and Desiree immediately released each other and moved apart.

"Who?" Carolyn asked, completely caught off guard by the announcement of a visitor. She hadn't told anyone she would be staying in the city. Everyone still expected them to be in Idlewild. Not many people would think to find her here. First of all, Carolyn hadn't been answering any calls from any of her nosy socialite friends. She was sure that she would soon be the talk of the town, so there was no need to feed them information.

The Gold Coast condo was one of the homes she and Ernest had considered putting on the market after Donna's stint in rehab. Carolyn had decided then that they didn't need to have so many places anymore. She had hoped it would force the family back together, under one roof. She had hoped being back in Idlewild this summer would've done that too. But everything seemed to be coming apart one thing at a time.

"Who would know I'm here and decide to pop in on me?" Carolyn mused.

"It's me, Carolyn," Aaron Collins, their lawyer, announced brashly, not bothering to wait to be announced. He nearly pushed Rebecca to the side as he forced his way into the room. "Look, we need to talk," Collins said gravely, holding back no punches, his face was stony.

Desiree stood up, her body language rigid. Carolyn grabbed Desiree's arm gently to comfort her.

"I'm sorry. I wasn't expecting anyone, and we can't be too diligent with all this media buzz around this story. You understand, I'm sure," Carolyn said to Collins with a nervous chuckle. "Please, Aaron, sit down."

"I can't stay," Collins said curtly. He looked at Carolyn seriously, and her facial expression folded into a frown, erasing the smile that she had painted on her face. "What's wrong? What is it?"

"Carolyn, I'm sorry to bother you at a time like this. I came to tell you that the check for the retainer and the court appearances was returned for insufficient funds," Collins announced gravely.

Carolyn's eyebrows shot up into arches on her face. Collins put his hand up before she could say a word. "I can give you a few days . . . You know I have worked with your family for quite a few—" he continued, but he was cut short.

It was Desiree's turn to speak now. "What do you mean, returned for insufficient funds?" she asked, incredulous. She knew that her parents had plenty of money . . . or so she thought.

Before Collins could answer, Carolyn spoke. "We have plenty of money. There must be some mistake. You have to be mistaken. You need to check your bank for the mistake. It couldn't be on our part. No, we have money," she said, her voice shaking. She didn't even believe that she was having to say this. Everyone knew they had money. Ernest had been born into money, for God's sake. This had to be some sort of mistake.

Collins didn't speak. He reached into his suit jacket pocket and pulled out a document, which had been folded to fit into his pocket. He offered it to Carolyn. "Carolyn, I don't mean to sound harsh, but I will not be able to render services to Tyree unless . . . ," he said, trailing off.

Desiree snatched the document from his hand. Her face was a bright shade of red, as if filled with blood. A vein in the side of her neck banged fiercely against her skin. Her health condition was secondary to the issue at hand.

"This is nonsense! Do you know who the Johnson family is? Do you know what we have? This is not a fly-by-night business venture family! This family has generational wealth!" Carolyn barked as she took the document from her daughter and scanned it with her eyes. She couldn't be reading that document correctly. Carolyn's head involuntarily moved back and forth. She didn't even realize she was biting her bottom lip until she tasted her own blood. She reviewed the document again.

Frozen, insufficient funds, seized account were the words that stuck out on the document. Carolyn's heart thundered now. She was suddenly freezing cold, like someone had pumped her body full of ice water. She closed her eyes to hold back the tears. She felt like someone had the strings to her life, and one by one, they were clipping them with scissors. She swallowed hard and looked up at Collins.

"I . . . I . . . don't understand. What does this all mean?" Carolyn asked a question she knew Collins couldn't answer. It was all she could manage. What else could she say to a prestigious attorney like Aaron Collins?

"Carolyn, it looks like the account has been seized by the federal government and all Ernest's assets have been frozen. I think you need to call Gus and ask what is going on," Collins said, his words dropping around Carolyn and Desiree like small atomic bombs.

Seized by the federal government! All the assets!
Carolyn's ears rang from the reality of those words. She
would definitely have to call Gus Beatty, Ernest's personal
accountant, to find out just what the heck was going on.
A few hours ago, she'd called the Idlewild house, where
Junior was supposed to be looking after Ernest until
Rebecca could get back there. No one had called her back,
which Carolyn now found strange. Maybe Gus knew what
was happening.

"I'm sure this is all some kind of mistake. Gus will get
back to me soon, and everything will work out," Carolyn
said, a cheery voice suddenly coming out of her mouth.
She plastered on a phony smile, her usual. It was the role
she'd played for so long that it just was second nature to
her now.

Act as if this bad thing is really not happening. Smile.
Keep up appearances. All the things she had practiced
over the years.

"You've known Ernest and me for years. We would
never pass a bad check. This is all some kind of fluke.
C'mon, you know us better than this," Carolyn added,
then laughed inappropriately.

Collins's facial expression was stoic. He let out an
exasperated breath. He really felt sorry for Desiree and
Tyree, and for Carolyn, for that matter.

Carolyn just didn't get it. Her life had changed . . .
something she needed to face. And face fast.

"I'll need a few days to arrange another payment. I'll
have to contact some of my other resources," Carolyn
said mindlessly as she stared down at the document she
had involuntarily crushed in her hand. Her mood had
suddenly changed again.

"I can give you until Friday, Carolyn, but after that, I
will have to move on to paying clients. Time is money,"
Collins told her, trying to keep his voice as soft as he
could without seeming insincere.

Desiree shot him an evil look. She couldn't believe how fast people turned on you when they thought you didn't have money to pad their pockets. She shook her head in disgust.

"You will get your money. I will do whatever I have to do to get your money," Carolyn said dryly. "Now you can see your way out. I wouldn't want to waste any of your precious and costly time." She was done with him.

Collins picked up his briefcase and headed for the door. Before he left the room, he stopped and turned toward Carolyn and Desiree again. "I know this may be the last thing you want to hear, Carolyn, but it's just the reality of the situation. You should protect yourself while you can. Don't be caught without some sort of protection, like Bernie Madoff's wife," Collins preached. "This is definitely just as bad."

Carolyn shot him a surprised look. She opened her mouth to tell him off for the insinuation, but she couldn't get the words out before Collins continued.

"Not to sound harsh, but it's the truth. The buzz is that Ernest is into something he won't soon be out of . . . even worse than Madoff. So, here's a friendly piece of advice. Stop living with your head under the covers, like you've done about his affairs and your son's and other daughter's problems over the years. This is far more serious . . . even deadly. You will be left with nothing, and your grandson will be left in jail to rot if you don't do something now. This one account being seized may just be the tip of the iceberg," Collins said gravely. Then he walked out of the room.

His words seemed to hit Carolyn like an open-handed slap to the face. She flopped back on the couch, as if she'd been gut punched. She knew that Collins was right. It was time for her to stop playing the victim role and protect herself. Carolyn quickly picked up her cell phone and stood. She needed to contact the keeper of her secret stash account. She had learned more than one lesson while being married to Ernest Johnson, Sr., but self-preservation and deceit were the two most important.

Just as Carolyn dialed the last number on her phone, she heard loud voices erupt behind her. Chaotic and loud, to say the least. Now was not the time; Carolyn needed quiet to concentrate.

"Shush, Rebecca and Desi. I'm on the . . . ," Carolyn said, annoyed, as she turned around slowly to scold them for making so much noise. Carolyn immediately dropped the phone on the glass top of the wet bar, where she stood, in response to what she saw in front of her. The loud clang sent a chill down her spine, but not more of a chill than what she confronted in front of her. It was as if a never-ending line of strange people were rushing at Carolyn at full speed. Her head whipped from side to side so fast, her eyes couldn't keep up with it. She couldn't focus on one face. They were all a blur, and so was the situation.

"What is going on here? Who are you? What is this!" Carolyn belted out. She was moving fast and furious now to stop these pillagers from invading her home. "Don't touch anything! Get out, all of you!" she screeched. Carolyn wanted to grab them all, stop this all-out invasion. Finally, someone stopped in front of her long enough to tell her what was going on. Carolyn's nostrils flared as she looked at the portly, balding man in a dark suit.

"Mrs. Johnson, I am Special Agent Craski from the Federal Bureau of Investigation," he said as he held his badge in his hand.

Her face went from burnt red to a gray shade of pale when she zeroed in on the badge. Then she clutched at her neck as she watched the gang of men and women rush around her home like scavengers on a hunt. Some wore suits, and others wore dark jackets with bright yellow letters on the backs. FBI. SEC. IRS-CI. To name a few.

"What is the meaning of this?" Carolyn managed to say to the ugly man. She felt faint again but was determined to stand her ground. "What legal right do you have to be in my home? Do you know who my husband is? His family?" she added weakly. It was the only defense she could muster. She had hidden behind the Johnson name for so many years that it was unfathomable now that it didn't even matter anymore. The name held no weight. A fact that Carolyn was not ready to live with at all.

"Mrs. Johnson, we have a search and seizure warrant for your home. Your husband, Ernest Sr., and your son, Ernest Jr., have been arrested. If you want to speak with us, we can go to another room . . . away from all this confusion. I know this is upsetting, but we do have a legal right to be here, ma'am," a man who called himself Special Agent Shore chimed in from behind his obese counterpart. "I think you'll be interested in what we have to say . . . if you give us a minute to explain," he added.

Ernest and Junior have been arrested? What! Carolyn felt so stupid. So betrayed. But she should have known better. Not long ago she had stumbled across some of Ernest's work when he was on one of his many business trips. After looking over the documents, she had suspected that he had been lying to his clients about their investment returns. Carolyn had kept her suspicions to herself; she had planned to use the information as leverage one day. Obviously, she wasn't going to get that chance. But she never could have imagined that it was *this* bad.

"Should I get an attorney? I mean . . . my husband . . . he ran his own business. I am just a housewife and a mother.

I don't know much about his dealings or his business," Carolyn lied, wringing her hands together from nerves.

Shore and Craski looked at one another knowingly. They had been watching Carolyn for months, too, so they knew she had more knowledge of her husband's business dealings than she was letting on. A devoted wife she was, but the role of unsuspecting wife didn't suit her that well.

"If I am guilty of anything, it might be shopping. Other than that, I won't be able to help you," Carolyn said, her words rushed and shaky. She wondered if they knew about her secret stash. There was no telling how far the feds had dug into their lives. Carolyn wondered if they knew her grandson had gotten arrested too.

"We can't advise you either way, but we can tell you that we have a legal right to be here. We will be searching and seizing any evidence that relates to our case. And we will be searching the *whole* property," Shore said, sounding official and stern. "Now, if you would follow us to the area we have set aside for you and your family to sit in while we search . . ." He stepped aside with his hand outstretched like a butler's so that Carolyn could lead the way. When she entered the condo's large foyer, she found Rebecca and Desiree sitting on the small shoe bench Carolyn had imported from Paris a few years earlier.

Rebecca's eyes were wide as dinner plates as she looked up at Carolyn.

"Mrs. J, what's going on?" Rebecca asked, worry furrowing her brow. "All these police . . . Why are they doing this? It's just so, so scary. Does this have anything to do with Tyree? Are Mr. J and Junior all right? Will they be here all night? Can we leave? Did we all do something wrong?" Rebecca shot questions at Carolyn fast and furious, like pellets from a toy gun.

Desiree opened her mouth to do the same, but Carolyn put up her hand to stop her. Carolyn felt like she was under fire. She didn't have answers herself to all those questions. She had no idea what the hell was going on. "Rebecca . . . please. Please. I have no idea. I have to sort all this out myself," Carolyn said in a low grumble, putting her hands up, as she sat down.

Carolyn looked around the foyer and then down a hallway for a few seconds. She squinted as she looked at one of the FBI agents. There was something familiar about the female agent. Something was different about her, but her face was unmistakable.

"Don't I know you?" Carolyn asked. Rebecca's and Desiree's eyes widened a bit. Carolyn's pulse quickened. All sorts of things ran through her mind. The familiar agent rushed past them. But like a bolt of lightning, it finally hit Carolyn.

"Bella? Rebecca, is that Bella? Is that the girl Junior brought to Idlewild?" Carolyn asked, her tone more frantic now. She was on her feet, standing now. She wanted to grab Rebecca's shoulders and shake her until she spit out the answer. "Rebecca! Is that her?"

"I don't know! But if it is, it seemed like she . . . she . . . ," Rebecca said, but she wanted to choose her next words wisely. She didn't want to ruffle Carolyn's feathers any more than they already were, but something had just not sat right about Junior and Bella from day one for Rebecca.

Carolyn wasn't letting up. She wanted to know everything. "She what?" Carolyn said to Rebecca. "What! I want to know what you heard or saw!" Carolyn grabbed Rebecca's shoulders and shook her.

Rebecca had a feeling she had already said too much. She swallowed the lump of fear that had formed at the back of her throat.

"Well, spit it out! What is it?" Carolyn said, noticing the look on Rebecca's face. She realized she was scaring the poor woman. Carolyn eased up a bit. "Rebecca, it is important that I know what you saw or heard," she said with as much calmness as she could muster.

"Well, Mrs. J, I hate to say this, but that is definitely Bella, and she came in with the FBI agents. She must be an FBI agent herself, which means she was probably lying to Junior all along," Rebecca replied, finally spitting out what she had been trying to say.

Carolyn's face folded into a frown. She twisted her lips, as if she didn't believe her son could be so stupid. "Are you sure? What makes you say that?" Carolyn asked brusquely, seeking clarification.

"I wasn't supposed to be listening, but I could hear Bella talking to them. More like arguing with them. She was saying something like . . . they should have called her before they came here. I swear, it was the strangest thing. She also no longer had an accent when I overheard her speaking with them," Rebecca reported, her words full of regret. She could see the anger streaking across Carolyn's face.

Carolyn was gone from in front of Rebecca in a flash. Carolyn stormed back into the part of the house where the federal agents were still sifting through her family's things. Her face was red hot with fury. She wanted answers, and she wanted them now!

"Bella! Bella!" she screamed as she angled around corners and went through doorways into the main part of the house. She didn't care that every area of her home was now swarming with law enforcement officers. "Bella! Where are you?" Carolyn shouted, garnering a few strange stares from some of the agents.

Shore finally came out of Ernest's office, where he had been searching, in response to Carolyn's screams. "What's the matter, Mrs. Johnson? Is there a problem?" he asked.

How dare he ask me if there is a problem while he is rummaging through my home like I'm some common criminal! Carolyn screamed silently in her head. Her cheeks were flushed red; her nostrils flared. She stormed toward Shore with her eyes squinted into dashes.

"Where is Bella? Why do you have her hiding from me? What, you don't want me to see her? What does she have to do with all of this? Where is she? Where is that traitor?" Carolyn shouted in Shore's face, her shaky finger jutting at him accusingly.

Shore let out a long sigh, like Carolyn was getting on his nerves. That didn't deter her one bit. It was bad enough they'd relegated her to the foyer of her own home. She wasn't backing down this time.

"I demand to know where she is! I need to see her face. I need to confirm what I know. Bella!" Carolyn shouted.

Agent Shore put up his hands in a halting motion. Just then Bella stepped up behind Shore, Craski right behind her. Bella's eyes were glassy, and her mouth was downturned.

"Bella! Oh my God!" Carolyn screeched, a look of disgust washing over her face. She moved forward and shot word daggers at the woman she knew as Bella. "Who are you? Where is my son? You did this, didn't you? You did all of this to my family!" Carolyn tried to walk into her, but Craski stepped in between them.

Bella stood there with her arms at her sides. It was like she couldn't move.

"Bella, is that even your name? Who are you? You came to my home with my son, you lied to us all, and I want to know who the hell you are," Carolyn persisted, noticing the other woman's body language. "Answer me," she growled with a sense of urgency.

Now the entire room seemed to be watching them. Carolyn couldn't understand what was going on. Craski stepped closer to them. Carolyn eyed him evilly, as if to say, "Stay away from me." Then she looked at Bella again.

Bella lowered her eyes to the floor. She had just gone through the same thing when they arrested Junior. The cat was out of the bag, and in the end, Agent Martinez was the one who'd broken this case, but she still couldn't denounce the feelings she had experienced when Junior found out who she was.

Chapter 16

Revelations

The stale air that clung to the cinder-block walls of the jail was like nothing Tyree had ever experienced in his life. It was stifling in there. He had never known he suffered from claustrophobia until now. The cell he was in was smaller than his closets at home. He didn't know how much more of being locked up he could take. Tyree hunched over the small silver metal toilet and dry heaved for the tenth time. The muscles in his stomach contracted painfully, but nothing happened. Again, for the tenth time, nothing came up. At least the day before he'd gotten some clear stomach bile to lurch up his esophagus and spew from his dry, cracked lips. Now, with his face so close to the bowl, the pungent smell of the toilet disinfectant settled at the back of his throat, making his empty stomach feel worse. He plunged his pointer finger into the back of his throat one more time. One more attempt to get something to come up. One more attempt to move himself closer to the death he'd been hoping for. Nothing happened.

Tyree knew then he was completely dry inside. That was exactly what he had wanted. Weak and dizzy, probably from dehydration, he crawled the two paces it took to get from the toilet back to his hard metal bunk. Tyree used what little strength he had left to climb onto the slab of metal. It was covered with a thin plastic mattress and a ratty, threadbare gray blanket. The smell of the blanket had made Tyree sick his first night there. It was what he would've imagined mildew or mold smelled like, if he'd ever had to imagine such a thing.

Tyree's head pounded as he tried to get into a position that was at least comfortable. That was nearly impossible on the hard bed. He grabbed the so-called blanket and pulled it over his arms. The blanket wasn't even big enough to cover his whole body, so he had chosen which part he was going to keep warm. Tyree had seen better blankets in the school nurse's office than the one they had given him at the jail.

Tyree let a soft moan escape his lips as his stomach roiled with hunger pains. Starvation was no easy way to die. He had never known until now what it even felt like to be hungry, much less starving to death. It even hurt to moan at this point. His head pounded, and his entire body ached. He was sure he'd probably lost more than ten pounds in the past week. Tyree balled his body into a tight knot and rocked back and forth with what little strength he had left.

"Please, God, just let me die today," Tyree rasped, barely able to get enough air in his lungs to get the words out. "Take care of my mom, and don't let her be sad forever after I die. Make sure she knows I didn't do what they're blaming me for. Comfort her the same way she comforted everyone else all my life."

Tyree wanted to cry—his face even folded itself into a crying frown—but he didn't have enough water in his body to even make tears. He was angry at himself after realizing he wasn't even good at killing himself. He had been on a hunger strike since he'd been brought to the solitary confinement unit inside the Cook County Jail, the famous Twenty-Sixth and Cal prison. It was taking way longer than he had expected for his body to finally give out. Each time the corrections officers slid the food tray into the slot in his door, Tyree would push it back out, causing the horrible food—usually thick, lumpy dark gray oatmeal for breakfast; hard bologna sandwiches on stale, moldy bread for lunch; and green slop for dinner—to fall on the floor. The corrections officers always yelled the same thing through the door.

"Food down! No meal in cell seventeen! Johnson, you won't get any more food until next meal call!" It was their procedure to make a recorded statement that Tyree had refused the food. They didn't want to be accused of starving him. Most of the corrections officers knew who Tyree was by now. A few of them cursed at him about the food trays, because they would be the ones responsible for getting the mess outside his door cleaned up.

Tyree had also refused to leave the cell for a shower each day. Most times they didn't force him, but after an inmate went four days without a shower, it was protocol that he or she would have to be forcefully showered. It had happened to Tyree already. The officers had stormed into his cell, restrained him, and dragged him into the in-mate shower stall, where he'd been soaped up and hosed down like an animal. Tyree had also refused to leave his cell for the forty-five minutes a day they wanted to give him for solo recreation. He didn't care to see the drab gray walls of the jail yard. That so-called recreation time was a joke in his eyes. The first time he'd gone outside, he'd been put in another cage that was open at the top. "What is the point?" he had asked the corrections officer. "It's still a cage." Tyree had seen the sky when he looked up, but he'd still been surrounded by gray walls on every side. It had been a big waste of time, in his assessment.

With no contact other than from the corrections offi-cers, Tyree felt most days like he was going crazy. He just wanted to die as quickly as possible. The last he'd heard from his attorney, he was waiting to hear back from the appeal about the bond. That seemed like an eternity ago. Tyree thought it best that he couldn't see his mother, because seeing her cry the last time in court had broken his heart and kept him awake at night for a week straight afterward.

Tyree felt himself slipping in and out of sleep now. Did that mean he was dying? He hoped so. He was praying that his body was finally breaking down before his death. But when he heard the cell-door locks clicking, he knew he was not dead yet.

"Johnson! Let's go! You got a visitor!" Tyree's favorite corrections officer yelled at him. He was the same grizzly bear of a man who had been guarding Tyree during the day since he'd arrived there. He'd told Tyree his name was Yusef.

Yusef had been the one to explain to Tyree that he had to be in solitary confinement for his own protection because of who his family was and his recent frequent appearances in the tabloid magazines. If the other inmates in the general population got hold of Tyree, he would definitely be assaulted or worse just because of his family's almost celebrity status. Tyree thought that it was horrible that he was being punished like a mass murderer just because he had been born into a family he hardly saw, barely knew, and now wanted nothing to do with. He wished that he and his mother had just stayed back in their little Indiana town, living life like regular people. Tyree was starting to understand why his mother had chosen to stay away from her family.

"I don't want to see anyone if it is not my mother," Tyree grumbled, pulling his blanket up over his head. His lawyer was the only person who had visited him and could visit him, and his lawyer never had anything good to say.

"You don't have a choice today. You need to get out of this cell before you wither away. Let's go, Johnson. Up, up, up," Yusef demanded, standing over Tyree now. "I'm not going to sit by and watch you kill yourself in here. You have way too much to live for. Now come on." The CO snatched the ratty little blanket off Tyree and urged him to sit up. Tyree moaned and groaned, but he listened to Yusef. Tyree had grown to respect him. He had come to know that Yusef's heart was just as big as his body.

"Who is the visitor?" Tyree whined as he stood up on achy, weak legs. He felt winded already. He managed to slide his feet into the horrible, cheap white jail sneakers he had been issued. Tyree felt like he could barely stand, much less move enough to walk to the visitation area. He was sure he'd faint before he made it there.

"Someone you need to see. At this point, beggars can't be choosers. A visitor is a visitor. Plenty of inmates in here never get visitors. You need to know that you have people that care about you. Look at you right now. Half dead from starving yourself. You need this visit today," Yusef said, his tone serious yet caring. It kind of made Tyree want to cry that a total stranger seemed to care more about him right now than his own family. Tyree had spent nights crying over the fact that he hadn't been able to see his mother, aside from in court, since he'd been arrested.

"All right. Let's go," Yusuf said, putting the handcuffs on Tyree before he led him out of the cell.

Tyree entered the small, cramped visitation area and looked around for the surprise visitor. He didn't see any familiar faces at first. Just a few prisoners sitting across from their visitors, who had sad faces, and speaking in hushed tones. The entire scene was depressing. Incarcerated mothers visited with their small children, unable to have real physical contact with them. Tyree hated this place with a passion. Figuring his visitor had not yet entered the visitation area, he took a seat and waited. A few minutes later, Tyree finally saw a door to the left of where he sat swing open. Tyree looked dumbfounded as he watched the familiar stranger stroll over to the other side of the table. Tyree immediately looked back and searched the room for the CO, but he had already stepped away. Tyree crumpled his face as the stranger took a seat.

The man's face was drawn tight with concern. Tyree could tell that the meeting was as uncomfortable for the man as it was for him. It was then that Tyree realized this man's face was similar to his own face. Tyree didn't know why, but in that moment he felt shame. At first, neither Tyree nor the man spoke. Tyree suddenly remembered that this man had been at his grandparents' party. His mother had stood speaking to this man and had seemed so distraught. Tyree's body grew hot, and he felt really uncomfortable sitting there now.

The man broke the silence. "Tyree, I . . . I . . . know you don't know me," the man said, his tone soft.

Tyree stared blankly at the man, his insides roiling.

"My name is Tyson Blackwell. I . . . I'm a friend . . . Well, I knew your mother," Tyson said, tripping over his words. He couldn't keep his hands still either. Tyree noted that immediately, because that was exactly how he was, too, whenever he was nervous.

Tyree stared at the man through squinted eyes. His head pounded even more now. The sick feeling seemed a thousand times worse now that he had to sit up on the hard visitation-room chair.

"I'll just get right to the point," Tyson continued, noticing that Tyree wasn't going to ask or say a thing. "Tyree, I am . . . I'm, um . . ." Tyson couldn't say it.

Tyree's nostrils opened and closed rapidly now. His legs swung in and out under the table.

"I'm your father," Tyson finally said.

Tyree's head jerked slightly, as if Tyson had just slapped him. The tears he'd tried to cry earlier, to no avail, had no trouble coming now. Tyree's mouth was pinched, and his fists were clenched. He couldn't speak. It was as if someone was ringing an alarm in his ears. He felt faint.

"I came to tell you because I think you have the right to know. And I also want you to know that no matter what happens, I will not give up on getting you out of here," Tyson said. Then he slid something across the table toward his son.

Tyree looked down. It was a newspaper clipping. Tyree's eyes couldn't help but read the headline that was in front of him. JUDGE TYSON BLACKWELL NAMED PRESIDING JUDGE OF COOK COUNTY'S CRIMINAL DIVISION. As Tyree read the big bold letters, he felt like someone was screaming the words in his ears. The pain in his head increased, and his heart pumped painfully in his chest. His long-lost father was a criminal court judge, yet here he sat, incarcerated for a crime he hadn't committed.

"I am going to do everything in my power. You will be exonerated. It'll take me some time, but I refuse to lose any more time with you, son," Tyson said, reaching across the table and putting his hand on top of Tyree's balled left fist.

Tyree was sure he'd have a heart attack when he let his eyes travel down to the picture under the headline. There he was, in all his greatness, looking like an older version of Tyree himself. Tyree blinked a few times, not knowing how to process what he was seeing in front of him. But it was there. Clear as day. A picture of his father in a judge's robe. Tyree stared at his father's face, his eyes in the photo. His eyes were so familiar. Tyree had the same eyes. And the goofy grin. He had grinned that way all his life, when he was happy or nervous. He had a father. All these years later, he had a father. This man must've been going about his life like he didn't have a care in the world, although his mother had clearly struggled alone to take care of him.

Tyree scanned the picture with his eyes one more time. Then he looked up at Tyson and searched for some sense of sorrow, but there was none. He couldn't see one bit of sorrow in his father's eyes. He lowered his eyes. He couldn't stop staring at the photo and then at Tyson.

"I know this is a lot, Tyree. I'm sorry to have to tell you like this. I just didn't want you to hear it from any other source. I wanted to be the one to tell you," Tyson said. "I am so sorry I let you down all this time, but I want to be here now. I want to help. I want us to be father and son."

"What does that mean? What does it mean for me? So, what, you're my father and you want to come act like you've always been around? What does it mean for me?" Tyree asked, forcing his words out of his mouth.

Tyson closed his eyes, and tears drained from the sides of them. He didn't really know the answer to those questions. Tyson didn't even know what his son's arrest would mean for his career, his marriage once everyone found out who Tyree really was. He couldn't even say where he was going to begin to try to help his son to get out of the mess he was in or how he would keep his own career intact while he did so. Tyson inhaled and came up with an answer for his son.

"It means that I am going to do everything in my power to make sure you are vindicated. It means that I will never leave your side while this is going on. Tyree, we may not have the father-and-son bond we should, because of all the lost years, but it is not going to change my love for you. I am not going to let you down any longer than I already have," Tyson said with feeling.

Tyree hung his head. He shook it back and forth. Things were getting worse and worse. "How could my mother do this to me! How could she know who you were all along and never tell me? And never plan to tell me?" he said angrily. The room was spinning around him. "I can't believe her! I hate her for this! My whole life has been a lie. I want to die!" he yelled, the weight of everything finally crashing down on his shoulders.

Tyson seemed taken aback. He leaned back in his chair and then moved the chair back from the table, his mouth agape. Yusuf appeared behind Tyree within a few seconds.

"I hate her and you! I want to die! I hate her! I hate you!" Tyree screamed over and over, never breaking eye contact with his father. A group of corrections officers surrounded Tyree now.

"Please don't hurt him," Tyson pleaded.

They pulled Tyree up from the chair. He continued to scream as they led him away. Tyree turned one last time and looked at his father. Tyson could see the sadness in his son's eyes, and for the first time since he'd met Tyree the other night, Tyson felt a deep connection with his child.

"I love you," Tyson mouthed, and he meant it. He could not remember the last time he had told anyone aside from Selena that he loved them. It just wasn't something they did in the Blackwell family. The thick metal door closed behind Tyree. Tyson stood up, feeling weaker than he had ever felt in his entire life. He would do whatever it took to get his only child out of this mess. Even if it meant destroying a career he'd worked his whole life to build.

Chapter 17

Consequences

Patrick blew the cigar smoke out of his mouth just as easily as he had taken it in. The gray haze from the smoke cast a gloomy cloud over the entire room. The mood in the room was the same: gray and cloudy. Patrick exhaled again. He had to take a few minutes to process the information he had just received.

He looked up at his main henchman, Declan, and spoke slowly, as if he wanted to emphasize his understanding of each word. "So you say that Johnson is in the hands of the feds now? Arrested? That he was running a scam with all his clients' money? Maybe even my money?" he said.

Declan nodded, his eyes wide, his heart hammering. All of Patrick's workers knew how unpredictable his mood could get. There was no telling how Patrick might react to this kind of bad news. Declan had once watched Patrick beat a man to death because Patrick had lost a hundred thousand dollars on a horse race. This was even worse. Much more money was at stake here.

"Declan, let's clear things up, eh? So you're saying that all the money I gave to Johnson is gone? And there's not a damn thing I can do about it?" Patrick asked. He was asking, but he already knew the answers to his own questions. The words made the acid in Declan's stomach churn. Patrick's stoic facial expression made Declan ball up his toes in his shoes.

"That's right. I followed the wife, like you said. The grandson has been arrested for murder. I found out that Johnson and his son have been arrested too. Ponzi scheme, they call it. Like Madoff, but worse," Declan related carefully.

Patrick listened intently as he stubbed out his cigar. He leaned into the mahogany-wood desk he sat behind. "What about the other daughter? The addict," he asked, steepling his fingers in front of him.

"Yes, I got her, like you asked. We have her in the van," Declan answered. He nodded at two men standing posted up near the door of Patrick's office. The men began moving, the rustle of their suits the only sound in the room. Declan looked at his boss seriously. "Before they bring her in, Patrick, I want to ask, what are you going to do with her?" Declan knew he was taking a chance by asking. Patrick shot him an evil glance. Declan felt the heat of Patrick's gaze bearing down on him.

Patrick knew that his hired help was trying to make the point that if Ernest wasn't around to pay the ransom for his daughter, they would most likely have to dispose of her. Patrick didn't like to be questioned. He also didn't like it when one of his lowly workers tried to point out the obvious to him before he could make the point himself. He flexed his jaw. "Why are you worried about it? You fancy her or something?" Patrick asked, annoyed.

Declan immediately knew he had said too much. He didn't mean to wear his feelings on his sleeve, but it had been hard when it came to Donna. The day he had snatched her, he'd found out exactly who she was and why Patrick wanted her. But Declan, being both equally romantic and stupid, had instantly fallen for her. She was stunningly beautiful to him. Her innocence in all this made him that much more attracted to her. It wasn't often Declan let himself form any attachment to what he called his "subjects," but he couldn't help it this time.

He was human, and his attraction to Donna was instant. That was a big no-no in his line of work. Falling for one of his victims could lead to big problems. Especially if Patrick got wind of it. Declan knew he couldn't look the least bit weak in front of Patrick, or else that could be bad news. Patrick had always said, "A hit man with feelings is too dangerous. That kind will turn on you in a minute."

"Patrick, go away out of that! I'd never catch a fancy for a bird! I know better than that!" Declan lied and looked away. He couldn't afford for Patrick to look in his eyes. Declan knew that Patrick was very smart and perceptive.

Before Patrick could say anything else, the other two men returned with Donna in tow. They dragged her into the room and closed the door behind them, and then they threw Donna to the floor. Patrick eyed her up and down. From the looks of it, his men had treated her decently. Well, as decently as a kidnapped drug addict could be treated. Aside from a few bruises on her shapely legs, Donna looked to be in good condition. Patrick could tell that she was afraid. Her entire body trembled like a leaf in a windstorm as she struggled to hold herself up. They had her hands bound in front of her, and her eyes were covered with a piece of thick black material. Typical. Patrick took a minute more to examine her before he spoke. He could tell that the girl was beautiful too. No wonder Declan liked her.

"Donna, is it?" Patrick said, trying to make his words as plain as possible with his thick accent.

"Yes," Donna said quietly. "Please! Please! Whoever you are, help me! Whatever you want, my parents will give you! They have money! They have jewelry! Do you know who Ernest Johnson is? Please, let me contact them! *Please!*" Donna pleaded, her voice hoarse from screaming and crying for days now. She didn't know if this would be her last chance to beg for her life or not. Donna was not going to let this opportunity pass her by.

Patrick chuckled a bit. Something about this pretty girl begging and offering him her parents' money amused him.

"Your parents have money, jewelry, and everything? Are you sure about that, my feek? Do you really think it's that easy? You just give us money and jewelry and you get to go home?" Patrick asked. He had crouched down so that he was level with her.

Donna was crying so hard now, she couldn't answer, but she shook her head up and down rapidly. The room was silent as Donna cried. Declan tried not to look at her. Patrick roughly grabbed her by the chin and held her face still.

"My darling, I think you and I need to have a very serious conversation. Your father, he's Ernest Johnson, am I correct?" Patrick said, circling the point. "Does he know where you are? Because my lads here called him. But where is he to save you? Where are his money and jewelry and all the fancy things you are used to, eh? Where is that when you need it?"

"No. No, please. My father—he . . . he is powerful! Whatever he did to you, please it has nothing to do with me! He will give you whatever you want," Donna cried, her tears spilling out of her blindfold and pooling in Patrick's hand. It was starting to sink in that her captors didn't care about money. They wanted some kind of revenge on her father. Her teeth were chattering so hard, she felt like her veneers would crack.

Patrick sucked his teeth. He felt bad for the girl; it wasn't her fault, after all. But, as was the custom in Ireland, she would have to pay for the sins of her father and the sins of his father before him.

"Donna, dear, I need you to relax," Patrick said, pulling her blindfold off gently. Declan's body tensed. Donna's lips were shaking, and her tears wouldn't stop. She was shocked that Patrick had allowed her to see his face, but it dawned on her that his decision to do that could only mean one thing: she wasn't going to make it out of there alive. Her whole body began to shake. She felt like she couldn't breathe. Patrick took his thumbs and wiped the tears and congealed mascara from under her eyes. Declan wanted to grab Donna and run, but he couldn't.

"Please, mister, I didn't mean to use drugs again. It just happened. I just want to see my parents. I just want to go home. I never meant to hurt anybody," Donna whimpered. Her neck was starting to hurt from Patrick holding her face for so long.

"See, darling, you asked me if I know who your father is, but"—Patrick suddenly gripped Donna's face so hard, his nails dug into her cheeks—"you haven't asked me who I am." Donna coughed, struggling under his grip. Her eyes went wide in fear, and Patrick shook her face again. "Do it. Ask me."

"Who . . . who are you?" Donna choked out.

Patrick smiled. He let go of her face. "I thought you'd never ask," he said. "I, Miss Donna, am Patrick O'Malley, the son of Darragh O'Malley, and our families have known each other a very, very long time."

Donna gasped and pushed herself away from Patrick.

Patrick laughed at her sudden fear. "So, I guess you do know who I am," he said.

"You're, you're the . . . the . . . ," Donna stuttered.

"I'm what, my sham?" Patrick cooed, standing up.

"You, you knew my father. My grandfather and your father were best friends. Your family helped us open the club in Idlewild," Donna whispered, slowly putting things together in her head. She was right; it wasn't about money. The O'Malleys were Irish mobsters, and they had just as much money as the Johnsons, or more. But even worse than that, the O'Malleys had the upper hand, because everything that the Johnsons had, they owed to Patrick's father.

"Exactly. So you see, you and I, we're close to family," Patrick said, extending a hand to pull Donna up. She rose to her feet on shaky knees, and Patrick helped her hold herself up. "So, you can understand how betrayed I felt when I found out your father had lost the money I gave him to invest for me. How could he, the son of the man that my father knew as a brother, betray my family?" Patrick looked at her, tilting his head.

Donna whimpered. There was something in his eyes that told her that his kindness to her was hiding something quite dangerous.

"You're going to help me, Donna," Patrick said. "You're going to help me because you owe me. So, what do you know about your father's business?" He wanted to get to the point of his meeting with her. He knew from watching Ernest and Junior all those days that Ernest's children knew quite a bit, more than Donna was letting on. Besides, he had seen Donna accompanying her brother to several financial institutions. So she had to know more than she was letting on. Patrick could have easily snatched Carolyn, the wife, but he had figured Donna would at least be out of her mind high and would tell them things they wanted to know.

"I don't know anything about my father's work, I promise. My brother, he's the one that handled some of the affairs, but I don't know much. I just always did whatever he told me to do so I could get money," Donna said, her words rushing out.

Patrick was shaking his head up and down while he contemplated what she was saying.

"But you must know something, then, if he was giving you all this money?" Patrick said, telling Donna more than asking her. He knew that she knew a lot more than she was letting on.

"I know some of it," she lied. She didn't know why she lied at a time like this. It had just slipped out. Donna had spent months digging into her father's finances and his business when she was siphoning off his money behind his back. She knew that he had been in the process of stashing money in offshore accounts and overseas.

Patrick tilted his head again. He put his hand up, so that his fingers were at Donna's eye level. He twisted his wrist quickly, and his men moved in on her like a pack of wolves to a piece of meat. Declan stood frozen.

"Ow!" Donna screeched as she was grabbed by her matted, tangled hair. "Okay, okay! I'm sorry! I'm sorry! I know a lot. I know a lot of things about what my father was doing. But he didn't tell me. I just kind of figured it all out, so I can't know for sure. I'm sorry, but I will tell you what I do know." At this point, she had to save herself.

Patrick cracked his neck and smiled. Then he reached a hand out to her. "There it is, darling. No sense in lying to me. Your father hurt both of us when he did what he did," he commented. "Let's sit down. I want you to tell me everything you know about the banks and the money."

The men brought Donna a chair, and she and Patrick sat down at his desk.

"Please, my feek, get comfortable, but before you get too comfortable, I want you to see what happens to people who lie to me in my face," Patrick said. He stood up, pulled a handgun from his waistband. Everyone in the room looked on with wide eyes. Patrick pointed the gun at Declan's head.

"It's all right, you muppet. She's a right fine ride. I understand," Patrick said.

Boom! He pulled the trigger, and Declan's brains flew out the back of his skull.

"Agh!" Donna screamed, then squeezed her eyes shut. It took everything in her not to vomit.

"Now," Patrick said, putting the gun away and wiping his hands on his pants, "let's get down to business. I need to know everything you know. But remember, don't lie to me."

Donna opened her eyes. "I won't."

Detectives Dietrich and Sharky stood in front of Desiree and Carolyn Johnson at the front door, letting the words they had just uttered sink in. Since the arrests and the FBI raid on the condo, Carolyn and Desiree had been staying in the Hyde Park mansion, and that was where the detectives had found them, waiting for news. The silence inside the Johnsons' home was shattered into a million pieces once the reality of what had been said finally hit home.

"No! No!" Carolyn screamed as Desiree held on to her to keep her from hitting the shiny white marble tile in their grand foyer.

It was like the detectives had just dropped an atomic bomb in their home. What did they mean, they had found Donna's car and belongings, but Donna was missing? What did they mean, Rebecca had been found dead inside Donna's car? Carolyn had to be having the worst nightmare of her life, and it was ongoing, never ending. It was all too much for her to process. Carolyn had spent the past two days calling Donna, with no answer. Carolyn had left so many messages for her youngest daughter that Donna's voicemail box was full and was not accepting any more messages. Carolyn had never imagined that something bad might've happened to Donna. In her view, things like that didn't happen to people like them.

"We are very sorry, Mrs. Johnson. We know this is hard to hear," Detective Dietrich lamented, trying to give Carolyn a few minutes to grieve before they continued with the details.

Desiree looked helpless, like she didn't know where to begin comforting her mother. She had never thought in a million years that coming home after all this time would be like this—first her son became trapped in a nightmare, then her father and her brother, and now her sister and Rebecca. Desiree hadn't felt comfortable when her mother sent Rebecca to look for Donna, but she had been too depressed about Tyree to protest.

Detective Sharky wanted to get on with this notification, but he also knew from years of experience that he had to give the grieving relatives a few minutes before he started bombarding them with questions.

"Can we come inside for a moment? We'd like to sit down and talk about some of the details. Maybe get a few questions answered?" Sharky said respectfully. "There is some very basic information about your sister and the deceased that we'd like to get from you both in order to try to sort this whole thing out," Sharky said to Desiree. Carolyn was clearly in no shape to give them permission to come inside the house.

Desiree nodded her agreement. She wanted to help the detectives as much as she could, especially if it meant that she would also get some information about her sister. She moved aside and invited the detectives inside.

"C'mon, Mother. Let's hear what they have to tell us so we can get Donna home as soon as possible," Desiree told her mother, trying to sound as hopeful as she could. Then she led the detectives to the living room, and her mother trailed behind them.

"Will this do?" Desiree asked, trying to be hospitable. She could see the detectives admiring the room like they'd never been inside a mansion before. She silently wished she wasn't in this mansion, but back in her modest home in a part of Indiana her family would've never stepped foot in.

"Perfect," Dietrich answered.

Desiree opened her arms invitingly. "You can have a seat. Make yourselves at home. Whatever you need to know to help the case, we will provide," she told the detectives.

Carolyn had finally calmed down a bit. Desiree sat her down on one of the Italian leather love seats, and Carolyn sat down next to her. As she and Sharky sat down in matching armchairs, Dietrich admired how the two women seemed to lean on one another for comfort. A nice mother-and-daughter moment. She also realized that they were the last two standing in the Johnson family.

"You say Rebecca was found in Donna's car? Dead? How? Why?" Carolyn croaked out. She still couldn't grasp the fact that Rebecca was dead. Rebecca had worked for the Johnsons since before Junior was born. The fact that Rebecca was dead was all Carolyn had heard when the detectives first arrived. It was enough. Rebecca was like a member of their family. Carolyn felt sick in the pit of her stomach.

Both detectives shook their heads in the affirmative.

"We were so worried about Donna. We didn't even think about Rebecca," Carolyn sobbed. "I sent her out there. This is my fault. I should've called the police when I couldn't get ahold of Donna. But . . . but she does this type of thing all the time, and Rebecca usually knew where to find her. Rebecca was more of a mother to my children than I could've ever been."

Carolyn and Desiree had been worried when they did not hear from Donna for a couple of days, but they had assumed she was staying with friends in the city and didn't want to be bothered with them until she was able to sort things out. They had thought that Rebecca would find Donna quickly, that she would come back with the news that Donna was safe, and that things would go along.

Detective Dietrich let out a long sigh. She never found it easy to deliver death notifications to the family of a homicide victim. "That is correct, Mrs. Johnson. The patrol cops found Donna's car abandoned in a parking lot on the West Side, and when they inspected further, they found Rebecca inside, dead from a gunshot wound to her temple," Dietrich said, breaking the news. She tried to sound as official yet sympathetic as she could.

"Oh my God! A gunshot wound?" Carolyn blurted, shaking her head left to right. "Rebecca wouldn't harm a fly! Why would someone kill her? And Donna? Where is my Donna!" It was all too much to hear.

"Where is my sister? What do you know about her? You said Rebecca was dead in her car, but what about Donna? What information do you have about her?" Desiree asked, her voice cracking, like she was on the brink. She had asked the questions, but she didn't know if she really wanted to know the answers.

"That's why we are here, Ms. Johnson. Your sister was not in the car. We found her pocketbook in the backseat, but no signs of her. We are guessing that whoever murdered Rebecca might have your sister. We have patrol cars out scouring the city for her. We've put out a missing persons alert, but there have been no leads yet," Sharky interjected. He wanted to be honest with the Johnsons. Things didn't look too good for their missing sister/daughter. Especially because Rebecca's murder seemed senseless. And there was nothing missing from the car or from Rebecca's purse. Donna's purse was also in the car. The detectives had already ruled out robbery as a motive.

"It's not looking like a robbery or a carjacking. Everything your daughter had—meaning her purse, money, credit cards—was still in the car. Rebecca still had money on her person and jewelry as well," Dietrich added. "We think that whoever did this might have other motives. It might be someone that knows Donna or Rebecca. That's why we are here talking to you. We're going to need all the help we can get if we have any hopes of finding your daughter." Dietrich paused for a moment to let those words sink in. "As you all might know, we are the detectives investigating a murder that occurred recently on the West Side. Your daughter was there at the scene, and so was her relative, who we have in custody. We don't know if there is a connection, but your daughter is a potential witness, and there seems to be no other leads right now."

Those words seemed to hit Carolyn and Desiree like an anvil dropped from the side of a tall building onto their heads.

"Oh God!" Desiree screeched, seeming to come alive. "If it wasn't a robbery by a stranger or a carjacking, and it has to be someone Donna knows, then it has to be him . . . the boyfriend! It has to be him! Oh God! It has to be him. He wanted Donna hurt . . . maybe even dead! He probably wanted to get rid of Donna! He committed the murder of that girl, pinned it on my son, and wants to get rid of my sister as a witness against him! I'm sure it's him!" Desiree roared, spewing wild accusations.

A sickening hush fell over the entire room. All eyes were on Desiree as she moved her hands wildly. Everyone was hanging on her every word. Carolyn was the first to break the silence.

"Desi! Stop! We don't know anything like that!" she barked.

Dietrich and Sharky both looked at the two Johnson women with raised eyebrows. Dietrich immediately pulled out her writing pad and a pen. She started taking notes furiously. She knew just who Desiree was talking about, but she wanted to hear it.

"Who? Who would want to get rid of whom? Who is this *he* you are referring to? Who wants your sister gone? What are you talking about, Ms. Johnson?" Dietrich asked, a bit too much excitement in her voice for Desiree's and Carolyn's liking. "We need to know everything."

Carolyn cleared her throat with a loud ahem, signaling to her eldest daughter to keep her mouth shut. But Carolyn knew Desiree had already said too much. There was no turning back now. Carolyn would have to explain everything to the detectives. Every embarrassing detail of her daughter's recent relapse.

"Detectives, you have to excuse us," Carolyn said, trying to sound lighthearted. "My daughter here is just upset. She is speculating right now. When she is upset, she tends to get a little crazy." Carolyn patted the air with her hands, as if to say, "Calm down and back up."

Desiree shot her mother an evil look. She was tired of hiding and acting like they had the perfect life, even under these circumstances. Donna was missing, and Desiree wanted to find her, but she also wanted them to know that the boyfriend had a motive. She wasn't about to act as if nothing was going on. Her son's life and now her sister's life were on the line.

"No! I'm not crazy! I know exactly what I'm saying!" Desiree blurted out, causing her mother to back down. Carolyn's eyebrows came together, and she flexed her jaw. Desiree didn't care. She turned toward Dietrich and Sharky and spoke to them directly, her voice stern.

"My sister has a no-good boyfriend that lives up on the West Side. She took my son to his house, and a girl ended up murdered there. They want to pin the murder on my son, and the boyfriend has been lying from the beginning. He didn't want my sister to be a witness, to tell about all the times he beat the victim and choked her until she passed out. We have hired a private investigator, and he's told us that the girl's cell phone is missing. We don't know what information could be on it, and we don't know who has it. This whole situation has been a lot for us to swallow, but I saw the look in that no-good boyfriend's eyes. I know when he wanted my sister out of the picture, like he wanted my sister dead! He wants my son to go down forever for something he didn't do, and without Donna to testify to everything that happened that night, he just might!"

The two detectives looked at one another. They had to be thinking about the absurdity of all this. Sharky moved to the edge of his seat. He had his palms on his knees and his eyebrows furrowed, in deep concentration. It was like Desiree was teasing them with the information she had. Dietrich's eyes were pleading with her to tell them more, so they could run it down too.

Sharky finally asked the questions that they all knew were coming next. "Who is this boyfriend? Who is it that you think wants your sister dead?"

Desiree swallowed hard. It had been hard enough for her to wrap her mind around what was happening to her family. She curled her hands into fists, just thinking about it all. If she could just get her hands on that scrawny-ass boyfriend now, there was no telling what Desiree would do. The tops of Desiree's hands ached, she had them balled so tight in anger.

"Oh, I'll tell you exactly who he is," Desiree said. "Tommy is the man my sister was with. He's a two-bit, murdering drug dealer. He stole money from my sister for years, convincing her to manipulate our father for cash. He is the one who murdered Lee Briggs, the same murder that they're holding my son for. Now, the only witness that can help my poor baby out of this, my sister, is missing! He has something to do with my sister's disappearance. I'd bet my life on it, since there's no one else that has it out for us like him!" Now it was like Desiree was dropping bombs of her own.

Sharky scrubbed his hands over his face and let out an involuntary groan. He closed his eyes and let the information he'd just heard sink in for a minute. Dietrich stopped writing; the pieces were coming together for her, and she needed a second to process everything. It was like they always said: *It's best to follow the money.* More eerie silence settled over the room.

Carolyn and Desiree watched both detectives' reactions to the information. It was clear that they knew something that the Johnsons didn't know.

"What is it? What is going on?" Desiree asked, dabbing at her face. She hadn't realized that she was crying in frustration. "What do you know?" she said, her voice forceful and her tone to the point.

Dietrich looked at Sharky. He looked back at her. With her eyes, Dietrich let her partner know that she wasn't going to be the one to answer the question. Dietrich's mind was too muddled to think straight. Sharky knew what he had to do. He was just afraid of the reaction Carolyn and Desiree might have.

"Detectives? What do you know?" Desiree repeated. She was growing a bit impatient with the waiting game.

"Well—" Sharky began, but Desiree cut him off.

"Well what!" she yelled.

"Tommy is not the only one who has something to gain from hurting Donna," Sharky said bluntly. There was no way they could beat around the bush anymore.

Desiree and Carolyn looked confused.

"When your father, and your husband, was arrested by the feds two days ago for running one of the biggest Ponzi schemes in history, and your son, his grandson, was arrested almost two weeks ago for the murder of a rock star's daughter, we didn't think that the two cases were connected, and up until now they weren't. However, as I sit and listen and string things together in my mind, it is clear to me that one of your father's enemies might be a suspect in your sister's disappearance," Sharky announced. He had to inhale after letting out that mouthful. The hunch had sounded ludicrous even to him as he recited it the Johnsons.

Desiree and Carolyn exchanged stunned glances.

"There could be some very dangerous people after you all," Shark informed them. "They may have snatched your daughter, Mrs. Johnson. And they may be coming after you two next."

Desiree and Carolyn looked at the detective like they weren't hearing him correctly. Carolyn's mouth was open, and Desiree's eyes were as wide as dinner plates. Detective Dietrich became very still for a few seconds. It was like something had hit her all of a sudden. She didn't even give the Johnsons more than a moment to react to what they had just learned.

"Ms. Johnson, does your daughter still have a bedroom here? Or do you have keys to wherever she was staying prior to her disappearance?" Dietrich asked, her mind racing in a million different directions. There had to be something about Donna's disappearance that was linked to Ernest Johnson's recent fate.

"She has a bedroom, but I don't know the last time she was here. But she's been staying God knows where since everything with Tyree blew up," Carolyn whimpered. The tears were back. "But I don't have keys to the new place my husband foolishly got her when she came home this last time. The keys might be in her purse. You said you recovered her purse, right?" The word *recovered* made Carolyn think of a disaster, and she lost it again. She began sobbing uncontrollably.

Desiree moved close to her mother and pulled her to her. She held Carolyn close, comforting her.

"How could your father have been so selfish? How did I miss the signs that things were going so badly?" Carolyn sobbed.

"Can we take a look around? We want to be sure we cover all our bases. There are just too many loose ends here," Detective Sharky said, taking the baton from Dietrich.

Desiree gently released her mother and looked over at her. Her mother nodded her approval. She wanted to do whatever it took to bring their Donna back home safely.

"I'll show you around," Desiree said, standing up and waving at the detectives to indicate that they should follow her.

Dietrich and Sharky looked at each other and exchanged a knowing glance. They stood and fell in line silently behind Desiree, hoping like hell they would find something that would verify that their hunch was right and they hadn't embarked on a wild-goose chase.

Detective Dietrich stepped into Donna's bedroom and looked around, amazed. The room was huge, its square footage greater than that of Dietrich's entire apartment. It was lavishly decorated in pink, black, and white. Beautiful silk curtains hung from the windows. Custom made for sure. Detective Dietrich knew expensive when she saw it. A pink-and-black zebra-print duvet covered the oversize king bed. Posters of boy bands hung on the walls, and fluffy pillows with Donna's initials on them covered the head of the bed. Detective Dietrich looked around for a few minutes, examining every inch of the room and picking up framed pictures of Donna and Carolyn and some of Donna alone. Before now she hadn't thought about how young Donna was.

She really is a beautiful girl, Detective Dietrich had to admit to herself.

She walked over to the vanity in the far left corner of the expansive room. All sorts of designer fragrances sat atop the beautiful white tabletop. Dietrich picked up several of the little bottles. She sniffed a couple. "Hmm. Expensive. Everything is expensive," she whispered to herself, placing the last bottle back down. She was preparing to step away from the vanity when something inside the garbage can caught her eye. It was a plastic drugstore bag. Dietrich grabbed the handles of the bag and pulled it up out of the can. She peered inside, and her heart immediately sped up. She turned around to where Sharky and Desiree were standing, talking about some of Donna's high school accomplishments.

"Hey, Shark. C'mere for one minute," Dietrich called, summoning him.

Sharky excused himself and walked over to Dietrich. "What's up?" he asked.

Detective Dietrich held the bag open and didn't say a word. Sharky looked inside the bag. He scrubbed his hands over his face.

"Dammit!" he grumbled.

"Who's going to tell them? You or me?" Dietrich asked.

Sharky shook his head from left to right. "I really don't think it matters at this point. Even flipping a coin to choose won't make a difference in how difficult this one is going to be," he replied.

They both looked over at Desiree. She was standing in Donna's old bedroom doorway, and Carolyn had joined her. Neither one of the detectives wanting to be the one to tell them that their missing and possibly dead sister/daughter might be carrying a baby of her own.

Chapter 18

Favors

Tommy's hands shook as he fished around in his pocket for the keys to his house. He was finally able to return to his West Side apartment after being banned while the police conducted their investigation. His return was bittersweet. Tommy thought about the fact that his girlfriend had died right in the loft, and he was immediately unnerved. Finally able to get the key in the lock, he inhaled and exhaled. After he turned the key and pushed open the door, he stood at the threshold, with his jaw slack and his eyebrows raised into arches. He blinked a couple of times, thinking that his eyes were deceiving him for sure.

"What the fuck?" Tommy gasped, trying to take in the disastrous scene. He couldn't absorb it all in one look. It took a few minutes before it all sank in. He slowly walked around the apartment. The police and crime-scene technicians had made a complete mess of Tommy's once posh, meticulously decorated place. The beautiful, expensive Italian leather sofa was turned over on its back, the cushions tossed on the floor in opposite directions like garbage. Black fingerprint powder stained the white leather of the sofa. The glass top of the coffee table, which Tommy had been so proud of when he purchased it, was shattered and had the same powdery black residue all over it. His ultramodern eggcup-white lacquer barstools were turned over, and one was even missing a leg.

The floor on which Lee had lain was still marred by dark burgundy bloodstains. White tape in the shape of her body outlined the place where she had been found. There was police tape, boot marks, and papers everywhere in the loft. The drawers and cabinets in the kitchen were all open, and the contents spilled out onto the counters and floors. Tommy's expensive artwork had been pulled off the walls and tossed aside like trash. One expensive painting was even ripped in the middle. Not one thing in the loft had been left in its place. Tommy kept walking around what used to be his beautiful home, disgusted. Glass crunched under his feet as he kicked his way through the debris, trying to decide where he was going to start to clean up. He picked up one of his famed pieces of art and tried to brush it off.

"Fucking cops. And they say *we* act like animals. Look at what they did to my fucking place. I should sue the fucking city for damaging my shit. Don't they know how hard I had to work to get all this?" Tommy mumbled aloud as he began picking other things up. He was so lost in thought that he didn't even realize he was being watched. Tommy bent down to pick up another shattered picture frame from the floor, but the crunch of glass behind him caught his attention. He whirled around on the balls of his feet. He was already paranoid. Tommy jumped fiercely.

"Don't even think about going for that little piece you keep in your boot," a strange female voice said calmly. "Put your fucking hands up over your head, where I can see them."

Tommy's eyes almost popped out of his head as he stood face-to-face with the end of a chrome .50-caliber Desert Eagle Special. He felt like his bladder would involuntarily release at any moment. Tommy raised his hands slowly, like he was told to do.

"Look, take whatever you want. I got money in my pocket and in the safe in the room," Tommy told the woman, his voice shaking like that of a coward. Tommy looked at the woman, with her long dark hair pulled back in a ponytail and her rugged clothes, and pegged her as a biker-chick gang member.

A meth head! Tommy screamed inside his head. He could come up with no other reason for the woman to be in his home, threatening him, except robbery.

The woman reached down and took the small .22 Tommy had stashed in the side of his boot. She ran her free hand around Tommy's waistband after that. Tommy got nervous. She was too clean for a meth head, and the way she was searching him reminded him of the cops.

"I'm clean, miss. I ain't got nothing else on me. Whatever you want, just take it. I got some new meth right there in my pocket. Just take it. It's like nothing you've ever experienced before, I'm telling you. You can have it," Tommy said, a bit more urgency lacing his words. That was one of the perils of being a two-bit drug dealer. People in the streets always wanted what you had and vice versa. Tommy had always known he was a target for robbery when he was on the streets, but he had never suspected that someone would find him at home. Especially some woman whom, without her gun, Tommy was sure he could take down.

"Oh, you think I'm here for your meth? I look like a meth head to you?" the woman asked, annoyed.

Tommy was taken aback. The woman didn't really look like a meth head. She actually was very beautiful.

"Well, no, I'm just trying to figure this thing out here. What can I do for you?" Tommy said, trying to get to the bottom of this invasion. He just wanted to get out of it in one piece.

"I'm here about the murder . . . you know the one with all the victims, including a dead girl and the girl that's missing and the little boy whose about to lose his freedom for a crime he didn't commit. I heard you were the state's main witness in the murder case, and you also might know where the counter witness has gone missing to," the woman said calmly.

Tommy shook his head back and forth rapidly. "Me? No. You got the wrong person. I'm not a snitch. I told those fucking detectives I don't know what happened here the night of that murder. I left the two bitches and the boy here. I told those pigs that. I wasn't here at all man," Tommy rambled, his lies spewing like hot lava from a volcano.

The woman chuckled at Tommy's response, her gun still trained on Tommy's head.

"You got to believe what I'm saying. I'm from the streets, and I would never snitch on anybody. I don't know who killed the girl, but it wasn't me. I'm not working with the police. Look at what they did to my house! You think I will work with them after this? Hell no! And . . . Donna . . . I . . . I haven't seen her. I swear to God," Tommy said even more urgently. He thought his street credibility was enough to convince one of his own that he was a good guy.

The woman looked at Tommy with a smirk on her face. She had just followed Tommy from a meeting with the dead girl's mother. Not only had Tommy agreed to testify against Tyree Johnson, but he was also being paid by Carly Shepherd, mother of the dead girl, to embellish the story so that there would be no doubt a jury would convict Tyree.

The woman was growing slightly impatient with Tommy's lies. She lifted the gun and brought it down on Tommy's head.

"Agh!" Tommy cried out. "Please . . . what do you want? Who are you?" he panted, holding his bleeding head.

"I don't have to believe anything you say. In fact, I don't believe anything you say. In my eyes, you are as low as they come. People have lost their lives because of you. So, I just came to make sure that you won't be able to ruin any more lives," the woman announced. "Let's call it returning the favor."

Tommy put his soiled hand in front of his face and examined the dark red blood running out of his head. Tommy could see the look in the woman's piercing eyes. It was cold and calculating.

"C'mon, man . . . you got to believe me. I am a lot of things, but I'm not a snitch and I'm not a murderer," Tommy said sincerely. "Don't do this. Just listen to what I have to say. I'm not snitching on anybody, and I swear I had nothing to do with Donna going missing."

The woman didn't seem fazed by Tommy's fake attempt at sincerity.

"Oh yeah, well, I think you're lying. I think you got paid to be a witness against Tyree Johnson, and I think you set Donna up to be snatched or possibly murdered. But since you weren't going to testify, like you said, you know what else you are not going to do?" the woman said to Tommy.

Tommy just stared at the woman. He didn't know the answer to the question, and he didn't want to take a chance by saying the wrong thing.

"What?" Tommy squeaked.

"Get out of this alive," the woman said as she raised her gun toward Tommy's head and pulled the trigger.

Boom! Tommy's body shrank to the floor like a deflated balloon.

There would be no testifying against Tyree Johnson. It was the least Liana Martinez could do for Junior after the pain she'd caused him in the name of justice. She knew how to commit a clean murder, and it was the last thing she did before she would shed her FBI credentials and badge once and for all.

Chapter 19

Loose Ends

Ernest Sr. could smell his own body odor so strongly now, his stomach did flips. He smelled like a combination of sickness and stale mold, like the inside the jail infirmary where he was being housed. He hadn't been able to have anyone change his clothes or wash him up since his arraignment. Ernest had made several phone calls since his arrest; none had been answered. He had held out hope that Gus or even Carolyn would come to his rescue. He lay in pain, without his expensive cancer treatment medications, on the hard jail bed, his eyes closed, despairing.

"Johnson!"

Ernest popped his eyes open and jumped at the sound of the corrections officer's voice. He struggled to sit up. He hadn't slept at all in the days since he had been arrested, so his head pounded from exhaustion. They had no mercy for a man who had months or even days to live. All they wanted was his head on a platter. No amount of money he had could get him out of this one.

"Let's go, Johnson. Someone posted your bond this morning. Let's go," the corrections officer grumbled. Two of them grabbed Ernest up roughly and damn near slammed him down into the wheelchair. No mercy at all. The word was out around the jail about Ernest and how many victims he'd left in the wake of his schemes. There were movie stars, movie directors, wealthy bankers, and businessmen who were all faced with the threat of losing everything. They had entrusted their entire fortunes to Ernest.

When Ernest heard that his bond had been posted, a warm feeling came over his body. Days earlier, he'd even been surprised that the judge gave him a bond at the arraignment, knowing his status in life. Now Ernest recognized the feeling that enveloped his body as pure relief. He knew his family wouldn't let him down, no matter how much he had done them dirty. Ernest's heart rate sped up from excitement at the thought of getting out of that hellhole.

Immediately, he wondered who would be waiting for him outside the metal doors of the jail. First, Ernest thought about Gus, his accountant, but his last conversation with Gus hadn't gone so great. Gus had figured things out a long time ago, and when he had confronted Ernest, things had gotten heated. *It can't be Gus*, Ernest surmised. There was only one other person that would care even a little bit about Ernest. He concluded quickly that it had to be Carolyn that had bailed him out. His parents had cut him off when they died, which was why he had resorted to the criminal activity that ultimately landed him in this predicament.

Ernest felt powerful as he was collected his scant belongings. In Ernest's assessment, wealthy people always got a chance to bond out. Ernest's bail was set at five million dollars, which would be five hundred thousand in cash. Ernest gathered up the newspapers he'd collected since his arrest. He had to admit to himself that he was secretly proud of gaining his celebrity back, although it was for other than savory reasons this time. Ernest had missed being the most popular man in Chicago like when he was younger. It only fed his ego that he was on the front page of almost all the newspapers and tabloids in the city.

"You collecting pictures of yourself, huh?" asked the officer who had called his name, a hint of sarcasm in his voice.

Ernest looked up at the officer from his wheelchair with a smug smirk on his face. Even now, as an inmate clinging to life by a thread, Ernest felt superior to even the guards and everyone else around him.

"You'll be back. Next time it will be after your trial, so you won't be smiling like this, I'm sure. Same things that make you laugh will make you cry. Next time, I'll be the one smiling . . . trust me," the officer commented as he pushed Ernest along like an orderly.

Ernest didn't comment. He had no time to argue with the likes of a jail guard. Ernest was a Johnson; he had a higher place in the world. Besides, coming back to jail wasn't an option in Ernest's mind. He had other plans. Or so he thought.

Ernest was led in handcuffs to the processing unit for out-processing. He couldn't wait to be free. He felt like an animal the way they treated him inside these walls. The whole time he walked through processing, Ernest was lost in thought about what he would say to his wife after everything that had happened. After how low Ernest had stooped with all of this, he still couldn't believe that Carolyn would come to his rescue. Ernest was glad that she was smart enough to have found the hidden money too, because from what he knew, after his arrest the feds had seized everything that was the least bit transparent.

Now his mind raced with questions. What could he possibly say to Carolyn that would suffice? Ernest silently rehearsed the things he would say. *Carolyn, you don't know how much I regret the past. I am going to be a better man.* Ernest rejected that statement; she'd heard all that before. *I'm just plain old sorry*, was the next thing that came to mind, but he knew that was such a cop-out. Ernest had said he was sorry to Carolyn so many times over the years that he was 100 percent sure that she would spit in his face if he said that. Ernest would have to do something so different from his regular self that she would be convinced that he meant what he was saying. He knew! He had an idea! This time he would beg her forgiveness for what he had done. That was his plan. He would wait until they got outside to their waiting car, and he would beg her forgiveness. He would grab her in a tight embrace and give her a long kiss, and he would beg for her forgiveness.

Ernest was pushed up to a table, where his things were sorted. The officer sorting things out in front of Ernest didn't even bother to make eye contact with him.

"One gold Rolex brand men's wristwatch! One black leather wallet with the word *Hermès* imprinted on the front! Ten one-hundred-dollar bills! One men's black leather belt with the words *Yves Saint Laurent* imprinted on the inside! Two gold-colored cuff links with white stones!" The corrections officer named all Ernest's belongings one by one. Ernest seemed proud of his collection of premier designer things. Junior had done a good job of helping him dress to go to the bank that day. They'd both agreed they needed to look rich. Ernest took satisfaction in knowing those jail guards couldn't even afford to have his belt. He felt superior. He was brimming inside with anticipation and anxiety.

"Is this all your belongings?" the officer asked when he was done sorting.

Ernest could care less about the stuff. There was plenty more where those items came from. If he had it his way, he'd leave every single thing right there. Ernest shook his head in the affirmative. The officer slid a piece of paper in front of Ernest, and without even reading it, Ernest mindlessly scribbled his signature at the bottom of the paper.

"Well, Mr. Rich, I guess you've been bonded out. We will see you after the trial. Trust me, it will be our pleasure to have you back," the correction officer said snidely, then spread an evil grin across his box-shaped face.

Ernest wondered why the officers all kept saying they expected to see him after the trial. What if he beat the case? They obviously had read too much of the media's take on his so-called crimes.

"You're right about one thing. I am rich, so when I beat this case with my high-paid attorneys, I'll be sure to send you a little note that says, *Kiss my ass*," Ernest replied, the heat of satisfaction settling over him like a warm blanket. He grabbed his things and was pushed through iron doors.

Ernest had a big winning smile plastered across his face when he entered the big empty room. He looked as if he had aged ten more years in three days, and he was exhausted, but that didn't stop him from smiling from ear to ear. He could hardly wait to see Carolyn's face. He would make it all right once he was face-to-face with her.

Ernest looked around; he didn't see her. Ernest furrowed his eyebrows in confusion. He turned back around to ask the corrections officer where his wife was, and that was when he heard a voice behind him. It sent chills down his spine.

"Daddy! I've missed you so much! Oh my God, I'm so happy to see you again," the familiar voice cried out. The familiar voice was like nails on a chalkboard in Ernest's ears right now. It was definitely not the voice he had expected to hear or even wanted to hear right then. Ernest whirled his head around so hard, he felt something snap at the base of it. His heart was thundering, and sweat immediately broke out all over his entire body.

"Donna?" Ernest said, a half-hearted, nervous smile on his face. He didn't have time to look closely at her. She was like a blur of hair and gangly arms as she rushed to him and threw her arms around his neck.

Ernest swallowed hard and tried to return her embrace, but his arms felt weak. His mind raced in a million directions. Donna wasn't supposed to be here. There was no way his wife would've sent their youngest daughter to bond him out. No! It was supposed to be Carolyn! How could Donna possibly be here? The last time Ernest had spoken to her, she was screaming on the other end of the phone, asking for money. He couldn't even return Donna's embrace: he was too nervous that something was amiss about her being there.

Donna pouted as she released her grip on her father. "Aren't you glad to see me? Aren't you glad I'm alive and that I came to get you out, Daddy?" she asked him. She wanted to slap the shit out of her father. It wasn't at all lost on her that if it were up to him, she would be dead at the hands of Patrick. Her selfish-ass father didn't even ask her if she was okay. The fucking nerve of him! Something inside her wanted to just squeeze his neck until the life left him.

Ernest laughed nervously as he looked around. He could smell a setup. He wasn't stupid. How would Donna have enough money to bail him out?

"Of course I am happy to see you, baby girl. It's just . . . I was expecting . . . Oh, forget it. I am happy to see you," Ernest lied, trying to tamp down his nerves. His hands trembled as he finally took a good look at Donna. She didn't look well. Although she had on makeup and nice clothes, her face looked sunken in. Her eyes were dark, sad. Something about her facial expression didn't sit right with Ernest. Her entire appearance, the entire scene—it all seemed somehow staged. His gut ached with the notion that something was not right.

"Let's go home, Daddy. We can catch up on everything. We can exchange our stories once we are all alone," Donna said, her words robotic, like she'd rehearsed them. She started pushing her father forward in his wheelchair, heading toward the exit. Ernest felt like impending doom was coming down on him.

What other choice did he have at this point? he reasoned with himself. It was either go with Donna or go back to jail. Ernest's body was numb as he was pushed along. Each spin of the wheels signaled doom for him, as if he was about to be sent right into danger.

Donna's heels clacked against the concrete floor, each bang seemingly signaling the awfulness that was to come. When they reached the door, Donna stopped pushing. Ernest's underarms were drenched with sweat, and his stomach was in knots. Donna sensed his trepidation, and she looked him in the face. She arched her eyebrows at him.

"What is it, Daddy? You can't be nervous about coming home to all of us, right?" Donna said, her voice phony and cracking. She looked like she couldn't take it anymore. Donna swallowed hard and moved her head from left to right. It was as if she was saying sorry to her father with her eyes. Her face folded into a frown.

Ernest figured it out! His daughter was trying to tell him something without saying it. Ernest looked at her seriously. Donna shook her head some more, and tears finally dropped from her eyes. She didn't say another word. She could no longer look at him. Donna abruptly turned around and pushed open the door. That was the signal. It had all gone according to plan. Her heart jackhammered against her sternum as she stepped aside. She silently mouthed the words, "I am sorry, Daddy."

Just then, two men rushed through the doorway and roughly grabbed Ernest on either side. They yanked him right out of the chair.

"Wait!" Ernest snarled. "Donna!"

He felt a gun suddenly being jammed into his side. Ernest tried to struggle, but his body was too weak to fight. Besides, when he looked out the door, he saw that a gun had been put against Donna's head. He knew that if he screamed for help or put up a fight, they would kill Donna right on the spot. Ernest relented. Donna didn't deserve to die like that because of his mistakes.

"Leave her alone! I will kill all of you!" Ernest growled in a last-ditch display of toughness. He had to go out with some kind of pride. The two men carried Ernest to a darkly tinted Mercedes S550. The back door flung open to invite him in. Ernest was forced into the back of the car. When he looked over, he almost fainted. Ernest felt vomit creeping up his esophagus, but there was absolutely nothing he could do now but face his consequences.

"Johnson. You don't look so happy to see me," Patrick said, then gave a small chuckle.

Ernest swallowed hard. He opened his mouth to speak, but Patrick put his hand up.

"No, no, let's not talk business, eh? All I need is a thank-you for bailing you out. But beyond that, there's nothing more to be said, you old codger," Patrick droned. He lit a cigar and offered one to Ernest, but Ernest felt like his throat would seize at any minute.

"Patrick, I can . . . I can explain everything to you," Ernest stammered, sweat dripping down the sides of his face now.

Patrick laughed. "Come on there, Johnson. You really don't look happy to see me. You're gonna hurt my feelings there," he said. Then he snapped his fingers, signaling to his men. Suddenly the car was moving.

Ernest balled his hands into fists so tight, his fingernails burned the insides of his palms. His eyes stretched to their limits. He had no idea what was going to happen next.

"If you just give me one more chance. They are mistaken . . . those things they said I've done. None of that is true. Patrick. If you would just give me some more time. I really can explain," Ernest pleaded, stumbling over his words.

His groveling tired Patrick to no end. He expected the great Ernest Johnson, Sr., to have some kind of bravado. Some kind of pride. In that moment, Patrick thought of Ernest as weak. He looked at Ernest with a concerned look. "Your time to explain is up, Johnson," Patrick said calmly. He raised his left hand slowly.

"Please!" Ernest managed to say, throwing his hands up in defense.

But then his world went black.

Chapter 20

What Goes Around

The interior of the Johnsons' Idlewild house seemed hollow, empty, and dreary. The federal agents who'd executed their search warrants had come there, as well, and had all but destroyed everything inside. Carolyn had cried for days after she saw the damage. All her family's summer memories had been obliterated. The agents had seized everything of value from the inside of the house. All Carolyn's expensive china and silverware, family heirlooms that the Johnsons had passed down to her on her wedding day, were gone. One of Carolyn's collections of vintage Chanel handbags, probably valued at over ninety thousand dollars, was also gone. All the antique artwork that Carolyn had collected during her and Ernest's trips around the world had been either seized or damaged. The reality of what they'd done had literally taken Carolyn's breath away when she arrived back in Idlewild and found the house in that condition. That first night she'd drunk herself comatose. She'd awakened on the floor with a horrible headache. That was when Carolyn had remembered what she'd come to Idlewild for in the first place.

Now she gathered the last of her stash and tucked it into an oversize Louis Vuitton luggage tote. She inhaled

and exhaled, as the experience was so final, so exasper-
ating. Carolyn stood in Donna's old bedroom, and she
felt her chest tighten. It was there that she had rocked
her youngest child to sleep. It was there that she had
read Donna stories and given her some of the finest
gifts. That room held so many memories that it made
Carolyn's head swirl. The room also held the most important thing that Carolyn would ever hide there—her
stash.

Taking one last look around Donna's room was
bittersweet. It was so final for Carolyn that she couldn't
help the tears that welled up behind her eyes. Desiree
stepped into the room. She had tears in her eyes as well.
It was bittersweet for her too. The reality of the situation had finally settled in on Desiree over the weeks too.
Carolyn turned around to meet her gaze. Desiree smiled
weakly.

"Oh, Desi. I'm so sorry about all of this. Having you
back home was the best thing that has ever happened
to me. More than I could have ever dreamed of when I
had Junior call you to come," Carolyn said sweetly, tears
flowing down her face now.

Desiree dabbed at her eyes. She didn't know what
she'd do without her son. Her entire family had been
completely blown up.

"I didn't get a chance to see Donna after she got home
from rehab until that night at the precinct. I feel so
badly that I abandoned her so many years ago. I should
have followed up and stayed in contact with her. If I
had, maybe she wouldn't be on drugs, and maybe none
of this would've happened to her or Tyree," Desiree
sobbed.

"No! Desiree, you stop it! None of this is your fault!"
Carolyn chastised through her own tears. She grabbed

Desiree by the shoulders. "You did all that you could do for all of us. I am forever grateful."

"It's just that all these bad things happened, and I feel like it has everything to do with me not wanting to be here or to come visit. Like some bad karmic consequence. I feel so badly," Desiree revealed.

"It's not your fault," Carolyn said.

"I wanted to tell you what happened today," Desiree said, changing the subject. "Tyson called me."

Carolyn froze. Her eyes opened wider.

"He was able to get Tyree freed on bond. You can go with me to bail Tyree out. But after that, we will be going to a location where no one will be able to find us, until his trial begins. He deserves a little peace of mind. Everything that he has been through is my fault. I owe him that much," Desiree told Carolyn.

"Oh, Desi, thank God! I will say my good-byes and say a prayer for you both," Carolyn replied, her face lighting up.

"Okay. Well, we've got to go quickly. I don't want any more unexpected surprises, and everything we all do is under watch now. They followed us here. I'm sure they are somewhere close," Desiree explained.

"Listen, Desi. I also want to say sorry to you for sending you away all those years ago. I want you to have something," Carolyn said as she picked up her oversize tote containing her stash of money and handed it to Desiree.

It was the last of everything they had. Every dollar Carolyn had left was inside that tote bag. She felt grateful to even have that. Years ago, Carolyn had taken to stashing bundles of cash in a safe she'd had installed behind a

Van Gogh that hung in Donna's summer-house bedroom. It was Carolyn's secret stash. A stash that she had never really imagined that she'd need. Especially not for something like this. Carolyn was so glad she had had the foresight to put something away. Originally, she'd started stashing the money after she saw one of her friends get nothing during divorce proceedings with her husband, who had secretly tricked her into signing a prenuptial agreement. After she saw her friend so devastated financially that the woman was forced to live in a shelter, Carolyn had begun putting away as much money as she could get her hands on without raising red flags in Ernest's eyes.

Carolyn had told herself that she would one day give the money back, that the money was there just in case Ernest and the Johnsons ever decided to turn their backs on her, like they were famous for doing to some of their own family members. But after Ernest began his affairs, Carolyn had stashed more and more of the money as a safety net for herself and her children. Carolyn was smarter than Ernest had ever given her credit for in the years they'd spent together. Carolyn wondered if he had a stash somewhere in Idlewild that she didn't know about. She didn't have any more time to look around the house. She wanted to get away.

"Desi, the car is outside," Carolyn announced. It would be the last time Carolyn would tell her eldest daughter those words. That was a sobering reality that trampled all over Carolyn's mood.

Desiree turned around, with tears in her eyes, then strode out of Donna's bedroom. She was prepared to walk away from here and go back to life as she'd known if for the past seventeen years. Carolyn knew what that meant too. Her entire family had been shattered, something she'd fought for half of her life to prevent. She stepped out of Donna's bedroom and pulled the door shut behind her. Desiree waited for her in the hallway. They smiled at one another and walked out of the Idlewild house together one last time. When the front door slammed behind them, Desiree closed her eyes and paused for a minute.

"Good-bye," she mouthed silently. Carolyn did the same.

Later that day, Carolyn stopped at the front desk of the building where she had once owned a beautiful condo. She thanked her doorman and the building staff. They all gave her hugs, and they were all sorry to see her go. Carolyn cut their good-byes short; she didn't need any long good-byes. She wanted to regain her pride and strength.

Carolyn rushed out of the building to the awaiting hired taxi. Carolyn hadn't ever had to order a car before, and she looked at the old black Lincoln Town Car and told herself it was something she would have to get used to—living like a regular person. It was a far cry from the privately owned Bentley she was used to being driven in. She inhaled the Chicago air one more time. She just loved Chicago, but Carolyn knew she couldn't stay here. She had set her leg to climb into the taxi when she heard it. She stopped cold in her tracks.

"Mrs. Johnson! Mrs. Johnson! Wait! Stop! Police!"

Loud screams came from her left. She stood up straight and whirled around on her feet. Her expression curled into a confused frown. Carolyn looked surprised. *Not again*! she thought when she saw Detectives Dietrich and

Sharky rushing toward her. Carolyn's face went stony. She flexed her jaw. *What do they want! I have nothing to say to them!* Carolyn's said in her head as she eyed the detectives evilly.

"Mrs. Johnson!" Detective Dietrich said breathlessly as she got right in front of Carolyn. Dietrich looked disheveled. She had big bags under her eyes, like she hadn't slept in days. Her hair was bushy, and her clothes looked like she'd had them on for weeks.

"How can I help you, Detective?" Carolyn said dryly. She eyed the detective up and down. Carolyn didn't like the woman. It was that simple. She saw Dietrich as her enemy.

"I don't know if you remember me! I am Detective—" Dietrich said as she pushed her wild mane of hair out of her face. She looked like she was on a mission.

"Of course I remember you!" Carolyn interrupted. "How could I forget the person that wants to put my grandson away for the rest of his life for something he did not do!" Carolyn gave her a hard stare. "What do you want?"

"Well, Mrs. Johnson, we are not here to speak to you about your grandson this time," Dietrich huffed.

At that moment, Detective Sharky stepped up to where the two women stood facing off. "Mrs. Johnson, we need you to come with us down to the station. We need to speak with you about the murder of Thomas Jackson, whom you may know as Tommy," Sharky said, his tone serious and demanding.

Carolyn looked like she'd seen a ghost. The detectives watched as the color drained from her face. She replayed the words in her head. *Murder of Thomas Jackson?* She felt like smiling.

"Yeah, we thought you'd have that kind of reaction. We advise you to come with us, Mrs. Johnson. We have surveillance tapes from Tommy's building, and we think you might have had contact with the woman we saw leaving around the time we think Tommy was murdered," Detective Dietrich said.

"No! I . . . I . . . have nothing to do with any of that. I don't know anything about a murder. I don't even know where Tommy lives. I have to go meet my youngest daughter. Whoever kidnapped her just dropped her off at a hospital," Carolyn said helplessly.

"I don't think so, Mrs. Johnson. Please don't make this harder than it has to be. We can get an arrest warrant for you, or you can just cooperate with us," Dietrich said, grabbing on to Carolyn's arm.

"And don't worry about your daughter," Sharky added. "We'll send a car to pick her up too."

"Wait! You don't understand!" Carolyn screamed, but Detective Dietrich wasn't letting up. She pulled Carolyn toward her and Sharky's unmarked police car. Sharky grabbed Carolyn's other arm.

"You can't do this! I need to call an attorney! You can't do this to me! I didn't have anything to do with any of this!" Carolyn screeched.

Detective Dietrich and Sharky held on to Carolyn like she was a mass murderer as they escorted her to their waiting car.

"Mrs. Johnson, there are lots of stones unturned right now. We need to find out what happened to Tommy. We need to find out what you know about the murder of the main witness in your grandson's case. And it all seems crazy, because your husband is the most hated man in the United States right now. I guess this is what happens when you want to be rich at any costs," Detective Dietrich said, a self-gratified tone lacing her words.

The story of the Johnsons was far from over. In fact, it had really just begun.